There had obviously been ▐ ▐ ▐ Nancy before, but Fred thought Adam had acted like a man enraged over something new. Old anger looked different. Old arguments had a weary sound, but Adam's words had held the edge of fresh pain.

Even so, Fred didn't think Nancy had been surprised by them. Whatever had pushed Adam over the edge tonight, Nancy knew about it—Fred would bet money on it.

He let himself out the back door and followed the uneven sidewalk to the gravel drive. He had a long trip home, and it would be dark in another hour. As he cranked the engine of his Buick to life, he glanced at Harriet and Porter's house again. It looked different now. It was a house of anger. A house divided. And he knew from long experience that what the Bible said was true—a house divided could not stand.

Don't miss Fred Vickery's
previous forays into murder in . . .

NO PLACE FOR SECRETS
and
NO PLACE LIKE HOME

MORE MYSTERIES FROM THE
BERKLEY PUBLISHING GROUP . . .

DOG LOVERS' MYSTERIES STARRING HOLLY WINTER: With her Alaskan malamute Rowdy, Holly dogs the trails of dangerous criminals. "A gifted and original writer." —Carolyn G. Hart

by Susan Conant

A NEW LEASH ON DEATH	A BITE OF DEATH
DEAD AND DOGGONE	PAWS BEFORE DYING

DOG LOVERS' MYSTERIES STARRING JACKIE WALSH: She's starting a new life with her son and an ex-police dog named Jake . . . teaching film classes and solving crimes!

by Melissa Cleary

A TAIL OF TWO MURDERS	SKULL AND DOG BONES
DOG COLLAR CRIME	DEAD AND BURIED
HOUNDED TO DEATH	THE MALTESE PUPPY
FIRST PEDIGREE MURDER	MURDER MOST BEASTLY

CHARLOTTE GRAHAM MYSTERIES: She's an actress with a flair for dramatics— and an eye for detection. "You'll get hooked on Charlotte Graham!" —*Rave Reviews*

by Stefanie Matteson

MURDER AT THE SPA	MURDER AT THE FALLS
MURDER AT TEATIME	MURDER ON HIGH
MURDER ON THE CLIFF	MURDER AMONG THE ANGELS
MURDER ON THE SILK ROAD	

PEACHES DANN MYSTERIES: Peaches has never had a very good memory. But she's learned to cope with it over the years . . . Fortunately, though, when it comes to murder, this absentminded amateur sleuth doesn't forgive and forget!

by Elizabeth Daniels Squire

WHO KILLED WHAT'S-HER-NAME?	REMEMBER THE ALIBI
MEMORY CAN BE MURDER	

HEMLOCK FALLS MYSTERIES: The Quilliam sisters combine their culinary and business skills to run an inn in upstate New York. But when it comes to murder, their talent for detection takes over . . .

by Claudia Bishop

A TASTE FOR MURDER	A DASH OF DEATH
A PINCH OF POISON	MURDER WELL-DONE

THE REVEREND LUCAS HOLT MYSTERIES: They call him "The Rev," a name he earned as pastor of a Texas prison. Now he solves crimes with a group of reformed ex-cons . . .

by Charles Meyer

THE SAINTS OF GOD MURDERS	BLESSED ARE THE MERCILESS

FRED VICKERY MYSTERIES: Senior sleuth Fred Vickery has been around long enough to know where the bodies are buried in the small town of Cutler, Colorado . . .

by Sherry Lewis

NO PLACE FOR SECRETS	NO PLACE LIKE HOME
NO PLACE FOR DEATH	

NO PLACE
FOR DEATH

SHERRY LEWIS

BERKLEY PRIME CRIME, NEW YORK

07018181

NO PLACE FOR DEATH

A Berkley Prime Crime Book / published by arrangement with the author

PRINTING HISTORY
Berkley Prime Crime edition / July 1996

The Putnam Berkley World Wide Web site address is
http://www.berkley.com

ISBN: 0-425-15383-5

Berkley Prime Crime Books are published by
The Berkley Publishing Group,
200 Madison Avenue, New York, NY 10016.
The name BERKLEY PRIME CRIME and the BERKLEY PRIME CRIME
design are trademarks belonging to Berkley Publishing Corporation.

PRINTED IN THE UNITED STATES OF AMERICA

10 9 8 7 6 5 4 3 2 1

For Gordon
This one's for you.

Keep looking forward—
that's where the adventure lies.

one

Fred Vickery followed his brother-in-law, Porter Jorgensen, from the Jorgensens' kitchen into the living room. In the nearly fifty years since they'd each married one of T. S. Cooper's daughters, they'd done this hundreds of times—a big meal in the kitchen, after which the men had been shooed into the living room while Phoebe and Harriet had cleared the table and chatted.

In the beginning Fred had often tried to help, but Phoebe had always sent him away. He'd finally given up after she explained it was her only chance to spend time alone with her sister and that the dishes provided a convenient excuse.

Settling into an easy chair, he listened to the clatter of silverware, the rush of water, and the low murmur of conversation. If he closed his eyes, he could almost believe nothing had ever changed. But the kids were all grown and out on their own—except Douglas, who'd moved back home in the spring—and Phoebe was gone. Had been for nearly three years now. Fred had grown used to living without her—almost. But times like this brought the pain back so sharply, Fred wondered if he'd ever truly adjust.

The past three years he'd avoided Phoebe's family almost entirely—four sisters all too much like Phoebe in one way or another and one brother. And too many children among them all to keep an accurate count. But Porter and Harriet lived the closest to Fred, and he'd missed the times they used to spend together. So when Harriet called last Sunday with this invitation to dinner, he convinced himself he'd healed enough to make it through the evening without trouble. He'd been wrong.

Stifling a groan, he patted his stomach. "Harriet sure hasn't lost her touch with a meal."

"Nope, I'll say that for her. She's still one of the best cooks in the county." Porter's ample frame provided silent proof of his words. He dropped heavily into his chair and picked up the remote control from the TV tray beside it. Almost instantly, a picture popped onto the screen, and Porter settled back in his chair as if he'd been watching the blasted thing all evening.

From the kitchen, a burst of laughter erupted and Fred's heart twisted. But it wasn't Phoebe's laugh. Tonight, Harriet and Nancy Bigelow, the Jorgensens' youngest child, had joined forces and kicked the men out of the kitchen. The laughter drifted away, then erupted again before fading into muted conversation. Nancy's voice blended with Harriet's like Phoebe's had. Both voices soft and melodious. Both a little husky. Both pleasant and soothing.

He leaned his head back against the chair and tried to push away the longing for the life he'd never know again. He'd had forty-seven years with Phoebe. This year would have been fifty. But no matter how much he longed for the past, he couldn't bring Phoebe back. All he had was the here and now. Tonight.

Tonight he'd shared some pleasant company and eaten a good meal for the first time in years. Obviously, Harriet and Phoebe had learned to cook from the same teacher. His daughter Margaret had cooked this well once, but she'd let her fear of fat grams and cholesterol drive all the spice from her food. So the only flavor he got these days was what he snuck into his own recipes. He glanced toward the kitchen and said, "It's good to see Nancy again. I didn't expect her to be here."

Porter grunted. "We all thought Douglas would come with you, and she was looking forward to seeing him again."

"I can't predict what Douglas'll do now any better than I could when he was a boy."

Porter nodded, no doubt remembering the younger Douglas and his tendency to leap from one interest to another without warning. "Did you say he's working now?"

Fred's mouth tightened into a frown. "He's still looking."

With an expression full of understanding, Porter leaned back in his chair. "If it's not one thing it's another, isn't it?" He shot a quick glance at the kitchen door. "Nancy's been on my mind a lot lately. She comes by more than she ought to, but that husband of hers spends all his time working, so she'd be alone if she didn't."

Fred heard disapproval in Porter's tone. He knew how it felt to object to a son-in-law, but Phoebe hadn't liked him to voice his opinion in front of Margaret, and he figured Harriet would feel the same way about Nancy's marriage. Besides, he'd known Adam Bigelow since childhood, had watched him all through school, and he'd always kind of liked the kid, so he tried to keep his next comment neutral. "What's Adam doing now? Does he still have that government job?"

"He's a subcontractor. Soil and water testing, that sort of thing. What it amounts to is he plays in the dirt and mud." Porter made a noise at something on the television and leaned slightly forward. "For hell's sake—" he muttered, then dropped back again and looked at Fred. "So, are you and Douglas coming to our picnic on Labor Day?"

"I don't know," Fred admitted. "Douglas could have found a job and left town by then."

"The real question is, what about you?" Porter asked. "We've missed having you around."

But Fred didn't want to make a promise he might not keep. "I don't know," he said again. "There are lots of memories in this house. More than I'd expected."

Porter studied the living room as if he could see the memories if he looked hard enough. "Well, I suppose there are, and I'm sure it's tough. But you can't make yourself a hermit forever. Just because Phoebe's gone doesn't mean you're not one of the family anymore."

"I know that."

"You should have been at Bev's for the Fourth of July. We had quite a party, and everybody asked about you."

Fred nodded. "Margaret told me."

Phoebe's eldest sister, Beverly, had long ago claimed the Fourth of July as her exclusive bailiwick, but Fred hadn't joined them at one of her parties since Phoebe passed on.

Chuckling at some picnic memory, Porter adjusted his shirtfront over his stomach. "Viv brought a date—did Margaret tell you that?"

Vivien, the sister between Phoebe and Harriet, had divorced her husband more than twenty years ago. Every year or so she'd date someone. Nothing serious had ever developed with any of her callers, but her descriptions of the dates kept the family in stitches.

Fred smiled. He'd missed Vivien's stories. "Do I need to run out and buy a wedding gift?"

Porter snorted in reply. "No, not yet. She called the next week and said the guy turned out to be the Date From Hell." He changed the channel on the television. "So, what about Labor Day? I've got to warn you, Bev said if you didn't show up this year she'd drive down and drag you up here by the seat of your pants."

Fred grinned at the image. Beverly had been a year ahead of Fred in school, so he knew she had to be at least seventy-four, but he had no trouble picturing her carrying out her threat. "Labor Day's still over two weeks away. I'll think about it and let you know."

In the other room, water shut off and chairs scraped against the floor. Porter jerked his head in the direction of the kitchen. "Sounds like they're coming. You know Harriet's not going to let you rest until you give her the answer she wants."

Before Fred could respond, footsteps clattered on the hardwood floor behind him. A second or two later, Harriet and Nancy came into the room. Harriet still wore her apron, and she'd left a kitchen towel over one shoulder. She had lighter hair and eyes than her sisters, but there was no mistaking which family she came from.

Nancy followed her mother, carrying a tray loaded with steaming mugs of coffee. She must have been about thirty, Fred calculated—give or take a year or two. The only girl out of the Jorgensens' five children, she had her mother's light hair, but her eyes were the same honey brown ones Phoebe'd had and that marked the family connection through several generations.

Harriet beamed at them and waved Nancy toward the coffee table. "Well, here we are. Anybody want coffee?"

"It's not decaf, is it?" Fred asked.

She handed him a mug and jerked her head toward her husband. "Are you kidding? Porter'd divorce me if I made decaf." She perched on the edge of the couch and let her gaze linger on Fred as he sipped cautiously. "So, did he talk you into coming for Labor Day?"

"I don't know—"

She touched one hand to his knee. "Please, Fred? We've missed you. Holidays aren't the same without you."

"They're not the same without Phoebe," he said.

He half expected Harriet's eyes to grow misty, but in her typical bullheaded way she refused to let the emotion take hold. "No, they're not. But we can't change that, can we? This is ridiculous, Fred. We live less than thirty miles apart, but we've hardly seen you the past three years."

"I'm here tonight," he protested.

"Yes, you are," she admitted. "And it's a good thing. I've just about reached the end of my patience."

Nancy grabbed a mug and wedged herself into a corner of the couch. "Come on, Uncle Fred, admit it. You've missed us, too."

He had. No denying it.

As if sensing his hesitation, Harriet touched his knee again. "Dorothy's bringing that casserole you like so much—"

Against his will, a laugh escaped. "You're fighting dirty."

She pushed at his knee and chuckled. "The best way to win you over has always been with food. Why do you think Phoebe spent one whole summer learning how to bake? We all thought we'd die in that hot old house before you got around to proposing."

Porter flicked through another couple of channels with the remote control. "You might as well give up, Fred. You don't stand a chance. They've been planning the menu all summer, working in your favorite dishes—"

Fred started to reply, but at that moment the front door slammed open and cut off his answer. Nancy's husband, Adam Bigelow, stood in the opening, his chest heaving from exertion or emotion, Fred couldn't be sure which. At just about six feet tall, Adam wasn't a small man. He had the broad-shouldered build and weathered complexion of a man who worked outdoors, and now that he'd reached his early thirties, he had a fine sprinkling of gray in his dark hair and beard.

Pausing only a second to get his bearings, Adam stormed into the living room toward Nancy. His dark eyes glinted and his breath came unevenly.

Nancy's smile faded. "Adam? What's wrong?"

He jerked his head toward the door. "I want to talk to you right now. Outside."

A flicker of uncertainty crossed Nancy's face, but she stood to face him. "*Now?* Adam—"

"Right now." The angry look he gave her spoke volumes and made Fred uneasy.

"For Pete's sake, boy—" Porter began.

"Don't get involved, Porter," Harriet interrupted. "Let the kids work out whatever it is."

Nancy looked at her parents and managed a weak smile in Fred's direction. "I'm sorry—"

"I said *now*." Adam grabbed her arm roughly and tried to pull her toward the door.

But she jerked away. "Let go of me."

Porter struggled to his feet and tried to step between them. "Whatever you're upset about, there's no need to get pushy—"

Ignoring the interruption, Adam grabbed for Nancy again, but this time she managed to sidestep him.

Looking decidedly upset, Harriet scrambled for Porter's remote control and aimed it toward the television. But when she turned up the volume on her first try and changed the channel on her second, she tossed it aside with a cry of frustration.

"Are you coming with me?" Adam shouted.

"Not while you're acting like this." Nancy tossed her head, but her eyes betrayed her anxiety.

Fred wondered if he should leave. But Harriet blocked the entrance to the kitchen, and Adam stood between him and the front door. Leaving right now would call more attention to himself than he wanted. But since he'd recently seen his son, Douglas, through a divorce, he didn't have the stomach for more angry accusations and bitter recriminations. And he didn't have the heart to witness a love die again.

When the television show gave way to a commercial, the volume jumped. With a growl Porter marched toward the set and turned it off manually. "Don't go with him, honey. Wait until he calms down."

Adam's face distorted. "This isn't your concern, Porter."

Harriet fluttered her hands toward the couch, and her mouth turned down at the corners. "Why don't you sit down, Adam? I'm sure you two can work out whatever's wrong."

But Adam laughed bitterly. "It doesn't matter anyway, Harriet. There's nothing to work out. I'm talking to an attorney first thing tomorrow."

It had gone this far, then. Fred sure hated to see it. He knew how deep the scars of divorce could run.

Harriet cried out as if Adam had struck her. "What? Oh, Adam. You don't mean that." She turned to Nancy and grabbed her arms. "He didn't mean it, sweetie."

Nancy's eyes filled with tears, and her face crumpled in pain. "Yes, he does."

"No," Harriet insisted. "You'll see." She reached a pleading hand toward her son-in-law. "Maybe you and I should talk about it, Adam."

But Nancy tugged her back. "No, Mom. Adam's right. This is between him and me——"

Adam barked another angry laugh. "If that was true, we might have a chance. But it's been a long time since things have been between the two of us, hasn't it?" Adam grabbed her arm and jerked her toward the door. But he must have gripped her arm too tightly or pulled her too roughly, because she cried out in pain.

That's all it took for Porter to lose his temper. Red-faced, he lunged toward his son-in-law. "You hurt her again, and I'll take you apart."

Nancy tried in vain to pull away from Adam. "Please don't, Dad."

But Adam held tight and jerked her toward the door again. "*Now*, Nancy. I'm not waiting all night while you milk your parents for sympathy."

Embarrassed to witness the argument and concerned for everyone involved, Fred wished they'd stop, that they'd separate and discuss it later. If they let this go on too long, it would be hard to repair the damage later.

Nancy bit her lip as if Adam had hurt her again, and Porter's round face darkened with anger. "Let go of her, you little son of a bitch—"

Adam whirled to face him. "Stay out of this, Porter, unless you want to hear things you'd rather not know about. Nancy can tell the whole damned lot of you about it later—" his mouth twisted into an ugly smile "—*if* she wants to."

As if she'd suddenly regained control, Nancy jerked her arm away. "Stop it, Adam," she snapped and strode toward the front door. "You want to talk? Fine. But leave my family out of this."

At least she was willing to talk, Fred thought. Maybe they'd discuss it rationally, once they were alone.

And they might have if Porter hadn't rushed after Nancy. "You're not going anywhere with him," he shouted. "Not unless he calms down."

Adam's face darkened dangerously. He leaned too close to Porter, and when he spoke his voice came out low and frighteningly controlled. "If you had any idea—"

Harriet looked at Fred as if she thought he should do something. But much as he hated watching this, he had no intention of getting involved. He'd learned his lesson with his own children. He worked hard not to interfere in their lives, and he wouldn't step into the middle of his niece's troubles.

"All right, you want a divorce?" Nancy shouted. "You've got it. Just get out of here before you do any more damage."

Fred bit back a groan of dismay. Assigning blame wouldn't fix anything.

"Before *I* do—?" Adam demanded. He laughed bitterly. "You're something else, you know that?"

Nancy turned away from him, and Harriet started to say something, but Porter put one arm around Harriet's shoulders and glared at Adam. "You heard her. Get the hell out."

Adam's lip curled. "That's the way you handle everything, isn't it? Can't even *think* about telling you the truth about any of your precious children because you wouldn't believe the truth if it hit you in the face. Well, they're not the angels you think they are, Porter."

As if Adam had given him an idea, Porter shot out his fist and connected with Adam's face. And when blood spurted from the boy's nose, all hell broke loose. Nancy cried out in shock, Harriet ran toward her husband shouting something, and Adam answered with a right hook to Porter's stomach.

Porter jerked to cover himself too late and groaned as Adam's fist knocked the wind out of him. Fred worked his way to his feet. Now that things had gone this far, he couldn't just sit back and watch. He had to do something, he just didn't know what. But someone was going to get hurt, he could feel it in his bones.

Before he could reach the fight, Nancy threw herself between her father and husband. Harriet shouted and Adam tried to hit Porter again, but because Nancy had planted herself between them, he struck her arm and shoulder instead. She cried out and gripped her arm with her other hand.

Porter pulled himself upright, still trying to catch his breath. "Call the sheriff, Harriet."

Harriet said something Fred couldn't quite hear, and Nancy sank onto the couch and buried her face in her hands.

Adam let his gaze wander over Nancy slowly, and Fred saw bare hatred there. "Congratulations," Adam said softly. "You've got what you wanted. I don't ever want to see you again."

"Adam, no—" Harriet cried and tried to grab him.

But Adam shook her off and slammed out the door.

Rounding on Porter, Harriet shouted, "Now look what you've done. Go after him."

"The hell I will, and neither will anyone else." With his dark red face a sharp contrast to his snow white hair, Porter dropped into his chair. His jaw worked overtime and his expression left no doubt he meant what he said.

Harriet glared at him. "You've ruined everything. The kids could have worked things out if you hadn't jumped into the middle of it. Did you hear what he said to her? Did you *hear*?"

"I heard. And I say, good riddance to bad rubbish," Porter grumbled.

Harriet shoved her hands onto her hips. "You're going to have to apologize to him tomorrow, you know."

Porter glared at her. "I'm not apologizing. I'm not sorry for a single thing I said. *Or* did."

Harriet stared at him for one long moment as if she couldn't believe her ears. "One of these days you're going to go too far." And without another word, she walked out of the room.

two

Fred wondered whether he should sneak away during the uneasy silence that filled the room in the wake of Harriet's departure. Nancy struggled to control herself, and as Porter watched, the anger slowly began to fade from his expression.

"Nancy?" Porter said softly.

She didn't look up.

"What's going on with you and Adam?"

She didn't answer, just shook her head and cried.

"Why's your mother blaming *me?* You saw what he was like. What does she think I should do when he barges in here acting like a maniac?"

That brought a reaction. Nancy sent her father a scathing look that lasted about three seconds. Then she sobbed, "Oh, Daddy," and raced into his arms, sounding for all the world like a little girl.

Porter returned the embrace, patting her back and smoothing her hair. "I'm not going to let that jerk treat you like that. Not anymore. You've been unhappy for a long time, and it's finally come to an end."

Nancy sobbed noisily and gulped air every few seconds. She nodded without speaking and leaned her head against his chest.

Having found an appreciative audience at last, Porter warmed to his theme. "He'd better not come around here again, that's all I can say. He shows his face on my property again, he'll be sorry. I don't care what your mother says."

"Oh, Daddy, *I'm* sorry."

Porter patted her shoulder. "Nothing for you to be sorry about, honey. It's not your fault."

Realizing there wasn't a thing he could do to help, Fred wandered slowly into the kitchen. He didn't agree with Porter's actions, but he understood only too well his need to help a child in trouble.

There had obviously been trouble between Adam and Nancy before, but Fred thought Adam had acted like a man enraged over something new. Old anger looked different. Old arguments had a weary sound, but Adam's words had held the rage of fresh pain.

Even so, Fred didn't think Nancy had been surprised by them. Whatever had pushed Adam over the edge tonight, Nancy knew about it—Fred would bet money on it.

He let himself out the back door and followed the uneven sidewalk to the gravel drive. He had a long trip home, and it would be dark in another hour. As he cranked the engine of his Buick to life, he glanced at Harriet and Porter's house again. It looked different now. It was a house of anger. A house divided. And he knew from long experience that what the Bible said was true—a house divided could not stand.

When the telephone rang at nearly ten o'clock that night, Fred dropped the *Denver Post* onto the floor beside his rocking chair and pushed to his feet. It had to be Margaret checking on him. She was the only one he knew who'd call this late.

He crossed the room and caught up the receiver on the fourth ring. "Hello?"

"Fred?" Even across the wire, Harriet's voice sounded unsteady.

"Harriet? What's wrong?"

"Oh, Fred," she wailed, and for several seconds he listened to the muffled sound of crying.

She'd called for sympathy. To talk to him about the argument the way she used to call Phoebe. Of all Phoebe's sisters, Harriet most often asked for a listening ear.

She sniffed loudly. "Oh, Fred. What am I going to do?"

Fred didn't want to get involved. He'd told Phoebe a

thousand times nothing good ever came of getting in the middle of a family squabble. He opened his mouth to tell Harriet so, but the image of her face, swollen and tearful and so like Phoebe's in distress, flashed through his mind. So he cleared his throat and said, "What's wrong?"

"Porter and I had the most dreadful argument, and he took off out of here in a rage. But I'm worried what he'll do."

Fred had to admit that being married to Porter probably gave Harriet more than her share of reasons to need a listening ear. Porter tended to get worked up fast and cool down slow, and Fred didn't like the idea of Porter in a temper roaming the countryside any more than Harriet did. "Do you have any idea where he's gone?"

"No. He's in one of his moods—you know how he gets. He said he wasn't going to stay here and be insulted, and he left."

"What did you say that made him think he was being insulted?"

"I didn't say *anything* insulting. You know me better than that."

Fred knew her, all right, but he didn't correct her.

"All I said was that he'd been a darned fool to step in between Nancy and Adam. You know as well as I do, Fred, those two could have worked things out if Porter hadn't stuck his big nose in where it didn't belong."

Fred didn't agree. There was something seriously wrong between Adam and Nancy. But he was smart enough not to correct her on that point, either.

"Porter does the same thing with the boys," Harriet fumed. "He's never learned to let go. Still thinks he needs to call all the shots. But he's *much* worse with Nancy."

Fred didn't want to listen to an inventory of Porter's weak points. "Well, you know how it is with fathers and daughters."

"I know how it *ought* to be. Especially after the daughter's all grown up. Did you ever see anything so ridiculous as that old fool starting a fist fight with a man half his age?"

Fred couldn't see what age had to do with anything. "Well, now—" he began.

But Harriet had worked herself up, and she didn't hear him. "What earthly good did he think interfering would do? That's what I want to know. Did he think he could force Adam and Nancy to stay together? I'm telling you, he should have kept his nose out of it."

Fred pulled in a deep breath and tried to use a note of reason. "I don't think the idea of a divorce was what really set him off."

But Harriet kept right on as if he hadn't spoken. "No! The silly old fool had to punch his son-in-law right in the nose and then kick him out of the house. I can't even imagine what's going to happen now. And to make matters worse, I just tried to call Nancy, but she's not home. I have no idea where she is, either. Have you heard from her?"

"Me? No. Why should I?"

"Well, you *were* here this evening. You saw everything that happened. I thought she might stop by to talk to you."

Fred hoped she wouldn't. He was already more involved in this family argument than he wanted to be. "She's probably at home but not answering the telephone," he suggested.

Harriet sniffed her disapproval. "She'd be a fool to go home tonight."

"Well, maybe," Fred hedged. "But if she thinks her marriage is in serious trouble—"

"It's *not* in serious trouble. At least it wasn't before her father got involved." Harriet's footsteps shuffled across her kitchen floor, and the sound carried through the wire. Pacing. "Tell me, Fred, what makes a man act like that?"

After over forty years of marriage, Fred would have thought she'd be used to Porter and his ways. Even he knew Porter well enough to not be surprised by tonight's events.

"*You* wouldn't have done anything so foolish," Harriet said.

"Well, you never know. I might have."

"Nonsense. You're too level-headed."

He grinned and wondered what Margaret would think if she heard that. Harriet certainly knew how to swing support in her favor, he'd grant her that.

She sighed softly. "I hope Nancy's all right."

"I'm sure she is."

"You don't think Adam would hit her again—?" She hesitated, then stated more firmly, "No, I'm sure she'll be fine."

"Of course she will. There's nothing to worry about."

"I'm sure you're right." Harriet's voice begged reassurance, but Fred was beginning to see that nothing he could say would provide it.

They'd reached the point of impasse. In a minute, she'd start rehashing, but Fred had no intention of going through it all again. "You'll hear from her in the morning, I'm sure."

She sighed deeply. He could picture her standing in her big old kitchen with her robe drawn up to her chin and a hairnet covering her faded blonde curls. She'd be staring out the kitchen window into the side yard as if she could see something that would help. "I can't believe this," she said. "I don't know what's happening to this family lately."

"Same thing that's happening to all of our families," Fred said. "Kids grow up. Personalities clash. It happens."

"But Nancy's been acting different lately, and tonight—" she broke off as if she couldn't stand to go on.

He tried using his most reassuring voice. "I'm sure you'll hear from her as soon as she and Adam work everything out." He hoped he sounded more convinced than he felt.

"If that darned fool husband of mine keeps his nose out of their business, they might," Harriet snapped, but at least she sounded a little less shaky. She drew in a steadying breath. "Well, I suppose I ought to let you get to bed, but thanks for the listening ear, Fred."

"Promise me you'll go upstairs and get some sleep yourself."

"I will," she vowed.

But he didn't believe her. Still, she did sound grateful and reassured, and it hadn't required much from him after all. Feeling suddenly generous, he said, "Call if you need anything else."

Smiling, he replaced the receiver and snapped off the

living room light. And he told himself there was nothing to worry about. By morning, everything would be fine.

Fred pulled open the kitchen blinds to let in the morning light and shoved the coffeepot under the cold water tap. He had a lot to do today—his morning constitutional around Spirit Lake, a tune-up and oil change on his car, and an overdue visit to his granddaughter Alison.

He worked to separate a coffee filter from the stack in the box, but his fingers wouldn't perform this morning. Blasted arthritis. Inhaling, he battled the filter again. He didn't understand why somebody couldn't make the silly things so they'd come apart easier.

When the telephone's ring broke the early morning silence, startling him, he dropped the whole stack on the floor and glanced at the clock on the wall. Just before eight—a little early for a social call.

Stooping slowly, stiff-kneed, he picked up the filters as the telephone rang again. It must be Margaret, but why would she call this early? She didn't usually check on him before she got the kids off to school.

From down the hall, he heard his son Douglas stumble around in his bedroom. The telephone must have wakened him. Fred straightened, hating how slowly he moved, dropped the filters onto the table and picked up the receiver.

Hearing Harriet's voice across the wire surprised him, and her hysterical sobbing surprised him even more.

"Harriet?"

She managed to croak, "Fred? Have you seen Nancy?" Then she broke down again.

He felt a twinge of sympathy for Harriet and a surge of anger toward his niece for not letting her mother know where she'd gone after the scene last night. "No. She hasn't called?"

Fred could hear Porter talking in the background, but he couldn't make out a word. But at least he'd come back home, and Harriet wasn't alone.

"We were hoping maybe she'd gotten in touch with you," Harriet said. She made a few attempts to quiet Porter, then pulled in a ragged breath. "Listen, Fred. We've got to find her. Immediately!"

"Why? What's happened?" Probably nothing, he told himself. This was most likely the result of a sleepless night and an overactive imagination. He waited patiently while Porter rumbled in the background again, and Harriet pulled herself together.

"A couple of deputies from the sheriff's office were just here," she said at last. "Oh, Fred, I still can't believe it."

"What happened? Did Porter punch Adam in the nose again?"

She didn't laugh. "No. Adam's been shot."

Shot? Fred's pulse beat an uneven rhythm. "How bad is he hurt?"

A pause, then she said in a too-quiet voice, "He's dead."

Fred dropped onto a kitchen chair and struggled to draw his next breath. "What happened?"

"They shot him in the back of the head," Harriet cried. "Somebody at EnviroSampl found him at his desk when they opened the office this morning."

"Do they know who did it?"

"No."

"Any suspects?"

"They're looking for Nancy, that's all I know."

Fred's fingers numbed and his blood ran cold. "Surely they don't think *Nancy* did it?" She might be young and spirited and occasionally unwise, but Nancy wouldn't purposely hurt another living soul.

"No! Of course not. But I don't know where she is! What if something's happened to *her*?"

Fred's kitchen door slammed open and he twisted toward it, startled, to find Douglas framed in the opening. The boy's dark hair tufted around his head, and his lean face looked puffy from sleep. He scowled at the telephone for waking him and shuffled toward the coffeepot.

When he saw the pot empty and the filters on the table, he set about making it himself. Good. Fred could sure use a cup.

He gave Douglas a weary smile and turned his attention

back to Harriet. "I guess Enos has already checked Nancy's house?"

"Of course he has," Harriet snapped. "But she's not there, and I'm worried sick that something's happened to her."

Porter must have moved closer to the telephone because his voice rumbled—"told you a dozen times already, Harriet—" before he faded out again.

Porter didn't sound worried, and neither was Fred. Not about Nancy's safety, anyway. He couldn't let himself seriously consider the possibility that she'd been killed. No, he worried that with Adam dead and Nancy nowhere to be found, people would begin to speculate about her part in it.

Douglas ran his fingers through his hair and leaned one hip against the counter, obviously interested in Fred's conversation.

"If you hear *anything*, you'll let us know, won't you?" Harriet pleaded.

"Of course. And don't worry. I'm sure she's fine."

"She has to be, Fred. I don't know what I'll do if anything's happened to her."

The telephone changed hands, and a second later Porter's voice boomed at him. "Sorry to bother you, Fred. You'll let us know?"

"Of course," he promised again.

"This is the damnedest thing."

"Is Harriet all right?"

This time Porter lowered his voice. "She's nervous as a cat, but she'll be all right once we find Nancy."

"Keep me posted."

"You bet. And Fred? Thanks for everything."

When Porter disconnected, Fred replaced the receiver slowly and turned toward Douglas's curious stare.

The boy paused in the act of spooning sugar into a mug. "What's up?"

"Nancy's husband's been murdered."

Douglas let the spoon clatter against the ceramic. "No kidding? Adam? Why would anybody want to kill him?"

Fred couldn't even begin to guess.

At thirty-seven, Douglas was the one closest in age to

Nancy and Adam of any of Fred's kids. He shook his head slowly as if he could make sense of it that way. "Adam's a great guy. Everybody likes him."

Somebody obviously didn't. But Fred didn't point that out. Instead, he said, "Enos will find whoever did it." And he tried to believe it.

Fred trusted Enos Asay. Absolutely. He was as good a sheriff as they'd had in Cutler in the past forty years. But he did have an annoying blind spot that kept him from seeing the truth at times. Because of it, he'd arrested Douglas for murder a few months ago, and Fred couldn't shake the uneasy feeling that he might do something equally misguided in this case.

Douglas dropped two slices of bread into the toaster and started rummaging through the refrigerator. "Did Uncle Porter or Aunt Harriet say anything about Adam at dinner last night?"

"No, but he stopped by for a minute after."

Douglas found the tub of margarine and straightened. "How did he look? Okay? Upset? Frightened?"

"Angry." Fred tried to ignore a rising sense of dread. Surely Enos had enough common sense not to suspect Nancy. Didn't he?

"About what? Work?"

Fred wished that were the case. "At Nancy."

Douglas frowned, and Fred could see the boy reaching the same conclusions he'd drawn himself. When the toast popped up, Douglas buttered it generously and ate it in speculative silence.

Fred poured a cup of coffee to soothe his nerves, but snatches of the argument at Harriet and Porter's echoed through his mind, and the image of Adam's angry face refused to fade.

At last unable to fight it any longer, he dumped the rest of his coffee into the sink and rinsed his cup.

Douglas frowned up at him. "Where are you going?"

"The sheriff's office."

"Why?"

"I was one of the last people to see Adam alive. I might have information they need."

Douglas looked skeptical.

"I have a civic duty to report everything I know to the authorities," Fred argued as he crossed to the back door. And he had a personal duty to set his mind at ease.

Douglas didn't look impressed by his argument. "Or you could be trying to get involved in the investigation."

"But I'm not."

Douglas's lips curved in a disbelieving smile. "No, I'm sure you're not."

Fred yanked open the door and glared at him. "I think you've been spending too much time around your sister."

Douglas laughed. "Yeah. Probably. But don't tell me I'm wrong, because I won't believe you."

Fred didn't answer. He just pulled the door closed behind him. Forcefully.

He marched up Lake Front toward Main Street, angered by Douglas's accusation, but more annoyed at its accuracy. He told himself he didn't want to get involved. He only wanted to reassure himself that Enos didn't suspect Nancy or Porter. And once he did that, he told himself, he'd be fine.

three

Halfway to town, Fred began to calm down a little. With the morning sun warming his shoulders and reflecting off the lake's surface like tiny golden mirrors, he couldn't remain agitated for long. And the half-mile walk to town was just long enough to calm him.

Fred loved mornings. Always had. He loved the way the sun painted the sky with its pastel brush. And he loved the way the scent of the forest always seemed more distinct. Earthy. Mossy. Fresh. He could almost smell the dew.

Cutler sat in the bottom of a narrow valley surrounded by forest. It nestled on the shores of Spirit Lake, high in the Colorado Rockies. Even in its most densely populated section it felt more like a nick in the timber than a town. Lodgepole pines towered over most of the buildings, aspen trees shimmered in the high mountain breezes, and the chatter of forest creatures broke the silence almost as often as sounds of human occupation.

With the nearest large city over a hundred miles away, Fred had always felt safe here. This was a good place to raise a family. A good place to call home. But the anger that seemed to infest society everywhere had invaded Cutler, too. And he didn't feel safe here any more. Not the way he used to.

He reached the intersection with Main Street and looked for Enos's truck on the street, but his usual parking spot stood empty. Enos figured since everybody in town knew where to find him, it didn't make sense to show up before breakfast, so he didn't usually show up until after ten. After coffee. But because of the murder, Fred had expected today to be different.

Deciding to take his chances, Fred crossed the street and climbed onto the boardwalk. The murder had taken place on the other end of Enos's jurisdiction—over forty miles away. Maybe he'd come in early and gone out already. But surely he'd left one of his deputies in charge, and a deputy could set Fred's mind at ease as well as Enos could. Maybe better.

Fred pushed open the office door and looked around, hoping he'd find Ivan Neeley and not Grady Hatch. Grady'd shown a distinct lack of patience with Fred's questions when Garrett Locke was killed—Ivan would probably be a little more receptive.

He was in luck. Ivan sat in Enos's chair, feet up, hands linked behind his head. When he saw Fred, he sat up slowly and lowered his feet to the floor. "Can I help you?"

"Ivan," Fred said in greeting.

Ivan narrowed his eyes in return.

"I just heard the news. It's terrible."

"It sure is," Ivan agreed, but he didn't sound very eager to discuss it.

Fred lowered himself into one of the battered old chairs in front of Enos's desk. "I thought I'd better come by right away."

"Oh? And why's that?"

"Well, I was one of the last people to see Adam alive. I figured Enos would want a statement."

"He might," Ivan conceded. "I'll let him know. We can give you a call when he's ready for you."

Fred nodded as if that sounded like a good idea. "I guess he's probably out investigating—?"

"Yep." Ivan kicked his feet back up.

"Any idea who did it?"

"Nope."

"I heard Adam was killed at his office. That's that little place up on the highway just outside of Mountain Home, isn't it?"

"Maybe."

Fred would take that as a yes. "Guess there must have been trouble there."

Ivan didn't answer. He was as closemouthed this morning as Grady.

Fred crossed an ankle over his knee and smiled. "Guess this'll keep you busy for a while."

Ivan shrugged. "I'm just making a few phone calls. Grady and Enos are up there with Robert."

Ah, yes. Robert Alpers, Enos's man-on-the-spot in Mountain Home. When Robert and his wife divorced, he'd quit his job with a police department somewhere in Utah, pulled up stakes, and moved to Colorado. And Enos had snapped him up the second his application for the newly created deputy sheriff position arrived. Since Mountain Home was even smaller than Cutler, the young man probably spent most of his time writing traffic citations and settling family squabbles, but Fred figured he'd likely been first on the scene of today's tragedy.

Ivan readjusted his position on the chair, but Fred thought he detected a bit of jealousy in his expression. Well, of course Ivan would feel left out. Relegated to manning the phones while Enos and the others investigated the murder—Fred knew *he* wouldn't like it one bit.

He looked supportive. "Seems to me Enos could use your help out there in the field."

Ivan didn't say anything, but he seemed to like that.

"After all," Fred pointed out. "You've been through this before. You know what you're looking for."

Ivan nodded. "That's the thing, see. Sometimes you can tell more by what's *not* at a crime scene than what is. It takes a while to learn that."

Fred looked understanding. "I suppose Enos thinks Robert knows what he's doing."

Ivan made a noise that sounded like disagreement. "This is a *lot* different than what he's used to."

Fred couldn't see how, but he tried to look sympathetic. "Well, it does seem to me Enos would want to use his best men on a case like this."

Ivan stared at him for a long moment. His lips curved. "What do you want, Fred?"

Fred looked magnificently innocent. "Want? I want to give my statement."

Ivan shook his head. "You want me to tell you something. What is it?"

Fred hesitated. If Enos didn't already suspect Nancy, Fred certainly didn't want to point the finger at her.

Ivan swung his feet to the floor again and stood. "Let me think. You're here because Adam was married to your niece—"

"Has Enos found her yet?"

"I'm working my way through a list of friends I got from her mother. Nothing yet."

"So she doesn't know about Adam?"

"Not that we know of. 'Course, she *might*—" Ivan broke off, but his implication was clear enough to Fred.

"I could help you look for her," Fred offered. Ivan shook his head and opened his mouth to protest, but Fred didn't let him. "Give me half your list. I'll make some calls and free you so you can get out there on the scene."

Ivan scowled. "You never give up, do you?"

Not if he could help it. Follow-through was one of his best qualities. "I'm just offering to help."

"I can't stop you from calling people, but I sure as hell can't give you half my list."

"Then tell me who you've called already."

"Can't do that, either."

Stubborn whelp. Here Fred was with an offer of help, and the young fool couldn't see what it would do for him. Fred shrugged and tried to look as if he didn't care one way or the other. He didn't like wasting time on the telephone, anyway.

He pushed to his feet and crossed to the door. "You'll tell Enos I came by?"

Ivan grinned. "Absolutely."

Without an answering smile, Fred stepped outside and started back down the boardwalk toward the intersection. If he were Nancy, where would he be? With a friend? Obviously not one Harriet knew. Family? All her brothers lived too far away to think she'd gone to see them. None of her other aunts and uncles lived close enough for Fred to believe she'd gone to them. So where?

Frustrated, he had to admit he didn't know enough about her these days to have any ideas. He started back down Lake Front, walking slowly and pondering. Had Harriet been right? Had Nancy been hurt? Or killed?

No. Adam was killed at his office, so the murder probably had nothing to do with Nancy. And she was fine. She had to be.

Fred supposed he should go back home and wait to hear from Harriet again, but he didn't want to wait. He hated waiting. He passed the Kirkhams' cabin and waved to Loralee, and he wondered how Harriet was holding up.

Maybe she'd already heard from Nancy. If so, she'd be fine. If not, she was probably worried sick, and Porter wouldn't offer much comfort. If Phoebe'd still been here, she would have insisted on rushing to Harriet's side.

When that realization hit him, Fred beamed a smile and almost missed a step. Of course that was where he needed to be. With Harriet, offering moral support. Or more.

Phoebe'd been good at hand-holding; Fred wasn't. But he *could* help look for Nancy. After seventy-three years, he knew the area better than most people, and he'd watched darned near everybody grow up and pass through school right under his nose. Those kids had a hard time refusing to answer his questions.

He walked a little faster, anxious now. Of course he'd check with Douglas first to make sure he hadn't heard from Harriet again—or from Nancy. Then he'd drive up to Harriet's and offer to look for his niece.

And maybe he'd swing by EnviroSampl on his way up the mountain—just to make sure Nancy wasn't already there. No use spinning his wheels.

Satisfied with his decision, Fred turned his face into the warm summer sun as he walked back home. Enos might argue with Fred for wanting to help find Nancy, but he couldn't stop him.

* * *

Knowing he must be getting close to the small office building that housed EnviroSampl, Fred let off the accelerator. He'd noticed the place before—one of dozens of similar warehouselike buildings nestled along the highway—but he'd never paid particular attention to it. He just didn't want to overshoot the turnoff and have to double back, because he'd have trouble explaining that to Enos.

He rounded a curve, and the road straightened for several hundred feet ahead. Bright orange cones partially blocked one lane, and flares burned near the side of the road. The flashing blue lights of an ambulance contrasted sharply with the dark green forest. It looked like he'd found the place.

Grady Hatch, tall and slim in his deputy sheriff's uniform, stepped toward the car and pumped his hands up and down as a signal to slow further. Grady had to be around thirty, but Fred still saw him as the gangly twelve-year-old who'd shot up faster than any other boy his age and who still towered over almost everyone.

Recognizing Fred's car, Grady frowned and lifted one hand as a signal for Fred to stop. With his eyes narrowed, he approached and waited for Fred to lower the window. "What do *you* want?"

Fred gave him a little smile. "Just passing by. Is Enos still here?"

Grady looked wary, but he nodded. "Yes."

"Where?"

The young man squinted into the hot August sunlight and looked toward the building. "Inside."

"I need to see him."

Grady shifted position and stared into the interior of the car again. "I can't let you go near the building, Fred, and you know it. What do you want?"

"I need to give him my statement. He probably doesn't know I was with Adam for a while last night."

Grady seemed to hesitate for a split second, but his face tightened and his eyes narrowed. "I can't let anyone near the murder scene, especially you."

"What do you mean, 'especially me'?"

Grady's frown deepened. "I mean you have a habit of getting yourself involved in official police business, and Enos doesn't like it."

"I'm here to give him a statement. What's wrong with that?"

This time Grady didn't refuse outright. He squinted at the building again and looked back at Fred. "He can get it from you later."

Fred leaned back into his seat with a shrug. "I might be able to tell him something that would help him find Nancy."

Grady hesitated and made a few noises of protest, just to assert his authority, but Fred kept smiling until he finally weakened. "All right, I'll check with him."

"Wonderful."

Grady stepped away from the car and hunched over his walkie-talkie for several minutes. Someone official-looking rushed from the front door of the building and disappeared into the back of an emergency vehicle. A woodpecker attacked a tree, and somewhere nearby a chipmunk voiced his opinion of all the ruckus.

Gesturing broadly with one hand, Grady explained something into the radio and looked back over his shoulder as if making sure Fred hadn't sneaked past him. Distrusting soul.

Fred settled back to wait, but less than ten seconds later the front door of EnviroSampl's small aluminum building burst open, and Enos stormed outside. He charged across the parking lot wearing a very unhappy expression.

At nearly fifty, Enos still had the stocky build of his youth. Broad-shouldered, round-faced, and sandy-complexioned, he walked with a quick, heavy step Fred never mistook for anyone else's. "What in hell's name are you doing here?" he demanded even before he reached the car.

"Like I explained to Grady—" Fred began.

"Save it. What are you *really* doing here?"

Fred struggled to keep his patience in check in the face of this unwarranted attack. "I'm *really* here to offer my statement and my help."

"Your help?"

Fred nodded. "Finding Nancy."

"Have you heard from her?"

"No. But—"

"Then I don't need your help. Go home."

"I can't."

"Well, you can't stay here."

"Did I ask you to let me stay?"

Enos rubbed his face with one big open hand and glared at him. "I don't have time to play games, Fred."

"I'm not playing games."

"Why don't you go home and wait in case Nancy calls?"

"Douglas is there."

"Well, I'll bet he's real happy about that. Look—I don't want Nancy to hear about Adam through the grapevine, and it's going to be damned hard to keep it quiet for long. But I *don't* need your help finding her."

When Enos stepped away, Fred caught sight of a small group of people clustered beneath the trees on one side of the building. "Who's over there?" he asked and nodded toward the group.

"Employees, business associates—people who belong here. Nobody who concerns you," Enos snapped, but curiosity got the better of him. "Why?"

"Just wondering."

"What are you up to?"

Why in the world did everybody accuse him of being "up to" something when he only wanted to help? "Nothing."

Enos barked a laugh. "I wish I could believe that, but I've got a real sick feeling you've got something up your sleeve. What is it?"

Fred raised his hands in self-defense. "Nothing. I just came by to offer my statement."

Enos pushed his hat back and scratched his head. "I was under the impression that Ivan had already talked to you about that."

Fred frowned. The young whelp certainly hadn't wasted any time. "He did."

"So I'll get your statement later."

"Well, all right," Fred conceded. "But it beats me how

you can investigate such a serious crime without talking to a key witness."

Enos rolled his eyes. "I suppose you plan to keep pestering me and my boys until I hear what you have to say?"

"Probably."

Enos sighed heavily, but he looked resigned. "All right, then. Let's get it over with. But I'm right in the middle of something, so you're going to have to wait a couple of minutes."

"Fine."

"And you're blocking traffic. Why don't you pull into the parking lot and wait there." Enos pointed one thick finger at Fred. "But don't get out of your car."

Fred tried not to resent Enos's comment. "You're too suspicious, you know that? It can't be good for you."

Enos readjusted his hat and worked up a thin smile. "Well, I'll agree with you there. It's probably not. But if you didn't keep sticking your nose where it didn't belong, I wouldn't have to be that way." He patted the hood of Fred's car and jogged back to the building.

Fred drove into the lot and looked for a spot near the group of employees and business associates. The parking lot wasn't large, but he wanted to find a good spot—one where he could keep an eye on everything. Luckily, he found a space near the front of the building between a red Mustang and a white Celebrity.

He studied the group for a few seconds. About ten people, some of whom looked familiar, some of whom didn't. He recognized the Barker boy who'd been on the basketball team at Paradise Valley High a few years back and Pete Scott's new young wife.

But the one who caught his eye was a reed-thin woman of about twenty-five. Charlotte Isaacson. Short dark hair. Red puffy eyes. She'd obviously been crying. A lot. She stood between two men Fred didn't recognize.

One, a man of about thirty-five, kept one hand on her arm and whispered to her every few seconds. They stood at equal height, probably about five-ten. The man's pants hung below his stomach and his shirt pooched out around his middle, and he had the soft sort of build that would probably make all his clothes look just that sloppy. His blond hair had thinned almost to baldness on top, and he darted continuous, anxious looks at the building and at the deputies.

On the other side, a tall black man stared at Charlotte as if he wanted to argue. She seemed to be ignoring him. He wore an expensive-looking business suit that seemed out of place around the more casual attire of the rest of the crowd. He scowled at Charlotte, said something Fred couldn't hear that brought a flush to her thin face, and then paced a few steps away. At the edge of his imaginary boundary, he pivoted and paced back. He looked irritated, anxious to get away, and not personally affected by Adam's death.

Fred wondered about the two men, but before he could draw any conclusions, a shout from the highway caught his attention. He turned halfway around to see what caused the commotion and saw a dark-colored Isuzu Trooper stopped at Grady's barrier.

He watched as the driver's door opened and Nancy emerged. Relieved that she'd finally shown up, he climbed out of his car and hurried toward her. He didn't want her to be alone when she heard the news about Adam. But his knees twinged from the pace he set, and the pain forced him to slow down a little.

He watched Grady stop her and hold her back when she would have run toward the building. The young man used his walkie-talkie again, and Nancy looked totally bewildered.

She didn't see Fred until he'd almost reached the shoulder of the road, but the instant she recognized him her expression clouded in confusion and she started toward him. "Uncle Fred? What's going on?"

Grady tried to assert his authority. "Mrs. Bigelow, I have to ask you to wait here for Sheriff Asay."

But Nancy's eyes snapped with anger. "I don't want to wait for Sheriff Asay, I want to know what's going on. Now."

Fred reached her side and slipped an arm around her shoulder. "Can't you tell her?"

"The sheriff wants to talk with her first," Grady insisted.

"Tell me what?" Nancy demanded. "What's going on? Where's Adam?"

Neither man answered.

"Uncle Fred?"

He tightened his arm around her shoulder. "I'm sorry, Nancy—"

Enlightenment slowly replaced curiosity. "Adam? He's all right, isn't he?"

Grady looked so uncomfortable, Fred almost felt sorry for him.

Nancy pulled away from Fred and started toward the building, but Grady caught her before she'd taken more than a couple of steps. "Mrs. Bigelow, wait here. Please."

"Something's happened to him, hasn't it?"

Fred wrapped his arms around her again, and Grady relinquished her to him.

"Is he hurt? Tell me!"

Fred could only say, "I'm sorry."

Nancy's eyes widened and her face lost its color. "Is he dead?"

"I'm afraid so," Fred admitted.

"Adam!" she screamed and tried to tear herself away.

But this time he held on. He let her fight him until her energy flagged; he smoothed her hair and felt her tears wet the front of his shirt.

"Why?" she sobbed. "Why?"

But he had no answer. He could only hold her, and his heart twisted under the weight of her grief. Some sixth sense warned him this was only the beginning. She'd argued with her husband the night before he died, and she'd disappeared for hours after the murder. Fred knew Nancy well enough to know she couldn't have done it, but Enos wouldn't be so certain. If he didn't consider her a suspect now, he soon would. And Nancy would go through hell before this was all over.

four

When Enos charged out the front door a few seconds later, Fred struggled to keep his expression innocent. Enos might understand his reasoning, but he'd never willingly accept his decision to help Nancy. And after the two previous murder investigations Fred had been involved with, Enos would definitely be on guard. But that couldn't be helped. Fred would just have to find a way around him.

Enos reached them, obviously unhappy to see Fred out of his car but, to his credit, he didn't say a word about it. He reached one hand out to Nancy almost tenderly. "Are you all right? Should I call Doc to bring you a sedative or something?"

Nancy shook her head. "No. I don't want anything. I'm all right." But she had to struggle to hold herself together. "Will you tell me what happened?"

Enos studied her for a long moment, either trying to decide how straightforward to be or how much she already knew. "He was shot," he said at last. "At fairly close range."

Nancy's knees buckled and she sagged a little. "When?"

"Doc figures it was probably early morning. Two o'clock— maybe three."

"What was Adam doing here at that time of morning?" Fred asked.

"We don't know yet."

"Where did the bullet hit him?" Nancy whispered.

"In the back of the head."

"Do you think somebody broke in?"

Enos shook his head slowly. "No signs of forced entry. Looks like the murderer had a key or else Adam let him in."

Which told Fred the killer had to be someone Adam knew. A coworker, a friend—a family member.

Nancy's jaw worked as if she wanted to speak, but no sound came out.

Enos put an arm around her and gave her a gentle squeeze. "We'll find the person who did this, I promise."

She nodded, gulping back tears until she could speak again. "Do you have any idea who it was?"

"Not yet. It's still too soon. But I've got good men on it." He nodded toward a clump of undergrowth near the building, and Fred recognized Robert Alpers in the brush.

"Have you found the murder weapon yet?" he asked.

"Not yet. But if it's out there, we'll find it. All we know for certain is that the bullet came from a small-caliber weapon." Enos turned back to Nancy. "Do you feel up to answering a few questions for me?"

For Enos to push her now felt so intrusive, Fred wanted to protest, but he knew Enos wouldn't let arguments sway him.

"I'll just ask you a few questions," Enos promised. "Five minutes. Everything else can wait for a day or two."

She looked confused, grief-stricken, shocked. Fred hated to see her like this—so overwhelmed by Adam's death she couldn't take it all in. He leaned close and spoke so only she could hear. "You'll be all right. Go with Enos and answer his questions. Everything will work out."

She met his gaze uncertainly, but she finally managed a trembling smile before she turned back to Enos. "Okay. I guess."

Enos took her arm to help her over a patch of uneven ground. "Are the keys still in your car?"

Nancy nodded.

Enos gestured toward the Trooper. "Grady, pull Nancy's car into the parking lot and lock it up for her. And, Fred—go on home. We'll take care of her."

But Fred didn't intend to leave until Nancy was free to go. He trailed Enos for a couple of steps. "I don't mind waiting. I can give her a ride home when you're through."

"That's not necessary," Enos said without looking back.

He tried another tack. "I don't mind waiting a while longer to give you my statement."

Enos didn't look interested. If anything, he gripped Nancy's arm a little tighter. "I'm going to have to get your statement later."

"I don't mind waiting," Fred repeated.

Enos pivoted to face him, and the look on his face told Fred he meant business. "Well, I *do* mind. I want you out of here. Now. And don't try manipulating me into letting you stay."

"I'm not trying to manipulate anything," Fred protested.

Enos made a noise like a growl.

"Do you want me to wait, Nancy?"

Enos's face darkened. "Knock it off, Fred." Angry now, he pulled Nancy into step with him again.

And this time Fred didn't follow. But he watched until Enos and Nancy disappeared into the building.

He started back toward his car, wishing he could think of some way to stretch out the walk until Nancy reappeared. But anything he might do would only anger Enos further. He knew how far he could push Enos and still keep his friendship. And he knew he'd reached the limit. For now.

He crossed the parking lot, aware that the people in the little group by the building had begun to speculate on Nancy's sudden appearance. It seemed obvious to Fred that since Adam was murdered at work, the motive arose from work. And he hoped Enos had the good sense to recognize it.

Pausing midstep, he studied the Mustang on one side of his Buick, then the Celebrity, and he wondered whether either had belonged to Adam. And whether either contained any clue as to what had happened here last night.

He glanced around cautiously to make sure he hadn't attracted any attention before he headed to the Mustang and looked in the driver's side window. A light jacket that looked like the one Adam had worn the night before had been tossed across the passenger's seat, two pairs of men's shoes had been thrown onto the floor, and a duffel bag gaped open on the back seat. If it was Adam's car, it didn't appear likely to divulge any secrets. On the other hand, if it belonged to someone else—

He mulled over his options and possible ways of finding out when a woman's voice cut into his thoughts. "What in the hell do you think you're doing?"

He jerked back around to see Charlotte Isaacson marching across the parking lot toward him, and she didn't look happy.

Stepping away from the cars, he met her with a smile. "Morning, Charlotte."

She didn't return his greeting.

He let his smile fade. "I wonder if you know whose car this is."

She folded her arms across her chest and firmed up her stance. "Why?"

"I think one of the tires is a little low," he lied.

She looked at the tires and frowned back up at him. "They look fine to me."

He tried to look skeptical. "Well, they might be, but I probably ought to point it out to the owner—"

Her mouth tightened into an unhappy line. "Those tires are just fine."

"Is it your car?"

Her gaze slipped. "No."

He patted the car's side and looked meaningfully at the front tire. "Is it Adam's?"

"Does it matter?"

He didn't remember her as being such an unfriendly woman. "Only if the tires are a problem. Do you know who owns the white car over there?"

She smirked. "Why? Does it have a flat tire, too?"

"No. Do you know whose it is?"

The smirk slipped. "Why do you want to know?"

"I'm a curious old man."

She folded her arms a little tighter and glared at him, but after a long hesitation she said, "It's mine."

"Why are you parked clear over there? Who was in this spot when you got here this morning?"

Narrowing her eyes, she pulled back as if she needed

distance to see him clearly and shrugged one thin shoulder. "Nobody was parked here, and it wasn't a conscious decision on my part to park there."

"Nobody was parked here when you arrived?"

"No." She looked a little irritated with him. "Look, Mr. Vickery, when I got here this morning the building was locked and the parking lot was empty—except for Adam's car. I didn't see, hear, or smell anybody else around."

"So, you were the first one here?"

"Yes."

"What time did you arrive?"

"Just after seven-thirty."

That seemed awfully early to Fred. "What is it you do here?"

"I'm a chemist."

"You knew Adam fairly well, then?"

"We were good friends." Tears filled her eyes again and she tried in vain to blink them away.

"I'm sorry. I know this must be hard on you."

She didn't respond, only lowered her eyes.

"You must have a key to the building," he said when he figured enough time had passed for her to pull herself back together.

She jerked back up to face him. "Of course I do, but I'm not the only person with one."

"Who else has a key?"

Her scowl deepened and her eyes clouded. "You know, I don't think any of this is your concern."

Of course it was his concern. Anything that touched his family concerned him. But rapid footsteps behind them stopped Fred from responding.

Charlotte's dumpy companion joined them. A troubled look marred his features. "Are you okay, Char?"

She sent him a quick, reassuring smile. "Yes, thanks. Mr. Vickery's concerned about my car."

After studying Fred for a second, the man offered his hand. "Mitch Hancock. What's your connection with Adam?"

"Actually, I'm Nancy's uncle. Are you a friend of Adam's? Or a coworker?"

"Both, I guess. God, this is a horrible business. I can't believe it."

"So you work here, too?"

"Yep. In the lab with Charlotte. We're the ones who run the tests on the samples Adam collected." He turned back toward Charlotte and jerked his head toward the man in the suit. "I thought I'd better come and get you. It seems our friend's getting impatient again."

With a heavy sigh, she looked over her shoulder and when she faced them again, her eyes had grown cold. "I wish Roy'd shown up after the sheriff got here. They'd have sent him away, and *I* wouldn't have to entertain him."

Mitch shot a look toward the other man. "Well, I'm not going to make this easier on him. As far as I'm concerned—"

Charlotte touched her fingertips to his lips. "Yes, Mitch. I know. I'll do it." And with only a vague smile in Fred's direction she hurried away.

Fred expected Mitch to follow. Instead he stuffed his hands in his pockets and rocked back on his heels as he stared after her. "Poor thing. I don't know why she's taking Adam's death so hard."

"Had they worked together very long?"

"Longer than I've been here."

"And how long have you been here?"

"About two years."

Long enough to become close friends—or to grow to hate one another. Fred watched Charlotte reach the crowd, take their impatient friend by the arm, and steer him a few steps away from the others. "Who's that guy?" he asked.

"The black one? His name's Roy Dennington." The light died from Mitch's eyes, and his voice sounded flat and harsh.

"You don't like him?"

Mitch smiled, but it looked as if it cost him some effort. "I didn't say that."

"He doesn't work here?"

Mitch shook his head. "To tell the truth, I don't know

what the hell he's doing here. I had no idea Adam even
knew him."

"What does he do?"

"From what I hear, he's a big shot land developer out of
some place in the Midwest."

Fred's heart dropped. With miles of unspoiled forest and
a handful of clear mountain lakes surrounding them, the
threat of development always loomed in the background.
Fred hated the idea of losing the place he loved to
condominiums and ski runs, and a developer in the vicinity
could only mean trouble. "Has he been in the area long?"

"I don't know. I've seen his name around, but I'd never
actually met him until today."

"He hasn't said why he's here this morning?"

"Just that he had an appointment with Adam at eight."

"Is that unusual?"

"Well, yeah." Mitch nodded energetically. "We're supposed to be impartial in what we do. We're *never* supposed
to meet with a prospective purchaser. And to have an
appointment outside normal business hours— Well, it looks
bad, even if there wasn't anything going on."

"What time did you get here this morning?"

To Fred's surprise, Mitch laughed. "*Me*? A few minutes
before eight, I guess. I promised Adam I'd be here early to
get him the results of some samples I was testing, but—"
He leaned closer as if they'd suddenly become best friends.
"I spent the weekend with a lady friend of mine, and I had
a little trouble getting away this morning."

"When did Roy Dennington get here?"

"I don't know. Maybe five minutes after me. I know it
was early—we don't even open until nine. I think Charlotte
had already called the sheriff's department, but they hadn't
shown up yet." He stiffened suddenly at something he saw
over Fred's shoulder. "Oh, great. Looks like I'm going to be
in the hot seat now."

Fred turned around and saw Enos at the door with Nancy
at his side. He lifted his hand in a halfhearted wave, but
Enos just glared back.

Mitch gave an embarrassed laugh. "He's not going to be

happy with me for shooting my mouth off. He warned us not to talk about anything until he's questioned each of us."

"I don't remember you saying anything that he could find offensive."

Mitch smiled. "Let's both stick to that story," he said and walked away before Fred could respond.

Enos had already started toward them, bearing down on Fred like a heat-seeking missile. He passed Mitch on the way, but he was so busy glaring at Fred, he didn't even acknowledge the other man.

"I suppose you have a real good explanation for why you're still here," he said as soon as he got close.

"As a matter of fact—" Fred began.

"Spare me the excuses," Enos interrupted.

"I'll have you know, I didn't even approach those people," Fred snapped in self-defense. "I was getting in my car when Charlotte Isaacson came over here and talked to me."

Enos narrowed his eyes in suspicion, but he nodded slightly as a signal for Fred to go on.

"Then that guy—Mitch what's-his-name—came over to tell her Roy Dennington was getting restless, and we exchanged a couple of words. Before I knew it, you were standing there glaring at me as if I'd committed murder myself."

Enos looked a little sheepish. "Did anyone say anything interesting?"

Feeling a little better, Fred shook his head. "Not really. But I wondered if this car with all the clothes in it is Adam's, and I was trying to figure that out when Charlotte came up and accosted me."

"As a matter of fact, it is Adam's."

"Well? Have you looked at what's in there? Whether you can find some sort of clue?"

"No."

"Are you going to?"

"Fred—"

"You never know what you might find—"

Enos put on his long-suffering look and sighed heavily. "I

know my job, Fred. Now let me do it." He paused and looked back at Nancy. "Look, since you're still here, would you mind taking her home? I don't think she should drive herself."

"I'd be glad to."

"Thanks. But do her a favor. Don't badger her with questions on the way home. She's pretty shook up."

"Well, of course she is. I know that. I'd never *badger* her."

"Good. And don't get any ideas about getting involved in this one, Fred. I mean it."

Drawing himself up to his full height, Fred met Enos's gaze squarely. "You must think I have nothing better to do than to think of ways to irritate you."

"Oh, I know you better than that. You only get involved out of the best of intentions. But don't tell me you don't enjoy it. Just look at you—Adam hasn't been dead twelve hours, and here you are."

"For the record, I'm here because my family needs me, not because I think poking around in murder is fun." Fred reached for his door handle and whipped open the car door. "You know what I think? I think this job is warping you."

Enos chuckled. "That might be, but I still call the shots. And I don't want you involved. Period. Nothing more to discuss." He nodded toward the car. "Wait there. I'll go get Nancy, and then you can leave."

Fred slid behind the wheel and waited. He tried to pull his temper back under control, but the morning's events and Enos's accusations left him seething. Well, it didn't much matter what Enos said in the long run. He'd made up his mind, and he'd do whatever it took to keep Harriet and her family from suffering the way he and Douglas had. Period. Nothing more to discuss.

When Nancy opened the passenger door and climbed in beside him, he smiled his most reassuring smile. "How are you doing? Holding up okay?"

The smile she sent back trembled a little. "I guess so," she said softly, but her eyes filled with tears.

He patted her hand and started the engine. "Go ahead and

cry, sweetheart. I know how hard it is to hold yourself together at times like this, and you don't have to worry about it in front of me."

She nodded and leaned back against the car seat as he drove, and he left her alone for the first several miles. But he finally had to interrupt her thoughts to ask, "Do you want to go home or to your mom and dad's house?"

"Neither," she said quickly, then looked a little embarrassed. "I love my parents, you know that. But I can't stay with them right now. I'm just not sure I want to be alone, either."

"Maybe you should stay with them. Just for a few days."

But she shook her head firmly. "No. I can't."

"Then where do you want me to take you?"

She didn't answer for a long time, and when she finally did he could barely hear her. "I don't know."

He didn't want to push, but he couldn't just drive around aimlessly. "Do you want to talk about it?"

She shook her head and stared out the window. "I'm just tired, and I guess I'm in shock."

"Of course you are."

"And I wish I could turn back the clock."

"Because of the argument you had with Adam?"

She nodded. "He'll never know how much I loved him."

"He knows."

"No, he doesn't. The last time I saw him everything was so ugly. He doesn't know. He—" She broke off and began to cry in great, gulping sobs that shook her slender frame and broke Fred's heart. "Oh, Uncle Fred, it's all my fault."

He reached over and took her hand, and he squeezed it hard enough to be sure she felt him there. "Now you listen to me, Nancy. Adam's dead, but no matter what happened between the two of you last night, his death isn't your fault."

She didn't answer, but she didn't argue, either. Sighing softly, she squeezed his hand. "Now I remember why you're my favorite uncle."

"Flattery will get you anything you want," he said in an attempt to make her smile, if even for a moment.

"Really?"

"Absolutely."

She stared at him, as if trying to decide whether he was telling the truth. And then as if she'd decided to test him, "Can I stay with you?"

Surprised at her question, he glanced away from the road just long enough to see if she meant it as a joke. She didn't.

"I'd be delighted. You can stay as long as you want. But let's stop by and let your mom and dad know you're okay first."

"All right." She turned back to the window, more relaxed than he'd seen her all morning. "Thanks."

With a smile, he leaned back in his seat and watched the countryside roll by. Porter and Harriet could relax, knowing Nancy was with him. And he'd be close enough to sense any shift in the direction of Enos's investigation.

He couldn't have set it up more perfectly if he'd tried.

five

Fred reached out for the mug of coffee Harriet held, but instead of handing it to him, she slammed it onto the kitchen table and sent nearly half of it sloshing over the sides. "How could you do this to me?"

He had to jump quickly to avoid the hot liquid. "Do what?"

Harriet jerked her head toward the living room door through which Nancy and Porter had disappeared a few seconds earlier. "She needs to be here. With *me*. I'm her *mother*, for heaven's sake."

"I'm only trying to help. You *asked* me to help."

"*This* isn't what I wanted you to do."

"It's what Nancy wants."

Harriet's eyes narrowed and her face flushed dark red. "I don't believe that."

Obviously, he'd upset her, so he tried backpedaling. "All right. It's my fault. I offered to let her stay, and she seemed to like the idea." And he excused the half-truth in the interest of family harmony.

Harriet snorted as if he'd proved her point.

"I was concerned about how much rest she'd get here," he said and held up both hands to ward off her attack. "Not because of you and Porter, but . . . well, the neighbors. You know how people are."

Harriet pulled her head back and glared, but at least she didn't snap at him.

"I know you and Porter will do everything you can to keep people from bothering her, but she'd still hear the phone ring. Still hear the doorbell."

Harriet still didn't say anything, but she looked a little less ready to attack.

"I figured my place would be the next best thing to home. Nobody has to know she's there—except Enos, of course. But she'll be close enough for you to call her often, and she can call you. You can come down. She can drop in here—"

That seemed to help a little. Harriet lost some of her steam.

"And I know how you are, Harriet," Fred went on. "You're a proud woman. You don't like asking for help. Phoebe was exactly the same way. I admire that, but I didn't want that to prevent you from asking me when *you* decided Nancy needed a place to stay. If I jumped the gun a little, I'm sorry."

Shaking her head now, Harriet dropped into a chair. "No. You did the best thing." She laughed, but it came out brittle and embarrassed. "I shouldn't have fired back at you."

It seemed to Fred she'd fired first, but he didn't think he ought to point that out.

"We're all a little edgy, I guess," she said.

Fred grabbed a dishcloth from the sink and mopped up the spilled coffee. "It's all right."

She twisted her fingers together and studied them as if she'd never seen them that way before. "Oh, Fred— What's going to happen?"

"I don't know," he said, but he suspected things wouldn't get any easier for a little while.

"I just can't believe Adam's dead. Murdered! Who could have done such a thing?"

"I imagine Enos will find a few people with motives. Then he'll have to figure out which one actually did it."

Her head jerked up, and she looked at him as if he'd crawled out from under a rock. "No matter what you saw here last night, Adam was a good man."

"I know that. But even the best of us make other people angry. This time someone stepped over the line and acted on it. We just have to wait for Enos to figure out who it was."

"I can't wait."

"It's hard to do."

"I'll bet you waited patiently when Douglas was in trouble." She sounded sarcastic.

"It *was* hard," he repeated.

She laughed outright. "I can just imagine. Everybody knows you're the very soul of patience."

He tried not to take offense at that. He could be very patient when the occasion called for it. But he didn't like to wait when something needed to be done. And he didn't procrastinate.

Harriet covered his hand with hers. "I haven't thanked you."

"There's no need," he said and got ready to drop back into his seat. Standing at the table, he could see over the half curtains at the window, across the side yard and the long gravel drive to the highway. Before he could sit down, a dark-colored sports car caught his attention. It slowed on its way past the house and stopped on the shoulder of the road.

A second later, a tall young cowboy complete with hat and boots climbed out, glanced both ways, and jogged across the highway toward the house.

"Who's that?" Fred asked.

Harriet stretched to see. Scowling, she shook her head. "I don't know. I've never seen him before," she said and dashed outside without another word.

Fred followed her as quickly as his arthritic knees would let him, and they met the young man halfway up the drive. He looked about thirty-five. Slim. Handsome. Sandy hair and moustache.

"What do you want?" Harriet demanded.

"I came to see Nancy. Is she here?"

"Why?" Harriet's curt tone and frigid expression set the cowboy back a pace.

"I heard about her husband, and I wanted to pay my respects."

But his expression of sympathy didn't thaw Harriet. "I don't know who you are, do I?" she demanded.

"No, probably not." He smiled, but he didn't offer his name.

Fred didn't want to overstep his bounds—he was teetering on the edge of Harriet's good graces already—so he contented himself with watching and being ready to step in if Harriet needed him. If she didn't, he'd keep his mouth shut.

"Well, I'm sorry," Harriet said. "Nancy's resting and she can't be disturbed."

The young man hesitated for half a beat. "Then I'll just try to catch her later." He turned and walked away quickly, and Fred couldn't be sure if he was running from Harriet or just anxious to cross the street before another car came.

"Wait a minute," she called after him, but he pretended not to hear. She scowled darkly. "I don't like the looks of him."

Fred put an arm around her shoulder. "He looked like a nice young man. Must be a friend of Adam's and Nancy's." He tried to steer her back into the house, but she wouldn't budge until the cowboy had turned his car around and passed the house again.

As he drove by, Fred noticed Nancy framed in an upstairs window, and he could tell by the direction of the young man's glance that he'd seen her, too. That didn't disturb him. But the way Nancy raised one hand to the glass and followed the car with her gaze did.

When the cowboy disappeared from view, Harriet relaxed. And Fred tried to follow suit. He'd obviously started seeing things that didn't exist. His imagination must be working overtime.

But no matter what he told himself, he couldn't shake the uneasy feeling that there was more going on here than met the eye.

Fred quickstepped down his driveway to Lake Front and turned toward downtown Cutler. He'd left Nancy asleep in Margaret's old room and Douglas in front of the television. He'd told Douglas he needed coffee and a quiet spot to gather his thoughts. And he didn't intend to let anything stop him from getting both at the Bluebird Cafe.

The summer sun beat down through the tall pines, filling him with energy as he walked. Surrounded by the forest and the sounds of home, he could almost forget this latest horror.

He turned east on Main Street and followed the board-walk to the far end of town where the Bluebird had taken up a corner as long as Fred could remember. He'd been coming here almost every morning since he was a young man.

Then, he'd stopped in to refill his thermos with coffee as he tracked problems from one school building to the next throughout the district. Now, he occasionally got a decent cup of coffee—if Doc Huggins or Enos or Margaret weren't there. If they were, Lizzie Hatch gave him decaf.

Pushing open the front door, he wiped his feet on the mat and scanned the room for an empty table. Since it was lunchtime, every stool at the counter held someone, but Fred's favorite corner booth hadn't been claimed. He nodded to George Newman and Grandpa Jones, who took up the first two stools, and quickly crossed to his own table.

When Lizzie Hatch bought the Bluebird a few years back, she'd ripped down the ivy-twined wallpaper that had been there since the beginning of time and replaced it with posters of Elvis Presley at various stages of his career. Over time she'd built a collection of the King's records on the jukebox, and now it held so many Elvis hits, there wasn't room for much else. She allowed about five current hits, over which she retained rights of approval, a few country western songs, and a handful that appealed to Fred's generation—Frank Sinatra, Rosemary Clooney, and Bing Crosby.

Lizzie saw him come in and lifted the coffeepot in his direction, a silent signal that Doc had come and gone and Fred was free to enjoy real coffee. He smiled and turned over his cup, savoring the smell of something wonderful coming from the kitchen. Lizzie featured chicken-fried steak with country gravy as the special on Thursday. One of his favorites. Maybe he'd have lunch, too.

Lizzie brought the coffee, filled his cup, and set the coffeepot on the table. She pulled out her order pad as if she'd read his mind. "Busy morning, I hear."

Fred nodded. News always sped through town, but Lizzie

usually got early wind of the goings-on at the sheriff's office from her son Grady.

"Is Nancy okay?"

Fred took a bracing sip. "She's doing all right. It's rough on her."

Lizzie nodded as if she agreed it must be and poised her pen over the order pad. She liked having people around her, but she didn't waste much time talking. "You want the special." It wasn't a question.

"With mashed potatoes and ranch dressing on the salad. And extra gravy."

She scowled down at him. "You want Doc to come after me?"

Fred snorted. "You know what his problem is? He's got too much time on his hands. If he had a few more patients, he wouldn't have time to follow me around trying to make sure I'm following orders."

Lizzie stuck the pen behind her ear and slipped the order pad into her pocket before picking up the coffeepot. "Maybe so, but you can't change what is."

Fred watched her disappear into the kitchen. Whether she meant he couldn't change Doc or he couldn't change his health problems, he didn't think his chances of extra gravy looked promising.

He'd had a little trouble with his heart a year or so ago. Nothing serious. He was fine. But he couldn't convince Margaret of that, and together she and Doc had drawn the rest of the town into a conspiracy to keep Fred's eating habits under surveillance. They tried to limit his cholesterol, sodium, and caffeine. They tried making him count fat grams and fiber content, as if such things mattered.

Fred had never been one to get caught up in the latest eating fads. He believed some joker would write a book in a few years claiming everyone needed cholesterol, sodium, and caffeine to be healthy, and the whole blasted country would race around trying to ingest as much as they could. But Fred figured if a man ate the way God intended, he could forget all the other nonsense.

Someone dropped a few coins into the jukebox, and Elvis

came to life singing "All Shook Up" just as the door opened
and Enos stepped inside.

Fred watched out of the corner of his eye, as if by looking
away he could keep Enos from seeing him. He didn't want
a lecture on murder investigation etiquette, and he didn't
want a bunch of accusations and speculations flung at him.

He watched while Enos greeted George and Grandpa and
shook hands and patted shoulders as he worked his way into
the main dining area. And he knew when Enos spotted him.

Enos crossed the room quickly and slid onto the bench
across the table, removing his cowboy hat and laying it on
its crown on the table. "Mind if I join you?"

"Of course not." Fred fiddled with the menu in its holder
and took another sip of coffee.

Enos flipped over his cup, signaled Lizzie, who'd come
to the kitchen door, and wiped his face with one big palm.
Shadows rimmed his eyes, and his coloring didn't look
good. "What a morning."

"You look tired."

"That's putting it mildly."

Fred lowered his cup and wrapped his hands around it,
waiting for the bomb to drop.

But Enos didn't even look angry. Just tired. "Adam's
death really shook me up. He and Matt used to hang out
together when they were younger, you know."

Fred had forgotten how close Enos's youngest brother
and Adam had been.

"And Adam practically lived with us that year Matt
stayed with Jess and me—" Enos broke off and looked
away again, but Fred saw an unusual brightness in his eyes
and heard his voice catch.

"You doing all right?"

Enos slid down in the seat a little and toyed with his
empty cup. "Yeah. Fine. But I'm not looking forward to
calling Matt." As if changing the subject would dull the
pain, he looked up again. "How's Nancy? Did you get her
home okay?"

Fred hesitated. He didn't want to actually *lie*, but telling
the truth didn't seem like a real good idea.

Enos raised his eyebrows. "Fred? You did get Nancy home all right, didn't you?"

He tried avoiding the issue. "She was lying down when I left."

But Enos must have picked up on something that made him suspicious. "Where?"

Lizzie slid a salad plate in front of Fred and a tiny cup of salad dressing. Grateful for the reprieve, he dumped the dressing on the salad, sprinkled it liberally with salt and pepper, and dug up a forkful as Lizzie poured Enos's coffee.

"Where?" Enos demanded.

Fred chewed.

Enos sat bolt upright and leaned a little too close. "Tell me you didn't take her to your place."

Fred swallowed. "She asked if she could stay."

Enos's face reddened. "Good billy hell, Fred—"

"She didn't want to stay alone."

Enos groaned and rubbed his face with his palm again. "I knew you'd find a way to get involved."

"Now just a minute," Fred protested. "She asked if she could stay with me. She's my niece—how could I say no?"

Enos glared at him, but he didn't make a comment.

"You know," Fred pointed out quite reasonably. "All you have to do is find the murderer, and this won't be a problem anymore. Any ideas?"

Enos kept glaring.

Fred laid down his fork and held the younger man's gaze. "We've been friends a long time, son. We used to be able to talk about everything. I don't want that to change."

Enos softened a little, but he tried to look angry for a few minutes longer before he finally answered. "I don't have a clue. Everybody I talked to this morning swears they loved him. He had no money trouble, no business trouble . . ."

But he stopped there, and Fred's stomach tightened in an uncomfortable knot. "Which leaves family."

Enos tore open two sugar packets and poured them into his cup. "Yeah. Which leaves family."

"But surely you don't think Nancy did it."

"I don't want to, but you've got to admit it looks pretty bad for her."

"Why? Because Adam asked for a divorce? That's not a motive for murder."

Enos gulped a mouthful of coffee and swallowed loudly. "It might be. But it's because she claims she spent the night with a friend in Estes Park."

Fred snorted. "Now that *does* look suspicious."

"But we'd already gotten the friend's name from Harriet." He pulled out a pocket notebook and consulted his notes. "Lisa Hickerson. And we'd already talked to Ms. Hickerson before Nancy showed up this morning. She told us she hasn't seen Nancy for a couple of weeks."

"Oh." Fred lowered his fork and battled the sick feeling in the pit of his stomach.

"And then, of course, there's Porter. We know he and Adam fought. We know Adam left the Jorgensens' house alive. But we also know Porter disappeared for several hours last night."

"But not at three in the morning."

"We don't know that. Harriet didn't hear him come in."

Fred's appetite evaporated, and he dropped his fork onto the table. "So you're looking at the family?"

"I have to, Fred. I'm sorry. I don't *want* it to be Nancy. Or Porter. And I hope we find something else soon. But if it *was* one of them, I won't hesitate to do my job."

"I wouldn't expect anything else." Fred's voice came out sounding small and tired, and unconvincing.

"Let's just hope something comes up when I talk to Charlotte again. Or Mitch. Or Roy Dennington."

Fred hoped. "What did that Dennington fellow want with Adam?"

Enos shrugged and drained his cup. "I'm checking on him. All I know is he's in property development." Signaling Lizzie for a refill, he pulled himself up into the seat a little straighter.

"So why did he want to see Adam?"

"I don't know. Yet."

Fred picked up his fork and stirred his salad. "Seems odd

you haven't heard about any trouble up at EnviroSampl.
Seems to me that's where you should be looking."

Enos's mouth tightened into a thin smile. "I *am* looking.
Don't worry." He drained his second cup and lowered it to
the table. "Well, I guess I can't sit around here all afternoon,
no matter how much I might want to. Give my best to
Nancy, will you? And Douglas." As he stood and worked
his hat into place, his face took on the soft expression it
reserved for Margaret. "And say hello to Maggie next time
you talk to her."

Fred nodded absently and watched Enos walk away as the
jukebox Elvis began to sing "I Can't Stop Loving You."

No matter what Enos thought, there had to be something
wrong at EnviroSampl. Nancy didn't kill Adam, and neither
did Porter. The murderer had to be someone connected to
him in some other way.

He told himself not to worry. Enos was good at what he
did. Competent, thorough, and ethical. He'd examine every
aspect of Adam Bigelow's life and his death, and he'd find
the murderer somewhere among the people he knew.

Just then, Lizzie interrupted his thoughts to deliver a
steaming plate of food smothered in gravy. It smelled
delicious, and Fred struggled to work up his appetite again
as he watched Enos cross the street and climb into the cab
of his truck.

Nancy was already devastated by Adam's death, but if
Enos came to arrest her, she'd be a whole lot worse off.
After lunch, Fred would get her to talk about Adam. He had
to know about the man and his work, and about the people
he worked with. Because there had to be something about
Adam's business Fred could use to point Enos in the right
direction.

six

Fred hurried down Main Street on his way home, mulling over the kinds of questions he wanted to ask Nancy. About Adam's business, his recent disappointments, triumphs, rivalries, arguments. About friendships turned sour or those recently developed. Anything that might be relevant.

She'd resist him pushing her to talk about it. But he couldn't let Enos keep going in the direction he'd started. Not when it led straight toward the family.

He passed the shoe repair shop and crossed Ash Street and wondered if he ought to pay a visit to some of Adam's coworkers. Maybe Charlotte Isaacson or that Mitch person. They might know a thing or two about Adam's life and if he had acted differently in the last few weeks.

Trouble was, Fred couldn't figure who'd want to kill Adam. He'd been a hardworking young man with a kind word for everyone. That's why his explosive behavior last night had been so surprising.

He passed the Copper Penny Lounge with its jukebox playing too loud in the middle of the day. Albán Toth, the Copper Penny's owner, must not be inside, or he'd never let them turn the music up like that. He must have gone out to the Four Seasons on Winter Lake to handle the lunch crowd.

But Webb would be inside. As usual. Fred tried to push aside the surge of resentment that always came when he thought of his own son-in-law. If they'd found Webb with a bullet through his head, Fred might have understood it. Webb spent more time at the Copper Penny than he did at home. He dropped in for lunch most days, and after work every day. And he spent the time telling stories—all of them somewhat entertaining and mildly amusing.

But Webb belonged at home, helping Margaret with their three children, fixing things around the house. Telling his stories to his wife and children, for crying out loud—

Fred pulled back on his temper and hurried past. It didn't do a bit of good to think about it, and even less to talk about it. Margaret would ignore his opinion. She always had.

Had Adam been more like Webb, Fred might have better understood his outburst last night. But Adam had never been one to let anger get the better of him. So what had happened between him and Nancy that pushed him so far? Fred knew he'd have to ask Nancy what was wrong between them, but he didn't look forward to it.

He trudged to the corner and stepped off the boardwalk to cross the street. But when he caught a glimpse of Janice Lacey sweeping the boardwalk in front of Lacey's General Store on the next block, he stopped. Of all the people to run into right now, Janice had to be the worst. Her sources of gossip worked faster than any other in town, and he had no doubt she already knew about Adam's murder. Worse, she'd be anxious to sniff out the details from anyone she ran into.

Well, she wouldn't get anything from him. Ducking around the corner quickly, he started toward the next block and hoped Janice hadn't seen him.

But before he'd gone a dozen steps he heard her running to catch up with him. "Fred? Yoo-hoo, Fred."

He pushed his knees to move faster and scanned the street for possible escape routes or hiding places. But he came up empty. He considered the auto repair shop. But he'd scolded Tito Romero last month for insisting Fred's brakes were in good working order, and Tito had been a little standoffish ever since.

He gauged the distance to the hardware store. But with this blasted arthritis, he'd never make it before Janice caught him.

Her rapid footsteps echoed on the Main Street boardwalk, and a second later she rounded the corner. Her short gray curls bobbed in the sunlight, her eyes glittered with the thrill of the chase, and her nose practically twitched with excitement.

She waved one hand in the air as if he might miss her. "Fred, wait. Please!"

Suppressing a groan, he waited. And he tried not to look as annoyed as he felt. "What is it?"

She reached his side and grabbed his arm to keep him from escaping while she struggled to catch her breath. She took several seconds to pull herself together before she gasped, "I heard the most distressing thing this morning. Tell me, is it true?"

"Is what true?"

"That Adam Bigelow was shot to death? Right in his own office?"

Fred wished he could deny it, just to keep her from spreading gossip, but he knew it wouldn't do any good. "Yes, it's true."

Janice clapped her free hand to her ample breast, but she clutched his arm tighter with the other hand, and her eyes widened in horror. "Oh, my goodness," she breathed. "I just can't believe it."

But she wanted to. Fred could see that.

"When Sophie Van Dyke called, I practically accused her of lying."

Sophie Van Dyke? How in the world had *she* heard already?

Janice fanned her hand in front of her face as if it would help. "What is the world coming to?"

Shaking his head, Fred kept his face solemn. Janice echoed his sentiments exactly, but he made it a habit not to agree with her out loud if he could help it.

"So? What's Enos doing about it?"

"Investigating."

"Does he know who did it?" she prodded.

"I don't know."

She narrowed her eyes and flicked her gaze at him as if she didn't believe him. "Come on, Fred. Everybody knows you've got an inside track into these things. Are you helping out again?"

"I've never helped out in the past," he insisted and tried to draw his arm away.

She winked, the merest blink of one eye. "Oh, of course not. I forgot. But who do you think did it?"

"I couldn't say."

"But you *do* have an idea, don't you?"

"I don't have a clue."

She frowned at him, and disbelief radiated from her.

He didn't argue. Janice always thought what she wanted without regard for fact. But he hoped she'd lose interest if he didn't fuel her curiosity.

He should have known better.

"I swear," Janice said after a long moment. "It's getting so a person's not safe anywhere. As soon as we heard about Adam, I told Bill I don't want him working late in the store anymore. You never know what might happen. Why, *he* could be next!"

"I really don't think we're dealing with a lunatic who's preying on people who work overtime, Janice."

She glared at him. "Do you know who did it?"

"No."

"Then how do you know Bill isn't in danger? How do you know we're not *all* in danger?"

"It is a worry," Fred conceded.

Janice sniffed, dissatisfied with his response but apparently ready to shift the conversation anyway. "How's Nancy taking it?"

"Hard."

"That poor girl. I just can't imagine what I'd do in her situation."

Fred couldn't imagine what Janice would be like without Bill to rein her in from time to time.

"How are Harriet and Porter taking all this?" Janice asked.

"It's hard on everybody. This sort of thing always is." He tugged his arm, and this time he managed to pull away from her grasp. "I need to get home. Say hello to Bill for me, won't you?"

He took a few steps away, but she trotted after him again.

"I admire you, Fred. You're certainly holding up well. I can't even imagine what I'd do if this sort of thing happened in *my* family."

Now, what in tarnation did she mean by that?

She tried to look innocent, as if her remark had been unintentional. "It's so strange that you get involved in these horrible, horrible things. I mean, two murders in such a short time, and both of them involving your family! And then there were the Cavanaughs—"

He tried to frame an appropriate response, but nothing sounded right. This new turn had the makings of some ugly gossip, and he didn't want to let it go unchecked.

"Some people are like that, you know," she insisted. "Some people attract evil. I've read about it somewhere."

As if that made it true.

Perking up at some idea that had just crossed her mind, Janice tugged at his arm. "You know what you need to do, Fred? Let Summer read your palm. Or she could read the cards for you."

Fred muffled a groan. Summer Day ran a New Age bookstore and art gallery a block or two down Main Street. She claimed to be psychic, but Fred thought it was a lot of nonsense. And he had no intention of letting her look at his palm—or at anything else, for that matter.

But Janice didn't seem to notice his hesitation. "I've been to her twice," she confessed in a near whisper. "You'd be amazed at how accurate she is. I mean, she told me things about my past you wouldn't believe."

Fred held back a laugh. Summer had lived in Cutler for fifteen years; Janice had been here all her life. Telling Janice about her past wasn't any great trick.

But Janice cupped her hand and shoved it under his nose as proof. "This is the valley of tears." She pointed at a spot where her hand creased into tiny lines. "All the heartache, all the troubles I've had—can you see them there?"

Fred could see a few age lines and some blue ink.

"And this—see how long my life line is? And that little glitch in the line right there? That's where Bill's going to die. I'm going to bury him."

"She told you *that*?"

Janice nodded and shoved her hand closer. "And right here? See those lines? That's where my kids were born. See? One, two, three. And she can see from my palm what sex they are, how old—"

Now *there* was a trick. Especially since her kids all lived within a fifty-mile radius. Fred stared at her, trying to decide whether she really believed all this nonsense or whether she was trying to set him up for something. But she looked absolutely sincere.

She uncupped her hand and lowered it to her side. "Anyway, Summer can tell you some pretty amazing things. You really ought to have her look at your hand and see if she can tell whether you attract violence or something—"

"Not interested."

"—or whether there's something you can do to avoid it."

Fred figured it was time to put a stop to that nonsense right now. "Listen, Janice, Cutler's a small place, and I've lived here for seventy-three years. I'm connected to darned near everybody around, and I don't need Summer or her mystical mumbo jumbo to tell me that."

Janice glared at him. "You are the most closed-minded man I've ever met."

"Thank you." He took a step away.

"Turning your back on someone who could provide you direction. Why, if Bill had an attitude like yours—"

Fred turned back to her. "Are you telling me Bill approves of this?"

Her face froze in disapproving lines. "I don't need Bill's permission. I work as hard as he does—harder, if the truth be told. And I have as much right to spend money on palm reading as he does on his ridiculous fly fishing."

"I can't argue with that."

His answer seemed to mollify her, and she thawed a little. "If you don't want Summer's help, I guess there's nothing I can do. Tell me, are any of Nancy's brothers coming home for the funeral?"

She flipped gears so quickly, Fred had to struggle to catch up. He didn't want to discuss family business, but refusing would only spark her overactive imagination. "I don't think anybody's even thought about a funeral yet."

"No, I suppose you're right." She dabbed the corner of her apron to her eyes. "You tell Nancy how concerned I am. And when it comes to planning the funeral, you tell her I'll be glad to help in any way I can."

He had no doubt of it.

Janice sniffed to prove how bad she felt. "That poor girl. This is going to be awfully rough on her. You know how people talk." She sent him a sideways glance. "Did I see her in the car with you a little bit ago?"

Fred nearly groaned aloud. "You might have, I guess."

"So she's staying with you?"

He tried hard not to move a muscle in response.

But her nose twitched as if she'd just smelled a morsel of gossip. "Well, I think that's wonderful. At least she'll be away from the gossip a little."

"That's what I'm hoping," Fred said, but he didn't hold out much hope now that Janice knew where to find her.

She lowered her voice and leaned closer as if she had a huge secret to share. "I'll tell you the thing that worries me. Sophie Van Dyke's sister, Louise, lives up in Mountain Home—you remember Louise, don't you? And you *know* how Sophie talks."

Fred knew that Sophie Van Dyke received regular updates from Janice. And he supposed she'd pass on whatever she heard to her sister.

Janice sighed as if she carried the weight of the world on her shoulders. "And after everything else poor Nancy's been through . . ."

Fred held his gaze steady, but she'd definitely caught him off guard with that one. What else *had* Nancy been through? He wanted to ask, but admitting he didn't know would be a terrible mistake. Janice would feed off that for weeks.

"Life's rough," he agreed. "I guess some of us have a worse time than others."

"Oh, my. Yes. The things I've heard over the years—" She bobbed her head in agreement with herself. "Owning the store puts us in a position of trust, you know. Almost like clergy. People tell us their problems all the time."

If they did, they made a big mistake. "Nancy *has* had a bad time of it," he agreed, still without a clue.

"Well, both of them had, poor dears," Janice said with a sniff. "I tell you, it's a sad thing to see a young couple go through so much."

"It is sad."

"And I shudder to *think* what Sophie will say about all that trouble they had. It'll be so hard on Nancy to rehash all her old heartache on top of this new—"

In spite of himself, he started to ask. "What—?"

"—but I promise you, if I hear a *word* about that old trouble, I'll nip it in the bud."

"But I—" Fred began, then broke off and bit back his question. "I'm sure Nancy will appreciate it."

"Well, of course she will. Why, I told Sophie this morning not to even think about bringing all that old stuff up."

This time Fred couldn't stop himself. "Just what is Sophie rehashing?"

Janice gaped at him. "*You* know. All that trouble they had a few years ago. You *did* know about it, didn't you?"

"Of course," he said. But if Phoebe'd ever told him anything about Nancy and Adam, it had gone in one ear and out the other.

"Well, then, don't you worry." Janice flashed a smile and glanced at her watch. "Goodness, I've been gone forever! I'd better get back, or Bill will be wondering where I ran off to." She took three steps away from him and looked back over her shoulder. "You will give your poor niece my regards, won't you?"

"Yes, of course."

She wagged her finger at him. "And don't you let Sophie Van Dyke get within a mile of her. I tell you, it's shameful the way that woman talks."

"I'll be careful."

Janice studied him silently for half a second before she turned away again. He watched her go and waited until she'd rounded the corner before he started toward home again. He breathed a sigh of relief that the interrogation was over, but he couldn't tamp down the curiosity about whatever it was Janice knew that he didn't. And he couldn't help but wonder whether it had anything to do with Adam's murder.

seven

By the time Fred reached home, the August sun had peaked high overhead. With the day hotter than usual, he'd worked up a bit of a sweat, and a pitcher of ice-cold lemonade sounded mighty tempting.

He turned into the driveway and stopped midstride. Margaret's Chevy stood smack-dab in the middle of the drive. Well, he wasn't surprised. In fact, he'd have been surprised if she *hadn't* rushed over the minute she heard about Adam's death. And he felt better knowing Nancy had Margaret with her.

He hurried across the deep front lawn, half expecting to hear laughter before he reached the front porch. Whenever Margaret and Nancy got together, there'd inevitably be laughter, and lots of it. But not today. Today cold silence greeted him as he opened the front door.

The women sat side by side on the couch, heads together— Margaret's dark and Nancy's light. Even with the difference in their ages, the resemblance between the two left no doubt they were related. They spoke too softly for Fred to hear, and both women started in surprise when he walked in.

Margaret worked up a smile, but her eyes reflected the pain she felt for her cousin. "Hi, Dad."

"Hi, sweetheart." He crossed the room, pressed a kiss to the top of Margaret's head and squeezed Nancy's shoulder. "Is everything okay?"

Nancy looked up with dull, lifeless eyes, as if she were still numb, but Margaret nodded and said, "Everything's fine. Where've you been?"

"The Bluebird." Fred settled into his rocking chair and

propped his feet on the footstool his son Jeffrey had sent for his last birthday.

Margaret rolled her eyes. "That figures."

"Enos was there," he said.

Even the mention of Enos's name made Margaret straighten her posture. They'd dated all through high school, and Fred had expected they'd marry when they reached an age for that sort of thing. But then Webster Templeton came along and swept Margaret off her feet. And Enos had countered by marrying Jessica Rich within months. But a spark still burned between them. You only had to watch one when the other entered the room to see it.

Margaret worked at not looking overly interested. "What did he have to say?"

"It's not good news," Fred warned.

Nancy shot Margaret a worried look. Margaret responded with a supportive nudge, and they faced Fred, ready to hear it.

"He said that Nancy and Porter are his main suspects."

"What?" Nancy's face lost its color.

And Margaret's face picked it up. "You've got to be kidding."

Fred only wished he were. "Apparently, nobody else admits to having any trouble with Adam. And evidently everything at the office was rosy."

"I don't believe it," Margaret said. "Is Enos out of his mind?"

"He's going on what he's been told so far."

"He's out of his mind," Margaret decided.

Nancy's fingers trembled in her lap. "He thinks *I* did it?"

"Either you or your dad." Fred hated to be so harsh, but they couldn't afford to waste time dancing around the truth.

"Is he planning to arrest me?"

"Not yet."

"He's out of his mind," Margaret insisted.

Nancy's eyes filled with tears, and she looked hopeless.

Holding her gaze, Fred leaned toward her. "I'm hoping it won't come to that, but it's going to be up to you. Where were you last night?"

"With my friend Lisa."

Fred shook his head. "No. They've already checked with her—"

"I asked her not to tell anyone where I was." She looked away, and Fred suspected she wasn't telling the complete truth.

"Why?"

"I thought Adam might call." Her voice came out clipped and stubborn.

"But why didn't she tell the sheriff the truth?"

"She promised she wouldn't tell anyone."

"Still, it seems to me—" Fred began.

"She promised," Nancy snapped, and when she folded her arms across her chest and clenched her jaw, Fred knew she wouldn't say another word about it.

He bit back a sigh and decided to abandon that line of questioning for now. "All right. Tell me everything you know about Adam's business."

Margaret looked suspicious. "Why?"

"So we can prove to Enos those people aren't telling the truth."

Nancy didn't respond at first, but after a long moment she said, "I don't know anything."

"*Think*," Fred urged. "We can't let you or your dad end up in jail."

Margaret looked shocked, as if he'd accused Nancy of murder himself. "You don't think it'll really come to that, do you?"

"Yes, I do."

"Surely—"

"Do you remember what happened with Douglas?" Fred argued. "How convinced we all were that nobody in their right mind could ever believe him capable of murder?"

Margaret nodded slowly. "Yes, but—"

"And do you remember the night they came to arrest him?"

She nodded again, and this time she didn't say a word.

"Good. Then let's get started." Fred looked back at Nancy. "Now, what was Adam working on?"

Without even taking the time to consider, Nancy shook her head. "I don't know."

"Stop and think a minute," Fred urged. "He must have said something to you."

"He never discussed his work with me."

Fred scooted to the edge of his chair and leaned a little closer. "Think about him coming home in the evenings. He comes in the front door and says—"

"He *never* discussed his work with me," she insisted.

Fred had trouble believing that, but if she didn't think Adam had discussed his work, she'd never remember anything. So they'd try another tack. "All right. Tell me about Adam's relationships with the people at work. Start with Charlotte Isaacson."

Nancy looked a little surprised. "With Charlotte? They're friends. They've known each other forever."

Fred waited for her to go on. When she didn't, he leaned forward another notch. "Tell me about it."

"They're friends. They worked together. She bought him lunch on his birthday and he always gave her something for Christmas. But I wasn't there. I don't know anything else."

He drew in a deep breath and tried to keep his voice level. "Did Adam ever talk about her? You know, tell you things she'd said or fill you in on what they'd talked about?"

Nancy stared at him. "No."

"Do you like her?" Margaret asked.

Nancy shrugged. "I don't really know her, but I guess she's all right."

"She wasn't a friend of the family?" Fred asked.

"No."

"Any special reason why not?"

"We just never got to know each other. I only spoke to her once or twice."

Margaret looked puzzled. "How long did she and Adam work together?"

"Six years. Maybe seven. They met when they worked at a lab in Boulder. Then when EnviroSampl opened, they both got jobs up here."

Fred hated to ask the next question, but he had to know.

"Did you ever wonder whether there was anything between them?"

Nancy's eyes widened, but instead of the reaction Fred expected, she laughed. "Adam and Charlotte? Heavens, no. Why do you ask that?"

"She looked pretty broken up today. Maybe a little *too* upset."

Nancy didn't let the suggestion upset her. "She wasn't his type any more than he was hers. Charlotte was too strong for him. He didn't like pushy women, and he definitely thought Charlotte was pushy. Besides, Adam would *never* have cheated on me."

Fred thought her certainty was a little naive, but he didn't say anything.

"Did they ever argue?" Margaret asked.

"Not that I know of."

"But if he thought she was too pushy—" Fred began, then stopped and shook his head in confusion.

"He *liked* her strength in business, but he didn't find it personally attractive," Nancy explained. "Besides, she had a steady stream of boyfriends, and I know Adam didn't especially like the current one."

Margaret sent a triumphant glance in Fred's direction. "Did he tell you that?"

Nancy shrugged as if she didn't remember. "I sometimes overheard them on the phone."

Now they were getting somewhere. "What kinds of things did they say?"

"I don't know. I remember Adam telling her she was getting in over her head."

Margaret looked excited. "What else?"

"He said she sure knew how to pick 'em, but he sounded sarcastic."

Fred waited for her to elaborate.

She didn't.

"That's it?" he pressed. Didn't she understand he was on her side?

Nancy shrugged. "I can't think of anything else."

"Just take your time," he urged.

But she shook her head and looked a little unhappy with him. "No, nothing."

"What about Mitch Hancock? Did Adam ever talk about him?"

"I've heard the name. He works at EnviroSampl, doesn't he?"

"He's another of the chemists there. What did Adam say about him?"

"Nothing specific."

That didn't help. He tried another name. "What about Roy Dennington?"

"Never heard of him."

Agitated, Fred pushed to his feet. "Did Adam ever argue with anyone at work? Did he come home angry or upset— especially recently?"

Nancy pressed her fingertips to her forehead. "I don't know."

Fred shot a glance at Margaret. At least she looked as confused as he felt.

She reached for Nancy's hands and gripped them tightly. "Nancy, Enos thinks maybe *you* killed Adam. Or that Uncle Porter did. Please, think harder."

Nancy's eyes puddled with tears, and she blinked furiously for several seconds before she pulled her hands away. "Look, I don't know *anything*. Adam and I were falling apart. We never talked anymore, and things were really bad the last few months."

Fred tried not to groan aloud. If Nancy's marriage had been falling apart over time, it would make her motive look stronger than it already did.

Margaret didn't seem to accept Nancy's answer. She'd been struggling with her own marriage for too many years. "Listen, Nancy, I know how hard it is to communicate when things are strained, but even under those circumstances people say things. Little things. I'm sure if you think harder, you'll remember—"

Nancy shot to her feet. "I *don't* know. I don't know what was going on at the office or what he was working on. I have no idea whether or not he fought with anyone. If you want to know what was going on at EnviroSampl, you're going to have to ask someone else."

"So he *never* discussed his work with you?" Fred asked, more to sum up the little bit of information Nancy had provided than to dig for more. But she didn't hear it that way.

"He never discussed the time of day with me." She took a couple of jerky steps away. "He hadn't even been living at home for the past few weeks. Before that, we hardly ever saw each other. And when he did, we fought. And telling Enos *that* isn't going to help me or my dad."

Her words faded into stunned silence. Fred met Margaret's surprised gaze and struggled to take it all in. "You mean you were separated?"

Nancy looked down at her fingers and her shoulders drooped. "Yes."

Well, for Pete's sake. "I take it your mom and dad don't know."

"No." She spoke so softly Fred almost couldn't hear her.

"Why didn't you tell them?"

"It was a trial separation. I didn't want to upset them unless I had to."

Margaret nodded as if she understood Nancy's reasoning. "It would have upset them, I'm sure, but it's a terrible burden for you to carry alone."

"I thought we'd work things out," Nancy said. "At least we weren't fighting as much."

"What did you fight about?" Fred asked.

"Nothing. Everything. We fought about the weather, about the way the living room was arranged. We fought about what I fixed for dinner and how much money I spent on a can of tuna. We just fought."

Margaret left her seat and crossed to Nancy's side. She wrapped her arms around her cousin and let her collapse against her. "I'm so sorry," she whispered.

Fred dropped into the rocking chair and stared at Nancy's back. No wonder she didn't want to stay with Harriet and Porter. But how did she hope to keep it secret from them now?

"You're going to have to tell them," Margaret said.

"Why? It'll just upset Mom and make Dad mad. What good will it do to tell them now?"

"If you and Adam weren't living together, Enos needs to know that," Margaret insisted. "And you don't want your parents to find out about it from somebody else."

Fred nodded his agreement. "Where was Adam staying?"

Nancy pulled in a steadying breath. "At the office until we decided what to do. They have a couch and a shower in one of the back rooms. He came home every few days for clean clothes."

Fred's stomach tightened. "Who else knew about this?"

"I don't know. I told a couple of my friends, but I have no idea who Adam told."

Margaret frowned at Fred. "What are you thinking? That whoever killed Adam knew he was staying in the office?"

He rubbed his chin. "Seems likely, doesn't it? They'd sure know where to find him at two in the morning."

Enlightenment dawned in Nancy's eyes. "Somebody he worked with?"

"I think so," Fred said.

Releasing Nancy, Margaret headed for the phone. "We've got to tell Enos about this."

But Nancy cried out and raced after her. "No, please. Not until I explain everything to my parents."

With her hand hovering over the receiver, Margaret glanced at Fred as if asking him what she should do. Now that was a switch. He nodded almost imperceptibly, and she lifted her hand to Nancy's shoulder.

"All right," she said. "But we can't keep this from Enos for long."

Nancy worked up a thin smile. "I know. And I promise I'll tell them tomorrow."

"Good." Fred set his rocker in motion again. But he didn't feel any better. Whoever killed Adam must have known he was staying at the office. But so far they only knew of one person who'd been aware of Adam's arrangement: Nancy. Porter didn't even know. And Fred didn't want to take this news to Enos unless he had at least one other name to go with it. Someone else who knew about Adam's living arrangements.

Margaret said something to Nancy and led her toward the kitchen, but at the door she paused and looked back over her shoulder. "You want a cup of herbal tea, Dad?"

In an effort to wean him from coffee, she'd brought him enough herb tea to supply an army. Raspberry, lemon, orange—every flavor imaginable. His cupboard looked like a blasted fruit basket inside. He'd tried a cup once to keep her happy, and he'd actually managed to choke down about half a cup of the vile stuff. But he hadn't made himself try it again, and he didn't intend to torture himself today.

He made a face and shook his head. "I'll pass."

Margaret made a face back and disappeared into the kitchen.

He watched her go and tried to relax a little. But if he hoped to keep Nancy out of jail, he had to know what was going on at EnviroSampl. She might not be able to tell him, but somebody could.

Charlotte Isaacson could.

He slowed the rocker and smiled to himself. She might not want to talk to him, but if he could get her alone for just a few minutes, he knew he could find something that would help.

If Margaret suspected he felt this way, she'd try to stop him. She might be willing to let him discuss the murder with Nancy, but she'd draw the line at him talking to anyone else.

But Margaret didn't understand how it felt to watch a child suffer—her own children were still too young. And Margaret had blind faith in Enos. So Fred would just make certain Margaret didn't suspect his intentions. He'd wait until tomorrow and pay a visit to Charlotte first thing in the morning.

eight

Fred walked as quickly as he dared around Spirit Lake the next morning. He followed the path from home, around the southern tip of the lake, past Summer Dey's still-dark cabin, and up the western shoreline to Doc Huggins's place before he turned around and headed back. He wouldn't dream of starting his day without his morning constitutional, but he wanted to head out in search of Charlotte Isaacson before anybody had a chance to stop him.

His feet kicked up dust, and his mind churned as he walked. Though it was still early, the temperature had already started to climb above normal. It would be another scorcher today. Another in a long line of hot, dry days in a drought year. They needed rain desperately. As desperately as he needed to learn something about Adam's death that *wouldn't* make it look as if Nancy had killed him.

He'd spent a sleepless night thinking about the murder, and his determination to help Nancy had grown with every hour that passed. It obsessed him now, to use Margaret's word for his ability to focus on a problem. He couldn't think of much else.

When he passed Summer Dey's cabin on the way back, he noticed a light in the kitchen window. He remembered Janice Lacey's willing acceptance of Summer's nonsense and shuddered. If Summer saw him out here, she'd waylay him; she'd done it before. She'd rattle on about Adam's aura or some such nonsense. She'd say that she'd seen death around him for weeks before the murder, and she'd jabber about how Adam had to die to pay a debt to a past life. Fred had heard it all before, but he didn't want to hear it today. It was nothing but hogwash.

He rushed past the open spot behind her cabin and kept going until the back deck of his own house came into view again. There he ducked off the trail and stole through the trees until he reached the side door of the garage.

He didn't expect Margaret for at least another half hour, and Douglas probably wasn't even awake yet, but Fred didn't want to risk running into either of them. Or Nancy. He didn't want to explain what he had in mind.

He lifted the garage door with as little noise as he could manage, and as he slipped behind the wheel of his Buick he fit the key into the ignition. It came to life quickly, quietly, and Fred once again acknowledged the wisdom of starting the engine three times a week to keep it in shape, whether he drove the car or not.

He backed onto Lake Front and sped away without even bothering to lower the garage door. He didn't usually leave it wide open, but he couldn't take the chance of disturbing Douglas and Nancy with it a second time.

Driving a little faster than usual, he made the trip to Mountain Home in just under an hour. At the first stop sign, he fished a deposit slip from his shirt pocket and double-checked the notation he'd jotted on the back. 392 Twin Creek Drive. The telephone directory said C. Isaacson lived there.

He found Twin Creek Drive at the edge of town and followed the winding street into the dense forest for about half a mile before he passed a mailbox with number 392 painted on the side. The forest closed in upon the property and made it impossible to see the house from the street, so he drove a little past the mailbox and parked on the shoulder of the road.

Hoping he'd found the right place, he walked back and peered down the shaded drive. But he still couldn't see anything.

He followed the gravel drive for several feet before he spotted Charlotte Isaacson's white Celebrity in front of the house. Well, good. He'd found the right place.

Blinds still blocked the windows, and the house looked asleep, but that suited his purpose. He wanted to catch Charlotte off guard. He'd hoped to get here before she left for work because he wanted to talk to her away from the office, where she might hesitate to tell him what he wanted to know. Away from the scene of the murder where she might be uncomfortable.

He climbed two narrow wooden steps, perched on a tiny front porch, and knocked on the door. Surprisingly, several seconds passed without an answer. Maybe she hadn't heard him. He rang the bell this time and waited. She must be inside.

A minute or so later he rang once more. He'd just about given up hope when the door creaked open, and half of Charlotte's thin face peeked out at him. "Yes? What do you want?"

Not a very friendly greeting, but he smiled anyway. "Good morning, Charlotte."

Recognition dawned in the one dark brown eye he could see. "Mr. Vickery? What are you doing here?"

"I wondered if I could talk to you for a minute."

A lengthy pause followed before the door creaked open another inch or two. "I guess so. Why?"

"I need to ask you a couple of questions."

"What about? My tires?" She smiled as if she'd made a joke.

"No. Do you mind if I come in?"

She hesitated so long he thought she'd refuse, but she finally pulled the door open the rest of the way and stepped aside to let him enter. "I guess not."

She wore a white terry cloth bathrobe and, he suspected, not much else beneath it. It didn't look as if she intended to go anywhere for a while. Padding on bare feet across the hardwood floor, she led him into a wide living room with gleaming wood everywhere and furniture in every shade of off-white imaginable.

She dropped gracefully into an off-white chair and gestured toward the off-white couch. Tucking a bookmark into an open paperback, she slid it onto the table beside her and retrieved a mug with both hands. "All right. What can I do for you?"

Fred lowered himself onto the couch and sank so far into the cushions he wondered if he'd ever get out. But he tried not to look too uncomfortable. "I'm trying to help Nancy find out what Adam was working on before he was killed."

She stared at him. "Seriously?"

"Yes."

"Why? She wasn't interested in his work before he died."

"Why do you think that?"

"I don't think it, I *know* it. Adam and I worked together for six years, and I know just how much his wife cared about him and his work."

"And you don't think she cared?"

"No." She smirked. "Besides, if she wants to know so badly, why isn't *she* here?"

Good question. Fred kept his face solemn. "She's very upset about Adam's death."

"I'm sure she is," she said, but sarcasm edged her words.

He decided to ignore it for the moment. "So, what was Adam working on?"

She shrugged lazily. "I'm not sure I could tell you about his projects, even if I wanted to."

"Why not?"

"We get a lot of government contracts for the Environmental Protection Agency. We often test sites that have applied for Superfund money. So much of what we do is confidential, I think it would be better to not talk about anything." Her face settled into determined lines that warned him she wouldn't go any further.

But he didn't intend to leave until he got what he came for. "I understand you and Adam were good friends."

She nodded. "Yes, we were. We'd known each other for years."

"This must be very hard on you, too."

As if she'd suddenly remembered she should be grieving, tears filled her eyes. "It's horrible. I'm okay when I'm here, but I don't know what I'll do when I have to go back to the office."

"Maybe you should take a few days off."

She snorted a laugh. "I called in sick today, but Philip will be furious that I did. I won't be able to get away with it tomorrow."

"Philip?"

"Philip Aagard. You know him, don't you?"

Fred tried to place the name but couldn't. He shook his head.

"He owns the place."

It didn't help. "He might surprise you and be more understanding than you think."

She laughed again. "Yeah. I'm sure."

"Did he and Adam get along?"

She lifted one thin shoulder. "I think Philip liked Adam as much as he likes anybody, but if he suddenly went into deep mourning, I'd be surprised. He's not a very compassionate person."

"You don't sound as if you care for him very much."

"Working for Philip's a little like working for Ebenezer Scrooge. Adam helped keep things tolerable. In fact, he's the only reason I've stayed as long as I have. He's the one who kept everyone from killing each other." She flushed deep red at her unwitting choice of words and said, "I really don't know what I'll do now."

Fred hadn't expected this reaction, but he tried not to show his surprise. "You and Adam were close?"

"Friends, Mr. Vickery. We were friends." As if he'd suggested something else.

"Tell me about the others at work," he said. "Did Adam get along with everyone?"

She looked a little reluctant to answer. "Yes."

"Including Mitch Hancock?"

"Yes."

"What about that other guy—Roy Dennington?"

She sipped her coffee and narrowed her eyes. "Are you *supposed* to be asking me questions like this?"

"I'm trying to help my niece."

"And she's trying to figure out who killed Adam?" She still didn't sound as if she believed it.

"Yes."

She tried to look amused. "And who does she think did it?"

"She doesn't know. That's why I'm helping her ask around. So, tell me about Roy Dennington."

"I'd never met him until yesterday."

"Had you ever heard of him before?"

"Never."

"Then how did Mitch know of him?"

She lifted one thin shoulder. "How would I know? Honestly, Mr. Vickery—"

Very helpful. "Tell me who usually tested the samples Adam collected."

"There are only three chemists at EnviroSampl, so it's either Mitch, Brooke, or me. We're not a very large outfit even though we do get most of the contracts for the EPA in this area."

Fred pondered her explanation for a few seconds. "What do you test for?"

"Possible contamination of land or water on potential construction sites. If the land's clean, the owners get the go-ahead. If it's not, the government tells them what they have to do before they can build. If there's a cleanup, we go back and gather more samples when they're through, and the whole thing starts over."

"What kind of test results would Adam have been anxious to get yesterday?"

She looked puzzled. "From one of our people?"

He nodded.

"None."

"You're sure?"

"Positive. We didn't have anything urgent pending. Besides, Adam wouldn't get the test results. Not directly. They'd go straight to Philip from the lab."

"But Mitch said he came in early to deliver some test results Adam was anxious to get."

Her eyes clouded. "Maybe you misunderstood him."

"Maybe," he conceded, but he knew he hadn't.

She sent him a look full of pity. "I really think you're barking up the wrong tree, Mr. Vickery."

"Maybe," he said again. "What about Roy Dennington?"

"Like I said, I don't know the man. He showed up for an appointment yesterday, and he ended up staying until the sheriff let us go."

"Any idea what he wanted to see Adam about?"

"None." She met his gaze a little too steadily, and Fred suspected she did have an idea. But he also suspected she wouldn't share it with him.

"Do you know where I can find him?"

"No."

"A telephone number?"

"No."

"Maybe there's something back at the office—"

"There isn't." She shifted position and recrossed her legs. "Look, I understand how anxious you must be to help Nancy, but I don't know anything."

"Do you think Roy Dennington was there to see Adam about something personal?"

She tried to force a laugh. "Like what?"

"You tell me."

She waved one hand at him as if discounting the idea. "You know what the sheriff thinks, don't you?"

"What?"

"He thinks Nancy did it. And it seems like you're going to an awful lot of trouble to divert suspicion away from her."

He met her gaze and held it. "She didn't kill Adam."

A look of malice flashed through her eyes so quickly Fred wondered whether he'd actually seen it. "I don't know how you can sound so certain. She's the only one who had a reason to."

Fred's throat tightened, but he tried to keep his face from showing any anxiety. "And what reason did she have?"

"He left her," she said as if that explained it all.

"They were separated," he admitted.

"She didn't want a divorce."

Fred thought back to the argument at Harriet's house. He'd been under the impression that Adam hadn't asked for a divorce before that night. But maybe he'd read the situation wrong. "Did Adam tell you that?" he asked.

Charlotte nodded. "He wanted out of the marriage, but she wouldn't agree to a divorce."

"Did he tell you why?"

"Why she wouldn't agree? Obviously, she didn't want to lose. If it had been her idea, I'm sure things would have been different."

So she killed him and lost him forever? Didn't make much sense to Fred. He allowed himself a tiny smile. "I meant, did he tell you why he wanted the divorce?"

She looked away as she readjusted the opening of her robe over her knee, then looked back up at him slowly. "Yes. But you'll have to ask Nancy about that. It's not my place to tell you."

"But Adam took you into his confidence. You must have been very close."

Her top leg jiggled nervously. "Like I said, Adam was my friend."

"I see."

"We worked together every day. We'd known each other for years. And he was staying at the office. Naturally, we talked about it."

Pay dirt! Another person who knew Adam was staying at the office. And *this* person had a key to the building. "Adam told you he was staying there?"

"Yes, he did," she said. "But it was pretty obvious. He had clothes and things around . . ."

"So anybody with access to the building would have known he was staying there."

Her leg jiggled a little faster. "I suppose so."

"Who else had after-hours access to the building?"

Her face darkened and her spine stiffened. "Honestly, Mr. Vickery, you sound as if you're interrogating me."

He held up a hand and smiled innocently. "Not at all. I just have a question or two."

She didn't look convinced. "I think I'm through answering your questions." She looked pointedly at the clock and stood. "Besides, I'm late for an appointment."

Pushing off with his fists, he managed to struggle back out of the couch. He followed her toward the door, but he stopped there. "I know *you* had a key. But besides yours, how many others were there?"

Anger pulled her mouth into a frown as she jerked the door open. "Everyone who works there has a key."

"I see." He stepped outside and looked back at her with a smile. "Well, thank you for your time. You've been very helpful."

She stared at him without moving for a very long time, then closed the door between them.

Fred walked away quickly, but he thought he could feel her eyes on his back until he turned onto the road. He didn't know a lot more about Adam or his work, but he knew somebody'd lied to him. And he intended to find out why.

nine

Once back inside his car, Fred retrieved the deposit slip where he'd written Charlotte's address from his pocket and jotted three more names on the back: Mitch Hancock, Roy Dennington, and Philip Aagard.

He wanted to talk to each of them, but he figured it made the most sense to start with Philip. If anyone could tell him what Adam was working on, the boss could. And Fred hoped Philip could also tell him where to locate Roy Dennington.

He made a U-turn and followed Twin Creek back into town. And he thought about Mitch Hancock's claim that Adam had been anxious to get some test results. Either Mitch had lied about that, or Charlotte had. But which had reason to lie? Both? Neither? Fred didn't know what either had to gain, but he certainly intended to find out.

Even driving at a reasonable speed, he reached Enviro-Sampl in just a few minutes. Adam's car had been removed, but Nancy's Trooper still held a spot near the highway, and there were only a few other cars taking up space. Fred guessed Charlotte wasn't the only staff member who needed a day off after yesterday's events.

He found a shady parking spot and hurried toward the building, anxious to catch Philip before he went out to gather samples somewhere. He pulled open the front door and stepped into a stuffy reception area refrigerated by a swamp cooler somewhere high overhead. The room held one tiny desk, two mismatched chairs, a filing cabinet, and Pete Scott's new young wife. Fred never could remember her name, but a nameplate on her desk reminded him it was Tiffany.

She tossed back a headful of blonde hair and looked up from her computer screen as he entered. "Good morning."

He smiled at her. "Hello, there. Tiffany Scott, isn't it? How's that husband of yours?"

She looked pleased that he'd remembered her. "Pete's doing great. He'll be back tomorrow."

Fred nodded as if he knew where Pete might be coming back from, but he couldn't remember hearing he was gone.

She didn't seem to notice. "Well, seeing you here is kind of a surprise. What can I do for you?"

"Is Philip Aagard in?"

Her brow puckered for half a beat. "Yes, but he's with somebody right now."

"What about Mitch Hancock?"

She looked confused, as if one request wouldn't usually follow the other. "That's who's with Mr. Aagard. Can I help you?"

"Well, I don't know." He pretended to consider her offer for a few seconds. "Do you know how long they'll be?"

"A few minutes, maybe. Do you want to wait?"

"If it's all right."

She nodded and went back to her typing, and Fred took a seat and watched her work for several minutes before she made a mistake, swore, and held her finger on one key while she scowled at the screen. "I can't believe how many mistakes I've made this morning."

"Some days are like that."

She frowned down at an open file on her desk. "I think it's because of what happened yesterday." With a guilty look around, she lowered her voice to a stage whisper. "I mean, it feels weird to even be here."

"Actually, I'm surprised to find you open today. I expected the place to be locked up tight."

"You don't know Philip very well, do you?" She gave a little laugh and glanced up at him. "Look, I hate to make you wait. If you'll tell me what you need, I'll be glad to help you."

"It's a personal matter."

She looked more than just a little curious, but she didn't pry.

Fred let her type for a few more seconds before he asked, "When did you start working here? Last time I heard, you were working at the bank."

She finished a word and smiled in his general direction. "About six months ago."

"Do you like it?"

"It's all right." She tapped out a few more sentences, swore again, and deleted the error.

"The murder must have bothered you a great deal."

"That's an understatement."

"Maybe you should ask your boss for a few days off."

She shook her head emphatically. "Not a good idea. Philip wouldn't be pleased that I even asked. You should have heard him when Charlotte called in this morning." She rolled her eyes to indicate exactly what she thought of Philip's reaction.

"He didn't like it?"

"No. He definitely did not." Mistake obviously corrected, she repositioned her fingers and started typing again.

He let her work for another few seconds. "I guess the murder was quite a shock to everybody."

"I'll say," she agreed. "I mean, I saw Adam night before last, and he seemed fine. But then yesterday—" She broke off and shook her head slowly.

Fred sat up a little straighter, drew in a deep breath, and tried not to let himself expect too much. After all, he'd seen Adam the night before he died, too. "Where did you see him?" he asked.

"Right here. I stayed late to finish up a contract Philip was working on, and Adam was here, too. We were both really busy, but he came out and talked to me for a few minutes. Then he got that phone call and . . ." She shook her head again. "It's just so hard to believe he's dead."

Fred moved a little closer. "What phone call?"

She shrugged an I-don't-know. "It came in on his direct

line. I couldn't really hear what he said, but he looked kind of upset when he came out."

"So you don't know who called?"

"No. But I wish I did. The sheriff asked me about it, too."

Good. She'd already told Enos about it. Maybe that would help Nancy. "What time did the call come in?" he asked.

She pursed her lips and darted a glance back at her computer as if the answer would appear on the screen. "I don't know. Seven-thirty, maybe."

"And what time did you leave?"

"A few minutes after that."

"Did Adam leave before you?"

She shook her head. "No, he was still here. Talking on the phone again."

"Any idea who the second call was from?"

"It wasn't *from* anybody. He made the second call."

"You're sure?"

"Yeah. The phone didn't ring again after that first time."

Fred leaned back in his seat. Were the two calls connected? Was there some way to find out who Adam talked to? Probably. But without official connections, Fred wouldn't have an easy time getting the information. "Was anybody else here when you left?"

"No. Just me and him. As usual."

"He stayed late often?"

Tiffany widened her eyes and looked as if she were about to impart a state secret. "All the time. But especially lately. A few people thought he was even living here."

"Really?" Fred worked hard to look surprised at the information. "Who?"

"I don't know who. But to tell you the truth, I think they're right."

"What makes you think that?"

"Well, you know, he had some of his stuff around, and he never seemed to go home. Besides, he'd changed so much the past few weeks."

"Changed how?"

Tiffany abandoned her typing again and rolled her chair

around so she could face him. "Little things. He'd stopped eating lunch in the break room, stopped talking to just about everybody. He looked preoccupied all the time. Lots of secret phone calls."

"Any idea why?"

She didn't even have to think about it. "Yeah," she said with a little laugh. "And who."

"What do you mean?"

She leaned a little closer and lowered her voice. "I saw him with another woman. Twice."

"You think he was having an affair?"

Nodding, she looked at him as if he'd lost his mind. "Well, yeah. I never thought Adam was that kind of guy, but the very minute—" She broke off and shook her head as if she couldn't bear to think about it. "To tell you the truth, the whole thing makes me sick."

"And you know who he was seeing?"

She nodded again. "Brooke Westphal."

Charlotte had mentioned a Brooke, but she hadn't given him a last name. Fred remembered Brooke Westphal as cute and blonde and a cheerleader all three years she'd been at Silver Mountain High School. She'd also been on the honor society, the debate team, and was president of some foreign language club. He remembered her well because she'd always been in the school after hours. She must have graduated ten years or more, which would put her in her late twenties by now.

"Adam was having an affair with Brooke? Are you sure?"

Tiffany stiffened, as if he'd called her integrity into question. And maybe he had. "I know what I saw," she said with a sniff and turned back to her computer just as the door to an office behind her opened. A tall, silver-haired man Fred guessed must be Philip Aagard led the way; Mitch Hancock and Deputy Robert Alpers followed.

Mitch mumbled something about needing to get back to the lab and darted around a corner.

But Philip extended a hand to Robert. "If there's anything else you need, just call."

Robert had an open, friendly face with a wide, moustache-adorned smile. He adjusted his deputy cap over his close-cropped curly brown hair and looked out at the world through a pair of wire-rimmed glasses. "Thanks, but I think I've asked everything I need to know for now." He tucked a notebook into his shirt pocket and readjusted his duty belt before he noticed Fred sitting there.

Fred smiled at him.

Robert did not look pleased. "Well. Mr. Vickery."

"Deputy."

"Enos warned me you'd probably come sniffing around, but I've got to confess, I didn't believe him. Are you waiting to see me?"

Fred stood and tried not to look irritated. He didn't *sniff*. "No. I wanted to see Mr. Aagard."

The silver-haired gentleman looked surprised. "I'm Philip Aagard. What can I help you with?"

But Robert piped up before Fred could even open his mouth. "Nothing. At least not if he's asking questions about Adam Bigelow's murder."

Philip's eyebrows rose a fraction. "Questions? What kinds of questions?"

Robert pushed his glasses up on his nose and grinned at Fred as if they shared a great joke. "What kinds of questions, Mr. Vickery?"

The young whelp couldn't be more than about twenty-five, and he had a lot to learn about respecting his elders. Fred ignored him as he held Philip Aagard's gaze and smiled. "Can you spare me a minute or two?"

At Philip's hesitant glance, Robert shrugged his approval. He hitched his duty belt again and tried to look tough. "You should know Sheriff Asay has authorized me to take anyone into custody who interferes with our official investigation."

Though Enos had threatened to lock him up before, Fred had never worried about it much. But this eager young whippersnapper just might take Enos seriously. "I don't plan to ask any questions at all about the murder."

"Good. Then you won't mind if I sit in."

Fred did mind. A great deal. But he shook his head and

smiled as nicely as he could. "I don't mind at all. How about you, Mr. Aagard?"

Philip Aagard looked even more confused. "I don't mind. Why don't we go into my office?"

Fred nodded and followed Philip. Robert brought up the rear and shut the door behind them.

The room wasn't large or well furnished or impressive in any way. But Philip Aagard presided over it as if it were the Oval Office. He gestured grandly toward the chairs in front of his desk and took his place only after Fred and Robert sat.

Folding his hands on the desk, he smiled benignly at them. "Now, Mr. . . . Vickery? What can I do for you?"

Fred had no idea. He couldn't ask the questions he'd come to ask, but he'd be dipped if he'd let Robert know he'd caught him. He tried a friendly sort of smile on his host.

Philip smiled back.

"I appreciate you taking the time to see me. I know how busy you must be, especially with Adam's untimely death."

Robert made a warning sound deep in the back of his throat.

Fred ignored him. He'd promised not to ask questions about the death, but it seemed unnatural not to mention it. "I don't know if you're aware that Adam's wife is my niece."

Philip's smile wavered. "Then let me offer my condolences."

Fred lowered his eyes and accepted Philip's offer, stalling for time and wishing he had some acceptable reason for wanting to be here.

"How is Nancy holding up?" Philip asked.

"Not real well," Fred said. "It's pretty rough on her."

Philip looked sympathetic. He nodded as if he understood how rough it probably was, refolded his hands on his desk, and waited.

"I'm trying to help her," Fred explained.

"She's lucky to have you, I'm sure."

A trifle impatiently Robert shifted in his chair and cleared his throat. He widened his eyes at Fred in a silent signal to get on with it.

"I wonder," Fred began and then hit on an idea. He tried

not to show his relief as he went on. "I wonder how soon you'll let Nancy clear Adam's things out of his office."

Philip looked surprised. "I don't think that's up to me."

"Oh. Whose decision would it be?"

"The sheriff's, I think. The room's still sealed off, and they're still investigating in there—" He broke off and looked to Robert for direction.

Robert tried hard to look official. "I can check with Sheriff Asay and let you know."

"Fine. Well, then, I won't take up any more of your time." Fred stood and held out his hand for Philip to shake.

Looking a little confused, he shook. "Give my best to your niece."

"Of course, and thank you." Fred started toward the door, pleased with himself for pulling this one off but still anxious to get away.

Robert bounded up, obviously a little disappointed at not being able to take Fred into custody.

But Philip hurried around him and reached the door first. "And if there's anything we can do to help her, I hope you'll let us know."

"I will. Thank you." Fred crossed back into the reception area with Robert a step behind, and Philip closed the door quietly but firmly behind them.

Robert reached the front door in three steps, tugged it open, and looked back at Fred. "You coming?"

Feeling benevolent now that he'd come through all right, Fred gave the boy one of his kindest smiles. "I need to call home. I thought I'd see if I could call from here. You'll have somebody let me know about Adam's things?"

"Yeah. Sure." Robert stepped outside, and with one last untrusting look at Fred, he slammed the door.

Fred turned back to Tiffany. She'd been watching their exchange with interest, and now she pointed toward a door that led into a small conference room. "You can use that phone over there."

Fred thanked her and started toward it, but before he'd gone ten feet, she jumped up from her desk and chased after him.

"Mr. Vickery?" she called softly. "Will you give Nancy a message for me?"

"I'd be happy to."

"Will you please tell her I'm sorry about Adam. I really liked him in spite of everything."

"In spite of everything?"

She nodded and looked a little embarrassed. "Well, you know, the thing with Brooke and all."

"Did Nancy know about Adam and Brooke?"

"She must have because her dad came in here a couple of days before Adam died, and they got into a horrible fight."

Fred's heart sank. "Porter?"

Tiffany nodded.

"Did they mention Brooke?"

Tiffany shook her head. "Of course the door was closed and I couldn't hear much, but I don't think so."

"Then what makes you think either Nancy or Porter knew?" Or suspected. Fred still had a hard time accepting the story that Adam had cheated on Nancy.

"Because I heard Porter tell Adam that he wouldn't let Nancy suffer just because Adam couldn't keep his pants up."

Fred made a mental note to add Porter's name to his list. What in blazes had the fool been thinking of?

"Of course I'd already seen Adam and Brooke together, so I knew what he meant." Tiffany averted her eyes and sighed. "It all seems so tragic—especially now."

"Why especially now?"

She checked the room behind her as if she didn't want to be overheard. "I know it's supposed to be a secret, but I kind of overheard Adam on the phone the other day talking to Dr. Huggins. But I haven't told anyone, I promise."

"You haven't?"

She shook her head and looked solemn. "Not a soul."

"I'm sure Nancy will appreciate knowing that." Since he had no idea what Tiffany was talking about, he hoped she'd break her rule for him.

"Like I said, I've always really liked Adam. But I don't know what got into him at the end."

"It's a real mystery." As big a mystery as all the things everyone but Fred seemed to know.

"Anyway," Tiffany said with a tight smile. "I don't know whether it's appropriate to say congratulations or not. But will you tell her I'm glad she still has the baby?"

Fred didn't know what he'd been expecting her to say, but it hadn't been that. Nancy pregnant? She had enough to deal with right now—the separation, Adam asking for a divorce, and his death.

He didn't want Nancy to be pregnant. Not now. Because if everything he'd heard today was true; if Nancy *was* pregnant, if Adam *was* having an affair, and if he'd left Nancy and demanded a divorce, his turning up dead looked bad for her. Very bad.

ten

Under normal circumstances, Fred would never have driven to Doc Huggins's place. He didn't drive anywhere his two legs could carry him. But if he took the car home, one of the kids would be there, and they'd find a way to keep him from doing anything else today.

So he drove through the side streets of Cutler, avoided Lake Front altogether, and pulled up to Doc's a little after eleven. With relief, he saw Doc's car in the garage, which meant he must be around. He left his own car in the driveway, as if he were paying a social call rather than a professional one, and followed the gravel path to Doc's office.

Doc had built his office onto the back of his house. A reception room, two examining rooms, one for his equipment, and another for his baseline lab work. He said he liked to keep his operation simple and friendly. That he liked people to feel at home when they came to see him. But Fred never felt at home sitting on an examination table while somebody poked around places that were no one's business but his own.

He pushed open the office door and peered inside. Empty. Good. He wanted to talk to Doc about Nancy, but he didn't want to run into anyone else while he was here. Even one other patient could carry away the news of his visit and start people wondering whether his heart was acting up again.

When he stepped into the reception area, his legs crossed a light beam and set off a buzzer somewhere in the front of the house. A few seconds later Velma Huggins rushed down the hallway wiping her hands on a towel attached to the front of her apron.

Fred had known Velma all her life. She was a few years younger than him, but she had almost as many grandkids as he did. But while gray had replaced nearly all the brown in his hair, Velma still took pride in her auburn curls. And nobody with a lick of sense ever questioned where the auburn came from these days.

When she saw him standing there, her step faltered. "Fred? Is something wrong?"

"No, I'm fine. I need to see Doc for a few minutes, though. Is he in?"

She nodded, but she didn't take her eyes from him. "Bernard's in the kitchen, pretending to be working on his billing. Let me go get him."

"Fine."

"You're sure you're okay?"

Exactly the reaction he'd expected. Hearing it from Velma was bad enough. He didn't want to risk running into anyone else, so he pointed toward the first examining room. "Do you mind if I wait for him in there?"

"Of course not. Go on in." She turned away, but Fred had seen the worry in her eyes. She was obviously afraid something was terribly wrong.

Well, good. That meant she'd convey her fears to Doc, and Fred wouldn't have to wait long.

He closed the door of the examination room behind him and settled onto one of those molded plastic chairs manufactured with the assumption that everyone's backside was built exactly the same way. Making himself as comfortable as he could under the circumstances, he scanned the titles of a few of the medical brochures Doc kept around. AIDS, breast feeding, and skin cancer. Smoking, diabetes, and glaucoma. Not exactly light reading.

For the umpteenth time he thought about forgetting this step and going straight to Nancy. But if she wanted him to know about the baby, she'd have told him already. She knew how to keep secrets. And if she hadn't told her parents about her marriage falling apart, she certainly wouldn't confide in him about her pregnancy.

He knew that getting the information he wanted out of Doc would require tact. Finesse. He couldn't just start demanding answers. Which was why he'd formed a plan. A bit drastic, but he figured the end justified the means.

Not three minutes later the door opened, and Doc rushed into the room. Doc shared none of his wife's pretensions of youth. He'd allowed most of his hair to fall out of the top of his head, and the fringe he had left was almost completely silver. Only his moustache and eyebrows still bore a trace of color. He'd packed on too many extra pounds over the past five years, which only made his restrictions on Fred's diet harder to tolerate.

He scowled at Fred and stuffed his stethoscope into his ears. "What's wrong? Your heart?"

"Nothing's wrong. It's just been a while since my last checkup, and I thought I'd beat you and Margaret to the punch."

Doc squinted at him as if trying to see through to the truth.

"Seriously. I feel fit as a fiddle. I just want to hear you agree with me."

Doc looked suspicious, but he nodded toward the examining table. "You want to hop on up there?"

Fred didn't, but he hopped anyway and unbuttoned his shirt so Doc could have easy access to his chest.

Doc took his temperature, then wrapped the blood pressure cuff around his arm. "Have you been having any unusual pains?"

"No."

"Are you sleeping all right?"

Fred waited until Doc had finished counting and his circulation started again and tried to figure out the best way to frame his answer. He'd slept fine for weeks until Nancy's trouble began.

Doc scribbled some numbers on a notepad and unwrapped the cuff. "You're not sleeping?"

"Dozing," Fred admitted.

"How much are you dozing a night?"

"A few hours, on and off."

Doc looked concerned and plucked the cold end of the stethoscope on Fred's chest. "Take a deep breath for me."

Fred breathed and Doc listened, first to his chest, then to his back before he pulled the stethoscope away.

"Everything sounds fine. Maybe we ought to run another EKG."

"I *am* fine, Doc. I don't need you to hook me up to that blasted machine again."

Doc stared at him for one long minute. "Then what's troubling you?"

"I've got my niece staying with me. You know Nancy Bigelow, don't you?"

"Very well. Is she doing all right?"

"I think so. I guess you've probably heard about Adam."

Doc nodded. "Enos called me to the scene. Terrible tragedy. Such a fine young man with so much to look forward to."

Fred let Doc ponder the tragedy and perform his medical wonders for a bit longer, then he spoke again. "To tell you the truth, I'm worried about her."

"Why? What's wrong?"

"She seems a little . . ." Fred let his voice trail off and searched for the right word. Upset? Too weak. Emotional? Well, of course she was.

"It's a terrible tragedy," Doc repeated and shined a light into Fred's ears so he could look inside.

Fred tilted his head to give him a better view. "She's having a rough time."

"I can imagine."

"She's a patient of yours, isn't she?"

Doc nodded. "Since the day she was born."

"Has she been in to see you since Adam's death?"

"No, and I really ought to drop by and check on her." He nodded toward Fred's shirt, a silent signal that he'd finished.

Fred rebuttoned and slid from the table. "I don't think she's feeling up to par."

"I imagine she's not." Doc ripped off the paper Fred had been sitting on and relined the table.

Fred tucked his shirttail back in and tried to keep his voice casual. "You know, Phoebe and I had the four kids, and I watched Margaret carry her own three and go through that one miscarriage."

Did he imagine it, or did Doc tense up?

"I know this sounds crazy, but I've been wondering if Nancy might be pregnant."

Doc's jaw set, and his eyes hardened. "Is that why you're here?"

"I told you why I'm here. To get a clean bill of health before Margaret decides to drag me in. So—did I check out okay?"

Doc's face didn't soften. "Why don't you ask Nancy if she's pregnant? Why come over here and pull a stunt like this to find out?"

"I'd rather not ask her just yet. Is she?"

Doc managed to look affronted. "I can't believe you're asking me that question. The patient-doctor relationship is a privileged one."

Well, it was certainly supposed to be. And Fred figured there might even be places where it was. But Doc didn't always honor it. "You didn't show any such qualms about sharing *my* condition with anyone who'd listen."

"If I thought for one minute you'd take care of yourself without help, I wouldn't have breathed a word."

Fred humphed to express his opinion.

Doc humphed back. "And as far as Nancy goes, I couldn't tell you, even if I wanted to—which I don't."

Fine. Fred figured he already had his answer. Nancy must be pregnant; otherwise Doc wouldn't refuse to answer. "How far along is she?"

Doc crossed his arms and clamped his lips together.

Further proof. "She can't be very far since she's not showing yet."

Doc glared at him.

"She's in good health, isn't she? No risks involved?"

No answer.

"Did you ever talk to Adam about the baby?"

"Who said there *was* a baby?"

"Who said there wasn't?"

Doc wrenched open the door to the examining room. "You're quite a piece of work, you know that? No wonder you can't sleep at night—your imagination's working overtime."

Fred chose to ignore that comment and followed him into the corridor. "Did you? Talk to Adam about it?"

Doc whirled to face him. "Why? Whether or not Nancy's pregnant, why do you want to know?"

Fred barely managed to avoid running into him. "Because Adam's dead."

"What does Nancy being pregnant have to do with that?"

"I don't know. I've heard a few things, and I've got to admit I'm a little worried. Trouble is, I'm not even sure the pieces I've managed to pick up are from the same puzzle."

For one long moment Doc didn't speak. He didn't blink, he didn't smile, he didn't move a muscle. "I can't tell you anything about Nancy's health."

"Okay. Tell me she *wasn't* pregnant. That'll do. If you can tell me that, it gets rid of one of the pieces."

Doc didn't look pleased. "I'm not telling you anything."

"I knew it. She is."

Doc fished Fred's file from the filing cabinet and made a couple of notations inside. "Does Enos know you're poking around in this murder?"

"I'm not *poking around* in the murder."

"He doesn't know, does he?" Doc slipped the file away and chuckled as if he'd just heard something amusing. "Well, he'll find out, Fred. And what do you think he's going to do then?"

"Nothing."

"Nothing? You're dreaming. He'll be livid." Doc started toward the front of the house again.

But Fred stepped in front of him. "Are you going to tell him?"

"I might."

"Well, you go right ahead and tell him I was here, but be

honest. Did I ask you even one question about the murder?"

Doc thought long and hard. "No," he conceded at last.

"I'm here because I'm concerned about my niece. Since she's staying with me, and since I'm the one providing her moral support right now, I figure the more I know about what she's going through, the more help I can give her."

Doc didn't say a word, but he did manage to look sheepish.

Indignant now, Fred pushed on. "I believe Nancy might be pregnant. And I've been told Adam wasn't happy about it. That's hard enough for a woman to go through, but now that he's dead, it'll be even worse."

Fred thought he had him, but Doc's face tightened again. "I might almost buy that answer, Fred. Except for one thing."

"What?"

"Adam wasn't unhappy about the baby. He was over-joyed." And with that, Doc tried to push past him.

But Fred held firm. "Are you sure?"

"Of course I'm sure. They'd been trying for years to have a baby." This time Doc managed to get around him.

Confused and frustrated, Fred started to follow, but he stopped after a couple of steps. He was going in circles. Everyone he'd talked to painted a different picture of Adam, of Nancy, and of their marriage. Were *any* of them accurate?

Doc reached the hallway back to the house and looked back over his shoulder. "Now what?"

"I don't know. I'm confused."

Doc's expression softened. "Look, Fred, I think you're a little paranoid. Nancy hasn't even been charged with any-thing."

"I know," he admitted. But he couldn't voice his great fear aloud. He knew she would be. Eventually.

"Listen, I know as well as you do that Nancy couldn't have done it. Adam's murderer stood less than three feet behind him, held the gun to the back of his head and pulled the trigger. Nancy's not that heartless."

Doc's faith heartened Fred a little. "Does Enos believe that?"

"Of course he does."

Fred's hopes soared. "Then he doesn't consider Nancy a suspect anymore? Or Porter, either?"

Doc looked away. "I didn't say that. I meant that in his heart, he knows. There's just no proof. But he'll find it."

Fred's hopes evaporated. "That's not good enough."

"He'll find it, just be patient."

Patient? While everyone suspected Nancy? While Adam's murderer got off scot-free? While Fred couldn't sleep?

Doc studied his face and frowned. "You can't get involved this time, Fred."

Turning away, Fred crossed to the outside door. "Did I say I was getting involved?"

"I've known you all my life," Doc called after him. "I know what you're thinking."

Fred grinned back over his shoulder. "You couldn't possibly know that, or you'd have kicked me out of here already."

Doc's frown deepened. "There's nothing you can do, Fred."

Fred pulled open the door and paused. "That's where you're wrong, Doc."

Letting the door close behind him, he rushed back up the path to where he'd left the Buick. He fished his list from his pocket and stared at the names left there. Mitch Hancock. Roy Dennington. He pulled out his pen and added two more.

Porter Jorgensen. Because Fred wanted to ask exactly what Porter knew about Nancy's marriage, what he and Adam fought about that day at Adam's office, and where Porter went the night of the murder.

And Brooke Westphal. Because Fred wanted to know the truth about the rumor concerning her and Adam. And he hoped with all his heart she'd deny it.

eleven

Fred drove back into town, debating whether to go home or try to talk to one more person on his list. Questions raced through his mind. Had Adam been murdered because of his personal life or his professional one? Was Mitch Hancock lying about delivering test results? Or had Charlotte Isaacson misled him about the test results going directly to Philip?

Who called Adam on his private line the night of his murder? And who did *he* call? Was Adam a faithful, loving husband excited by the impending birth of his first child? Or a cheating husband who didn't want the responsibilities of fatherhood? And why had he chosen that night to ask Nancy for a divorce? Did anyone know the real story? And would anyone tell it to Fred?

He wanted to pursue his leads, slender as they were, but he had no idea where to turn. Brooke Westphal and Mitch Hancock would still be at work—and even Fred couldn't justify visiting EnviroSampl twice in one day. He still had no idea where to find Roy Dennington. And he'd have to be awfully creative to come up with an excuse for approaching Philip Aagard again.

He felt restless. Anxious. Too keyed up to rest. Too agitated to sit around home and wait for Enos to do something. He cruised slowly past the Bluebird Café and thought about stopping in for lunch. But if Margaret started looking for him she'd head to the Bluebird first, and he wasn't in the mood for a confrontation today.

He drove out of the city limits and into the forest beyond, still without a destination in mind. When he rounded a curve

in the road, the towering red and white sign announcing
Jefferson's One-Stop caught his eye. He let off the accelerator and turned into the parking lot. Whatever he decided,
it couldn't hurt to have a full tank of gas. With all this
driving, he'd probably have to fill up twice this month.

Fred waved to Glen Jefferson as he pulled up to the
no-lead pump. Glen, tall, heavyset, dark-haired and blue-
eyed, waved back. He was a nice enough guy, but he had a
few ideas Fred didn't agree with.

He'd been heard to say that people were going to profit
from the growth around Cutler, and that he aimed to be one
of them. He felt so strongly about it, he'd sold his car repair
shop last year and opened the One-Stop in hopes of
cornering the market. He did a decent business during the
summer months when passing tourists stopped in for gas
and goodies, but Fred didn't know how he made enough to
support his small family the rest of the year. But no matter
how skewed their thinking, local people ought to stick
together, so Fred gave Glen his business.

After inserting the nozzle into his gas tank, Fred watched
the numbers flash across the digital display and names of
possible murderers flashed through his mind—Mitch Hancock, Brooke Westphal, Roy Dennington, Charlotte Isaacson, and Philip Aagard. Had one of them done it? And if so,
why?

He checked his watch again. He'd been gone since early
morning. Margaret would be worried about him. Douglas
would be trying to calm her down. Fred wondered whether
he ought to head back home. After all, Nancy was there, and
he supposed he *should* be with her.

But other than providing comfort, what could he do at
home? Sit in his rocking chair and stare out the window?
No, thank you. Comfort wouldn't get Nancy very far, and he
couldn't steer Enos in the right direction from his rocking
chair. He certainly couldn't ask Nancy to come with him to
question suspects, so the only answer was to let Margaret
and Douglas fill in for him while he was away.

Fred paced a few steps away from the pump and watched
a couple of cars pass on the highway. He admitted grudg-

ingly that Porter and Nancy might each *look* guilty—on the surface. With her marriage falling apart, a baby on the way, and her husband possibly carrying on with another woman, Nancy had strong enough motives for murder.

And Porter—Porter's tendency to fly off the handle certainly didn't help. And with the two arguments he had with Adam before he died, Porter looked like a prime suspect. Why had Porter gone to Adam's office? What had they argued about? And where had Porter gone the night of the murder? Shaking his head, Fred looked back at his car.

Obviously, he needed to ask Porter a few questions. And there was no time like the present for asking them. Leaving the tank filling on its own, Fred started across the parking lot toward the pay phone on the side of the building.

Glen Jefferson leaned against the door frame and studied him with interest. "Trouble, Fred?"

"Not a bit, Glen. Thanks. I just need to use the phone for a minute or two."

Glen pushed himself up and took a step or two after him. "You're welcome to use the one inside. I don't let everybody, but I don't mind if you use it."

Fred smiled and kept going. He appreciated Glen's offer, but he might be overheard in there, and he didn't want to start any fresh rumors. "This is fine," he said. "I'll just be a minute." He dropped a quarter into the pay phone but didn't dial until Glen took a few reluctant steps away.

Porter answered on the fourth ring.

"Porter? It's Fred. Have you got a minute?"

"For you? Anytime. What's wrong?"

"Is Harriet around?"

"She's outside hanging up the wash. Should I go get her?" He sounded apprehensive.

"No, that's all right. It's you I want to talk to."

"Why?" Porter's voice dropped. "Is something wrong with Nancy?"

"No. No, nothing like that. I just have a couple of questions about Adam."

A brief pause. "What about him?"

"I stopped by his office today, and one or two things came to light I wanted to ask you about."

Porter made a noise. "I don't suppose Enos has managed to make an arrest yet."

"Not that I know of."

"Well, I don't know what's taking him so long," Porter huffed. "I told him it's that boss of Adam's who did it."

At the possibility Porter might know something, Fred's pulse skipped. "Philip Aagard? Why do you say that?"

Porter barked a laugh. "You ever meet him?"

"Just this morning."

"What did you think?"

Fred considered for a second before he answered. "I didn't see enough of him to form a judgment, but he seemed all right."

"The guy's a dirtbag," Porter said. "He hasn't got any morals. Or ethics. He asked Adam to do things—" He broke off and breathed raggedly for several seconds. "Enos ought to park himself in that guy's office and not leave until he finds enough evidence to drag him away in handcuffs."

Fred glanced over his shoulder to make sure Glen hadn't moved any closer. He hadn't, but Fred kept his voice down anyway. "What kind of things did he ask Adam to do?"

"Work too late. Stay away from his family too much . . ." He drew in a deep breath. "If you ask me, this divorce business was all his fault. Adam was the best son-in-law a man could ask for—treated Nancy like a princess—until last year."

"What happened then?"

Porter grunted. "Philip Aagard took over EnviroSampl, that's what. Everything fell apart after that."

Fred wanted specifics. Something he could hang his hat on. But he wasn't likely to get it like this. He couldn't tell whether Porter's accusations had any basis in truth or whether they stemmed from a desperate attempt to fasten blame on someone.

He decided to try a new tack. "The receptionist mentioned that you dropped in to see Adam a couple of days before he died."

Heavy silence hummed between them. "I guess maybe I did. Why?"

"She said you and Adam had an argument."

"We may have. I don't remember."

"Porter, that was Monday. He turned up dead on Thursday morning—less than seventy-two hours later. How can you not remember?"

"All right, I remember. But it wasn't anything important."

Well, it seemed important to Fred. "If what's-her-name told me about it, she'll tell other people. I didn't exactly have to pry it out of her."

No response.

He tried to reason with him. "Look, Porter, I'm trying to help."

Dead air stretched between them for a few seconds before Porter said, "I don't need help," as only an extremely shortsighted man could say it.

Reason obviously wouldn't work. Pulling in a steadying breath, Fred decided to try fear. "What do you think will happen when Enos hears about it?"

"Nothing. Why should anything happen?"

"For Pete's sake, Porter. You had a fight with Adam at his office in front of witnesses. You fought with him again the night he died. How do you think that's going to look?"

Another few seconds passed, but just when Fred thought he'd struck out again, Porter asked, "What did the receptionist say?"

"She heard you tell Adam you wouldn't let Nancy suffer because he couldn't control himself—or words to that effect."

Muffled sound drifted through the wire, and Porter mumbled, "Hell's bells."

"What's wrong?"

"I can't talk right now. Harriet just came back inside."

"Then we have to talk later."

"Sure. Sure." Porter must have cupped his hand around the mouthpiece because the words sounded muffled.

"When?" Fred demanded.

A heavy sigh. "Soon."

"Tonight?"

"No, tomorrow." Porter paused, then said, "I promised Harriet I'd drive her down to see Nancy about noon."

Good. Fred thought Nancy needed her parents—whether she knew it or not. "Well, we certainly can't talk at my house. We have to meet somewhere. Where?"

"Hell, I don't know." The tone of Porter's voice changed so suddenly, Fred figured Harriet must have come into the room.

"How about the Bluebird?" Fred suggested.

"No, I'd rather not do that."

"The Copper Penny?"

A slight hesitation. "I guess that's all right."

"I'll see you at noon, then."

"Fine. Yes. I'll see you then." And before Fred could manage another word, Porter disconnected.

Fred ran a hand across his chin and slowly replaced the receiver. That conversation hadn't gone real well. Porter sounded as if he was hiding something, and Fred didn't like to think what that could mean.

For half a heartbeat, Fred wondered whether Porter had killed Adam, but he pushed the thought away as quickly as it formed. Porter might be a hothead, but he wouldn't kill anybody. Fred would bet his own life on it.

He started back toward the Buick, but stopped for a dark-colored low-slung sports car that pulled up to the pump. The driver, a sandy-haired young man, leaned over and opened his glove compartment. He dug around for a few seconds, then slammed it shut and straightened to look behind one of his sun visors.

Fred knew he'd seen him somewhere before, so he watched him closely. After a few seconds he recognized him as the cowboy who'd come looking for Nancy yesterday.

The young man apparently found what he wanted in his car and pushed open his door. But when he found himself face-to-face with Fred, he blinked in surprise. "Excuse me. I didn't see you standing there." He tried to walk around Fred, but Fred didn't budge.

Instead, he smiled. "Good morning."

The cowboy studied him as if trying to remember where they'd met before. "Do I know you from somewhere?"

"I think we met at Porter and Harriet Jorgensen's house yesterday."

The cowboy nodded. "Yes. Maybe that was it." He held out his hand for a shake. "Name's Kelley Yarnell."

Fred shook hands. "Fred Vickery. I'm Nancy's uncle."

When he moved aside, Kelley busied himself with his gas cap, but he spared a glance for Fred. "How's she doing?"

"About as well as you could expect. It's hard on her."

"Yeah. I guess it is." Kelley gave an embarrassed laugh. "I can't even imagine." He squinted into the hot August sun. "How's she feeling?"

Did he know about Nancy's pregnancy? Fred squelched that thought immediately. Of course not. He couldn't. Her parents didn't even know. "I think she's all right."

Kelley looked almost relieved.

"You were pretty good friends with Adam and Nancy?"

Kelley studied his fingernails. "Well, I don't know—I haven't seen them since I moved. But maybe you could tell her I asked about her when you see her again."

"I'd be glad to. Does she know where to find you?"

He looked away casually. "I've got a room at the Columbine Inn just outside of Granby."

Fred smiled. Nancy could use all the friends she could get right now. "I'll pass that on to her."

Kelley's face relaxed, and his eyes lightened considerably. "Thank you."

"No problem." Fred tucked his hands into his pockets. "How long will you be in town?"

"I don't really know. I, uh—I came up here on business, and I guess I'll stay until I've taken care of everything." He broke off at the sound of a vehicle slowing on the highway, and his face tightened noticeably. "Listen, I'm late for an appointment. Be sure to give Nancy my best."

Curious at what made Kelley freeze up like that, Fred looked over his shoulder. Enos's pickup truck bounced across the parking lot toward him, and Fred's heart sank. Just like a blasted bad penny.

Enos pulled his truck so close he almost hit Fred's bumper, then hopped out of the cab. "Well, well, well," he said. "Look who's here."

Kelly pulled the nozzle from his gas tank and stared at Fred with open curiosity.

Fred didn't even bother trying to smile. He'd seen Enos in this mood before.

Enos strolled a little closer. "I just tried to call you."

"I wasn't there."

"I know." Enos smiled, but his eyes didn't look especially friendly. "I heard a vicious rumor today. I kind of hoped you'd set my mind to rest."

"What did you hear?"

Enos adjusted his hat, hitched his pants up, and nodded to Kelley as the young man slid behind the wheel of his car. "Well, now, it's kind of silly, really. Deputy Alpers claimed he saw someone up at EnviroSampl who matched your description."

Fred didn't bother to deny it.

"Naturally, I didn't believe it," Enos said.

"Naturally."

Enos frowned at the highway. "You and I have been friends a long time, Fred. You know how I feel about civilians poking around in police business, and we *are* in the middle of a murder investigation—"

"I know that."

"So I know you wouldn't go nosing around the murder scene."

"Of course I wouldn't," Fred said with a tight smile. "Especially since you've got everything under control."

Enos pulled a pack of gum from his shirt pocket and folded a piece into his mouth. "That's what I thought."

"So, do you know who did it yet?"

Enos flushed ever so slightly.

"What kind of physical evidence do you have? Have you found the murder weapon?"

"You know I can't discuss it with you."

"You don't still suspect Nancy, do you?"

Enos glanced away while the cowboy revved his engine and drove off.

Fred tried not to panic. "You don't suspect Porter?"

Enos's jaw tightened.

"You do, don't you? What about the other suspects?"

Enos readjusted his hat. "You're pushing it, Fred."

Of course he was. He intended to push. *Somebody* had to. "Listen, Enos. I know Mitch Hancock's lying. And Charlotte Isaacson's not telling everything she knows—"

Enos made a noise like a low growl.

"And Philip Aagard—I've heard things have gone downhill ever since he took over at EnviroSampl. Have you checked him out?"

Enos's scowl deepened. "You've been busy, haven't you?"

Damn right, he had. "Tell me what Roy Dennington's doing in town. Why he's hanging around EnviroSampl."

"You're barking up the wrong tree, Fred."

"Horsefeathers. Have you checked out their stories? Do you even know where to find Dennington?"

"As a matter of fact, I have and I do. Dennington's staying at the Columbine. And yes, I've talked to him, too."

Fred hadn't expected that answer. It took a little of the wind out of his sails. "You've talked to all of them?"

"Of course I have."

"And?"

"And nothing."

"Don't be stubborn. What did they say?"

Enos pulled his hat off and turned it in his hands. A bad sign.

"What is it you don't want me to know?" Fred asked.

Enos looked away and stared at the tops of the aspen trees behind the One-Stop. "It's not good, Fred. Mitch Hancock swears Nancy was at EnviroSampl about midnight and that she had another argument with Adam."

twelve

Fred felt as if Enos had punched him. Hard. He tried to draw in a steadying breath. It didn't help. He grasped at the only straw he could see. "What was Mitch doing there?"

"He forgot his house keys and had to go back. When he got there, Nancy's car was outside and he heard her arguing with Adam, so he went in through the back, got his keys, and left."

Fred tried to keep his hands steady, to draw one breath after another, and to force down his rising panic. After all, he'd expected something like this. Just not so soon.

He shrugged, as if by refusing to take Enos seriously, he could erase his words. "So she was there. That doesn't mean she killed him."

Enos massaged his face with his open palm and looked incredibly weary. "You don't know how much I want to believe that."

"But you don't."

Enos shook his head slowly. "I can only deal with the facts."

"The facts? You're not dealing with facts. The *fact* is, Nancy didn't kill Adam, somebody else did."

Enos kept shaking his head. "Don't do this, Fred."

"Do what? Try to make you see reason?"

"I have to do my job."

"What's that? Arrest an innocent woman? A *pregnant* woman?"

Enos's head stopped moving. "Nancy's pregnant?"

"She sure is."

"You're sure about that?"

"Absolutely positive."

Enos glanced away, and when he looked back his face mirrored incredible sadness. "Ah, hell. Poor Adam. Did he know?"

Fred nodded. "Yes, he did. But not many others do. You, me, Doc, and Nancy—and Pete Scott's wife. As far as I know, that's it."

Enos struggled with himself for several seconds before his shoulders drooped and he said, "All right. Look. The evidence against her is strong, but I'll hold off bringing her in as long as I can."

Fred tried to smile. "Thank you, son."

"But pregnant or not, I'll arrest her if she did it."

"I understand that, but she didn't do it."

"You'd better hope she didn't." Enos turned on his heel and headed back toward his truck.

Fred watched him go. He lifted his hand in a halfhearted wave as Enos backed out and sped away. And he waited for a long moment before he took the hose out of his tank and paid Glen Jefferson for his gas.

All the while Enos's parting words echoed through his mind. *You'd better hope.* Well, he did hope. But hoping wouldn't get him anywhere. He'd have to do a sight more than that if he wanted to keep Nancy out of jail.

When Fred pulled into his driveway and found Margaret's Chevy parked there, he felt absolutely no surprise. He just hoped she wouldn't try to keep Nancy from talking to him about Adam and his death.

He made it only halfway to the garage before Margaret burst from the house and raced toward him. He could see her mouth move, and he knew she was demanding to know where he'd been.

Her anger didn't surprise him any more than her presence. But he didn't have the energy to deal with it, so he waved at her and pulled into the garage.

She followed him inside and positioned herself just outside his door with her hands parked on her hips. She waited until he'd rolled down his window before she started in. "Where in the hell have you been?" she demanded.

Fred pushed open his car door and climbed out. "I had a couple of errands to run." He leaned toward her, fully intending to kiss her cheek.

She pulled away and glared at him. "What kind of errands?"

He gave up on the kiss and stepped around her so he could get inside. "A bit of this and that," he said. "Nothing special. Where's Nancy?"

"In the house." Margaret followed him and tugged on his sleeve. "You're doing it again, aren't you?"

"Doing what?" He pulled open the back door and waited while she stepped through.

"Poking around where you don't belong. Admit it—you've been gone all morning, but you didn't go to the Bluebird, and you haven't been to Lacey's. And rumor has it you're poking around the scene of Adam's murder."

He didn't want to argue, so he snagged up the coffeepot and dumped the morning's cold coffee into the sink. He needed a cup.

Margaret was obviously spoiling for a fight. "Where have you been?" she demanded again.

"Sounds to me like you have an idea already." He rinsed the pot and filled it with cold water. "Where did you say Nancy is?"

"She's lying down. Why?"

"How's she doing?"

Margaret's eyes softened a little. "It's hard to tell. She acts numb."

"Well, that's normal, I suppose. The mind's way of protecting itself from the grief." Fumbling with a stack of coffee filters, he finally managed to peel one from the rest. "Where's Douglas?"

The minute he asked, Fred knew he'd made a big mistake.

Margaret's eyes glinted again, and her mouth puckered. "Who knows? He took off as soon as I got here." She shot Fred an exasperated look. "He takes after his father."

But Douglas usually disappeared to avoid responsibility, while Fred's heightened sense of it drove him to action. He measured coffee into the filter and shoved it into place. "Maybe he had a job interview." They could always hope.

"Maybe he didn't."

"Maybe he had to take Alison for therapy."

Margaret rolled her eyes. "And maybe he got bored and went to the Copper Penny to play pool."

"Now, Margaret—"

As if he'd reached for her, she backed away a couple of steps. "So, where *have* you been? You left early this morning, and I'll bet you never even gave Nancy a second thought—you just figured I'd be here with her."

Her words found their mark but, as usual, she'd misunderstood his intentions. "You didn't have to stay."

She pushed at the air between them. "Nancy needed somebody with her, and it obviously wasn't going to be you." She stuck a lock of hair behind her ear and paced a few steps. "Look, Dad, I might have stayed, anyway. But I don't appreciate you just assuming I'll take care of things while you race around getting yourself into trouble."

"I'm not getting myself into trouble, and I never asked you to stay here and take care of anything for me."

"Nancy's going through hell. She shouldn't be left alone."

He sank down onto a chair while the coffee perked. "Maybe you're right."

She dropped to the chair beside his, and her eyes brightened at what she obviously saw as his imminent submission. "Good. So you won't leave her alone anymore?"

"I won't leave her alone."

"And you'll stop poking around where you have no business?"

He should have expected her to sneak that one in. "I'm not poking around where I have no business."

She shook her head as if she could keep his words from landing on her. "Don't give me that. I know exactly what you're doing."

"What am I doing?"

"Sticking your nose into the murder. Again."

"I'm not *sticking my nose* anywhere."

"Do you have any idea how angry Enos is with you?"

Fred knew. He didn't comment.

Margaret leaned back in her chair and smirked. "So, what excuse are you giving yourself for getting involved this time?"

He scowled at her. "I don't have to make up excuses for doing what needs to be done."

She snorted in a most unladylike manner.

"Tell me, young lady, what do you want? For Nancy to wind up in jail?"

She sighed as if he'd asked an incredibly stupid question. "You know I don't. But I don't think that's going to happen."

"It *is* going to happen. I just came from Enos, and he's about ready to arrest her."

Her face paled, and she shook her head in denial. "No."

Her reaction soothed his feelings a little, but he kept the stern look on his face. "Yes."

Margaret started to say something, but before she could, the kitchen door creaked open and Nancy looked into the room. Margaret snapped her lips together and tried to smile.

But the effort appeared wasted on Nancy. She looked tired, worn, hollow-eyed, and pinched. Pushing open the door, she stepped into the room. "I thought I heard you in here, Uncle Fred."

Fred surrendered his chair to her and patted her shoulder as she sat. "How are you feeling, sweetheart?"

She shoved the fingers of both hands into her hair and held her head as she lowered it. "Horrible. I feel like I'm living in a nightmare, you know?"

He did. "Well, you're not alone. You know that, don't you?"

Her lips trembled. "I don't know what I'd do without you."

"That's what family's for." He patted her again and crossed the room to pour the coffee.

Nancy tilted her head back and slid down in her chair.

"I'd like to sleep all day, but I suppose I ought to pick up my car. I hate to leave it up at Adam's office any longer."

Margaret nodded eagerly and started to her feet. "I'll take you."

But Fred didn't want Margaret to take her. He wanted time alone with Nancy. Time to talk. Time to ask questions. He lowered his cup and tried to put on his most sincere expression. "Sweetheart, you've been here all morning. The kids will be worried, and Webb'll be wondering where you are. No sense looking for trouble, that's what I say. You go on home—I'll take Nancy."

Margaret's eyes flew to the wall clock, and she registered the time with a little frown, but she still looked hesitant. "Maybe you're right."

"No 'maybe' about it. Go on home. You can stop in again tomorrow."

"Please don't cause trouble at home because of me," Nancy insisted.

"All right," Margaret said, but she drew the words out as if she had to test every letter. She looked wary. "Why are you so anxious to get rid of me, Dad?"

"Rid of you?" Fred turned to Nancy for support. "See what I put up with around here? I try to do something nice, and just look what it gets me."

Nancy almost smiled at Margaret. "You've been wonderful, but please don't ignore your family because of me."

Fred figured that would get Margaret out the door, but she still hesitated. "He's up to something." When Fred pushed the air out of his mouth in a burst, she pointed an accusing finger in his face. "See? I *knew* it. What are you doing, Dad?"

"I'm not doing anything but trying to help you. It's not *my* fault your husband hasn't figured out how to make his own lunch, for Pete's sake."

Margaret flushed. "Don't start on that."

"Fine," he huffed. "Go home."

She snatched up her purse and keys from the back of the table and pressed a kiss to Nancy's cheek. "Watch him. He can't be trusted."

Nancy nodded and looked serious. "I'll be careful."

"And you—" Margaret pointed at him again, then thought better of it and yanked open the back door. "You'd better not do anything that makes Enos call me."

Seemed to Fred, she should be grateful to him for letting her talk with Enos once in a while, but he didn't point that out.

Nancy watched Margaret slam the door behind her, then turned to Fred with a curious expression. "You two seem a lot different than you used to."

Fred slurped a mouthful of coffee and gestured toward the door with his cup. "Well, we have been. Ever since Margaret decided I need a mother."

Nancy smiled, and her eyes looked more alive than he'd seen them yet.

"I ran into a friend of yours today," he said.

"Really? Who?"

"Some young fellow by the name of Kelley Yarnell."

Did he imagine it, or did her expression freeze? "Kelley? Where did you see him?"

"Over at the One-Stop. But listen, there's something I wanted to talk to you about—"

"What was he doing?"

"Putting gas in his car. He said to tell you he's thinking of you. But I wanted to talk to you about something Enos said—"

Nancy nodded reluctantly.

"We have to talk about the night of Adam's murder. It's important."

She scooted even further down on her chair and pursed her mouth. "I don't want to talk about it anymore."

Under other circumstances, Fred might have backed off. But this was too important. "What were you doing at Adam's office just before he was killed?"

She snapped back up. "Who told you that?"

"Apparently Mitch Hancock went back to the office and heard you there."

Nancy began to tremble and buried her face in her hands. "What a nightmare."

Fred sat beside her and touched her hand, less for comfort than for attention. "We have to talk about this, Nancy. Enos isn't going to arrest you yet, but the only reason he's holding off is because of the baby."

Her head shot up. "How does he know about that?"

"That's not important. Now, what I—"

"How do *you* know about it?" Her eyes snapped and her face closed down.

"It's not as big a secret as you think."

"Apparently not."

"So, what were you doing at EnviroSampl that night?"

"Fighting with my husband. Isn't that what Mitch told Enos?"

Fred nodded. "It is. But why?"

"Why? Because Adam didn't want this baby, that's why. He wanted me to have an abortion."

Fred's heart twisted. "Are you sure?"

"Of course I'm sure. It's why we separated. Why he wanted the divorce. He wanted me to have an abortion, but I refused. He didn't want the baby, and he didn't want me anymore."

Fred touched her shoulder tentatively, but when she flinched he pulled his hand away. "Doc told me you'd been *trying* to get pregnant. That Adam was thrilled."

"Doc doesn't know what he's talking about."

At a loss for words, Fred folded his hands together and studied them for several seconds. In the end, he could only manage to croak out, "I'm so sorry."

She flashed a tearful glance at him and shoved herself away from the table. "Just don't tell my mother. Please."

"You can't keep it a secret, Nancy. Secrets don't help."

"You're wrong, Uncle Fred. It's the truth that doesn't help."

Fred hated to hear such sentiment from someone so young. He shook his head and tried to understand where her bitterness came from, but he couldn't comprehend any of it. "Why did Adam want you to get an abortion? That seems so unlike him."

She shot to her feet and her face colored with anger.

"Why do you say that? Adam was a good man, but he wasn't a saint."

"I didn't say he was." Fred reached for her hand and held it gently. "Tell me what happened between the two of you."

She jerked her hand away. "I can't."

"I know it's hard to talk about, but if there's anything you can say that will shed some light on Adam's death—"

Anger snapped in her eyes. "You think Adam was killed because of me? Or the baby?"

"I didn't say that, either."

"Maybe you think *I* killed him."

Fred stood and met her gaze. "If I thought that, you wouldn't be here now. I'm trying to keep you out of jail. *Trying* to get to the bottom of this mess, but you're not making it any easier."

She didn't say anything, but her stare faltered just a little.

He put his hands on her shoulders and made her face him. "Was Adam having an affair?"

She stiffened, but she didn't try to pull away. "What makes you think that?"

"I can't think of any other reason he'd want you to have an abortion. Maybe he was in love with someone else. Maybe he left you for her, but then you found out you were pregnant. Maybe he resented the baby—even thought you were trying to hold him with it."

"Stop it—" she barely breathed the words. "Don't say any more."

Fred's heart sank. He hadn't liked the idea of Adam cheating, but her reaction convinced him. "Do you know who she was?"

She twisted away from him and shook her head almost frantically. "No."

But he didn't believe her. She knew more than she was telling him. "You can't keep the truth hidden any longer, Nancy. A man is dead—your husband is dead—and we have to find the person who's responsible."

"I don't know anything," she insisted, but her expression convinced Fred she knew quite a lot.

"Was it Brooke Westphal?"

Nancy's jaw tightened. "No. You're way off base, Uncle Fred. You don't know what you're talking about." She backed a few steps toward the living room. "I—I don't feel well all of a sudden. Maybe I ought to lie down again."

"You can't run away from the truth."

"You're not even close to the truth," she said.

"Then tell me—"

But she turned away.

"What about your car?" he shouted in desperation.

She pushed open the door. "I can get it later." And before he could say anything else, she let the door swing shut between them.

Fred stared after her for a long time, battling his emotions and sorting his thoughts. He hadn't intended to upset her; he'd only wanted to get to the truth.

He sighed heavily and poured himself another cup of coffee. He needed it now more than ever.

Brooke Westphal. He couldn't even imagine her as the "other woman." But she had the answers he needed, he was convinced of it. He longed to talk to her right now—this minute. But he'd have to wait until evening when he could find her alone, and when Douglas could stay here with Nancy. With any luck, he'd learn the truth about a lot of things.

He stared out the kitchen window and took a healthy swig of scalding coffee. And he prayed that Nancy would forgive him for bringing the truth to light.

thirteen

Fred waited until after dinner to bring up his idea. He waited until Nancy had eaten and disappeared into her room to rest. Until he'd cleared the table and Douglas had run the dish water.

He watched as Douglas rinsed a plate and stacked it in the drainer. "What are your plans tonight, son?"

Douglas washed another plate, rinsed, and shrugged. "I'm driving Alison down to Denver in the morning for an appointment with Dr. Shriver, so I think I'll hit the sack early. Why?"

"You don't mind staying here for an hour or so with Nancy, then?"

Douglas looked up at him. "Where are you going?"

"Out."

"That's all you're going to tell me? Out?"

"Out."

Douglas grinned. "You either have a hot date, or you're digging around in something that Enos isn't going to like."

Fred dried a plate and placed it on the shelf. "Well, I don't have a date."

"I didn't think so. You're trying to figure out who killed Adam, aren't you?"

"I'm trying to help Nancy stay out of jail."

Douglas leaned one hip against the counter. "And Enos knows what you're doing?"

"He suspects."

"What about Maggie?"

"She confronted me with her suspicions this afternoon."

Douglas's grin widened and he shook his head. "You're

one of a kind, Dad." He turned back to the dishes. "I suppose you want me to cover for you."

"I don't want you to actually *lie*, but you don't have to volunteer anything if one of them calls."

"All right. You got it—on one condition."

Bribery. Fred scowled. "What's that?"

"You tell *me* the truth. Where are you going?"

"To visit Brooke Westphal."

"Brooke? You're kidding? Why?"

"You know her?"

Douglas nodded. "I went to school with her oldest brother and I see her at the Copper Penny once in a while."

Fred dried another plate. "Tell me about her. I haven't seen her since she left high school."

"She's a nice kid. We've talked once or twice, and she bought me a beer one night."

"She bought *you* a beer?" Times certainly had changed. "Does she have a boyfriend?"

"I don't know. We didn't talk about it."

"Have you ever seen her with anyone?"

Douglas pondered for a second. "No. Not that I remember. Why?"

"Rumor has it that she and Adam were having an affair."

"Are you serious?"

Fred nodded. "Unfortunately."

"I don't believe it. She's not that kind of girl."

"I certainly don't *want* to believe it."

"But you do?"

"I'm beginning to. Anyway, that's why I want to talk to her tonight. I figure I'll either confirm the rumor or blow it out of the water."

Douglas loaded dirty glasses into the water almost absently. "Does Nancy know?"

"I'm afraid so."

"Oh, man— She must feel like hell."

"I think that's putting it mildly." Fred dried another dish and stacked it in the cupboard and tried to send Douglas an eye signal to wash a little faster.

Instead, Douglas added more hot water to the sink. "Do you think Brooke killed Adam?"

"I don't know. Maybe." Fred stacked another dry plate and shook his head. "No, I guess I really don't. Not unless she's changed a lot."

"Do you think she knows who did?"

"I don't know."

Douglas stopped washing altogether. "Listen, Dad. Why don't you just go? I'll finish the dishes."

"We're almost done, aren't we?"

"It'll take me less than five minutes, and you're chomping at the bit to get out of here. Go now, and maybe you'll be back before Margaret calls."

Fred didn't have to be prompted twice. He tossed his dish towel over the back of a chair and snatched his keys from the counter. "Keep an eye on Nancy. I'm worried about her."

"Don't be. I know what she's going through."

Fred squeezed the boy's shoulder. "I know. And thanks, son."

"Just don't get me in trouble with Maggie."

Fred opened the back door and stepped outside. "You can always claim I snuck out when you weren't looking."

Douglas pretended to scowl at him. "Are you kidding? Then I'd be in trouble for not keeping a better eye on you. Just hurry back."

With one last smile to cement their conspiracy, Fred closed the door and hurried to the garage. Less than a minute later, he pulled out of the driveway and started up Lake Front toward town. And within minutes he was following the highway toward Mountain Home for the fourth time in three days.

The sun had settled on the mountain peaks, and pools of shadow drenched the highway. Most of the time dense forest filled his vision, but every mile or so he drove out of the trees. Where meadows lined the roads, he could see distant wildlife taking advantage of Mother Nature's feeding time.

He drove slowly, aware that deer or elk could bound out

of the trees at any moment. Bear and moose were a little less likely, but not impossible. He'd driven these roads for many years as he'd crisscrossed the school district. They were like second nature to him now, and for that very reason he never made the mistake of thinking he knew what he'd find around the next bend.

He felt exactly the same way about life. He wouldn't have pictured Brooke Westphal and Adam Bigelow together in a million years, but apparently . . .

He just hoped he wasn't on a wild-goose chase, that he'd find Brooke home. Maybe he should have made an appointment with her, but he hadn't wanted to put her on guard. Still, the closer he got, the more anxious he grew.

If Adam had left Nancy for Brooke and then Nancy announced her pregnancy and refused to get an abortion, Enos might think Nancy killed Adam because he refused to come back to her. Or that Brooke killed him because he'd agreed to go back because of the baby. Fred didn't like either choice.

He reached Mountain Home as dusk settled and found Brooke's small blue house without trouble. It sat near the road, one of a long line of similar cottages nestled into the mountainside like kittens against a mother cat. A light burned in one of the front windows, and Fred's hopes kindled. With luck, he'd get to the bottom of this tonight.

He parked on the street and followed the sidewalk to the front door. He rang the bell and when the door finally opened, Brooke stood in the opening.

The last few years hadn't dulled her looks or diminished the life that burned in her eyes. Light spilled over shoulders and through her shoulder-length blonde hair. When she recognized him, she smiled as if she'd seen him just yesterday. "Mr. Vickery. What are you doing here?"

"I need to talk to you. Have you got a minute?"

"Sure." She stepped aside and let him enter, then shut the door and led him into the living room.

The room looked like her, tiny and bright, friendly and comfortable. Pink and yellow, green and blue tumbled over each other throughout the room—flowers on the couch, plaid on the throw pillows—none of the furniture had escaped the color. Tables were draped with it, walls splashed with it, picture frames lined with it. And somehow, with Brooke standing in the midst of that riot of color, the room looked exactly right.

She gestured toward an easy chair, then folded herself into a corner of the couch. "What do you need?"

"To ask you a few questions." He fit himself into the chair. It was wider, deeper, sturdier than it looked, and he settled into it eagerly.

"About what?"

"Adam Bigelow."

Her smile faded a watt. "What about him?"

"How well did you know him?"

"Very well. Why?"

Somehow the rumor was even harder to believe in her presence. "I'm trying to help Nancy find out why he was killed."

Her expression didn't falter, not even for a split second. "What do you think *I* can tell you?"

"Who do you think did it?"

She looked thoughtful. "I've been wondering that ever since it happened. To tell you the truth, I don't know."

"Surely you must have an idea, a suspicion—?"

"No. I can't think of anyone who'd want him dead." She tossed back her hair and knit her brows together. "Isn't it possible it was a stranger? Maybe someone broke in to the office and Adam surprised him—"

Fred shook his head. "The murderer either had a key, or Adam let him or her inside."

"Then it was someone he knew." She sounded incredibly sad.

"I'm afraid so."

She stood and walked to the window. Pulling back the curtain, she peered outside as if she'd find some answer there.

"Tell me about your relationship with him," Fred prompted after several minutes of silence.

She leaned her forehead against the wall, and when she

spoke again, her voice drifted softly across the room. "There isn't a lot to tell."

"You were friends?"

"Yes."

"More than friends?"

Her head whipped around, and her eyes darkened. "No. Absolutely not."

The intensity of her answer set him back a pace, confused him, and made him forget his next question. "No?"

"What made you think we were?"

"Well, I— Someone told me they'd seen you together. Alone."

"That doesn't mean anything. You and I are alone together right now."

She had a point. "It was more than that. They mentioned phone calls, secret meetings, that sort of thing."

To his surprise, she laughed. "You must have talked to Tiffany Scott."

"Well, yes."

"That explains it. She has the most vivid imagination of anyone I know."

"Then it's not true?"

"No."

He rubbed his forehead as if it would help order his thoughts. He'd been so certain. Even Nancy believed the rumor—didn't she? Or had he misread her reaction and jumped to that conclusion?

"So you didn't meet Adam away from the office?" he asked.

Brooke's smile slid from her face. She came back to the couch, dropped onto it, and leaned forward with her elbows on her knees. "The truth is, we did meet a couple of times, and we probably made a few phone calls that sounded kind of secretive. But it *wasn't* because we were sleeping together."

"What were you doing?"

She shoved her hair out of her face, but it tumbled right back. "Work."

"Then why meet in secret?"

"There wasn't anything secret about it. A couple of times we worked late on a test or something, but we didn't try to hide it from anyone."

"I didn't think Adam worked in the lab."

"He didn't, that's why he asked me to help a few times—when he had a special test to run."

"Why you and not Mitch or Charlotte?"

"I don't know. I guess because Adam and I were friends. We've known each other since we were kids, and I was willing to help him when he needed it."

"The others weren't?"

"I don't think Adam ever asked. Mitch is a nice enough guy, but he's not the type to go the extra mile for anyone else. And Charlotte—" She broke off and smiled coldly. "Well, Charlotte probably *would* have gone the extra mile if Adam had let her."

Now there was a new twist to the tale. "Why do you think that?"

But she just shook her head and gave an embarrassed laugh. "Forget it, I'm just being catty. Charlotte's okay, I guess. She's eager." Brooke definitely didn't mean it as a compliment.

"Tell me what Adam was working on when he died."

"We just got a couple of new contracts, and I know he wasn't satisfied with the results of his latest project. We went back into the lab a couple of days before he died to rerun the tests."

"I don't understand. I thought the test results were sent directly to Philip Aagard. How did Adam know what they were?"

"Adam always requested a copy of his test results from Philip. He was very thorough."

"Did he get them before they were sent to the EPA, or after?"

"I don't know. Why?"

"If he saw them before, I can understand why he'd want to run a second set of tests and make sure the right results were sent out. But if he got them after . . ." He shrugged and let her draw her own conclusions.

She obviously reached the same one he had. "He must have gotten them before, or it wouldn't make sense to gather new samples and rerun the tests."

"He gathered new samples?"

She nodded. "That's what he told me."

"I still don't understand why he had you working on it after hours. How many tests did you perform?"

"A couple. Three. I don't know. Not very many."

They sat in silence for several minutes until a new idea occurred to Fred. "Did you rerun tests that you performed originally?" he asked.

She met his gaze steadily, as if she'd already made that connection. "No."

"Whose tests did you redo? Charlotte's or Mitch's?"

"I didn't know whose they were. I only know they weren't on any property I'd tested already."

"How did you know that?"

"Adam told me."

"So he brought in new samples and got you to give him a second opinion? Did he ever ask one of the others to retest your results?"

"Not that I know of. But, then, I don't think they knew that I checked theirs."

Fred shifted position in the chair, rubbed his chin, and tried to pull his thoughts together. He thought about Mitch's story that he'd been delivering test results to Adam, and wondered whether Mitch had been telling the truth after all.

Half an hour ago he'd been convinced Adam was killed because of his personal life. Now he didn't know what he thought. "Why did he want the tests rerun?" he asked. "What did he hope to find?"

"I don't know."

"What property did you run the tests on?"

She untucked herself and shoved her fingers through her hair in a jerky, agitated motion. "I don't know. I just wish I did."

This time he didn't believe her. He'd struck a nerve. "Did anybody else know you were working nights?"

She shook her head. "I don't think so."

"If you had to pick one of the two—Mitch or Charlotte— which would you think Adam was double-checking?"

"I'm not sure. Mitch is terribly competitive, determined to be the best in his field. But I wouldn't put it past him to cut corners if he thought it would get him somewhere. Charlotte tries to be careful, but the quality of her work has always been inconsistent, and it's gotten worse since she and Mitch started seeing each other."

"Charlotte and Mitch are dating?"

Brooke's lips twitched. "If you want to call it that."

It took almost a full minute for her meaning to hit him, but when it did, Fred's face flamed. He pushed himself to his feet and crossed the room. "Weren't you curious to know which property you were testing?"

She shook her head quickly. "Adam didn't want to tell me."

That didn't necessarily eliminate curiosity—at least not for anyone Fred knew. And for the second time he had the feeling she wasn't telling the truth. This time he didn't let it pass. "But you knew, didn't you?"

She stared at him for several long seconds before she nodded. "All right. Yes. I saw the files."

"Which property was it?"

"Shadow Mountain."

Fred pulled back in surprise and stared at Brooke. "Shadow Mountain? Why did you run tests on that place?"

"Somebody must be interested in buying it."

"But there've been people interested in developing the property before now, and I've never heard about trouble with the EPA. I didn't think the property was contaminated."

Brooke shook her head. "Maybe they were thinking about a different kind of development. All I know is the original tests on the tailings, the quarries, and the sinkhole came out showing a lot of contamination. In fact, with that old mine there, it'd take a fortune to clean the place up enough for any kind of development, and I never could imagine anyone willing to put that kind of money into it. But some of the tests Adam had me run came out clean."

"Are you sure?"

She nodded soberly. "Yes. It surprised me, too."

"Why the difference?"

"I have no idea—unless the second set of tests weren't on Shadow Mountain property."

"Did you see any other files?"

"No, but that doesn't mean Adam wasn't working on something else."

Fred pondered that thought for a few seconds, more confused than ever. "Who wants to buy Shadow Mountain?"

She shrugged an I-don't-know.

He drew in a deep breath and tried to take it all in. He felt as if he were in the middle of an old nightmare. Shadow Mountain had been at the center of the first murders he'd been involved with. Now it looked as if it might be connected to Adam Bigelow's death, as well.

"Who ran the original tests?" he asked.

Brooke met his gaze steadily. "I don't know—really, I don't. But I always kind of thought it might have been Mitch because he stopped by the office late one night and found us there in Adam's office, and the next day he and Adam got into a terrible argument. I assumed he'd figured out what Adam was doing, and that he didn't like it."

"Why did you think that?"

She looked uncertain. "I've been trying to remember what made me think that ever since Adam died. Believe me, if Mitch killed him, I want his butt in jail—he's not my favorite person at EnviroSampl. But if it's all my imagination, I don't want to get him in trouble."

Fred put a hand on her shoulder and worked up a reassuring smile. "Don't worry. I've never known Enos to arrest somebody on speculation. What else can you tell me?"

Relief flitted across her face, but she shook her head. "Nothing. Honestly."

Fred waited a few seconds, hoping she'd think of something else, but she shook her head again. "I'm sorry."

He pressed her shoulder. "You've been a big help."

She stood and smiled tentatively. "Do you think this is why Adam was killed?"

"I honestly don't know," he admitted. "We can't assume anything."

"I can't imagine anyone killing Adam because of some reworked tests—I mean, it sounds ridiculous."

It did to Fred, too. But he knew he didn't have the whole story—yet. "If you think of anything else, will you let me know?"

"Of course I will." Walking slowly, she led him to the door and flipped on a light to guide him back down the path. "Be careful driving home."

"I'm always careful." Fred hurried through the shadows to his car and slid behind the wheel. Exhaustion swamped him suddenly, and his arthritis bothered him in the cool night air. He had a long drive home—plenty of time to think things through and reorder his ideas—and he hoped to put the time to good use.

He felt as though he'd stirred up the mud from the bottom of a pond and clouded the water. He knew too many things, and the truth lay somewhere in the middle of all of it. But would he recognize it when he saw it?

Longing for the comfort of home and the warmth of his bed, he drove out of town and started back down the mountain. He wished Brooke hadn't mentioned Shadow Mountain, because thinking it might be connected in some way to Adam's death left him with a very bad taste in his mouth.

fourteen

When the sun came up the next morning, Fred slid open his closet door as quietly as he could and reached inside for his boots. After the trip from Mountain Home, he'd fallen into bed exhausted, but he hadn't slept well. Too many things battled for his attention: too many ideas, too many possibilities, too many concerns. So when the first rays of sun peeked through his curtains, he'd abandoned all pretense of sleep and climbed out of bed.

He told himself he wanted to take his morning constitutional early and that walking around the lake would help him pull his thoughts together. But he wanted to get outside without waking Nancy. In her condition she needed all the rest she could get.

Pulling the laces tight on his workboot, he looped one end around his finger. But arthritis refused to let his fingers form the laces into a bow, so he abandoned his first effort and started again.

When he heard footsteps in the hallway, he glanced at the clock beside his bed. It sounded like Douglas getting ready to drive Alison to her appointment with Dr. Shriver.

But a moment later someone knocked on the door. "Uncle Fred? Are you awake?"

Leaving his boot untied, he slopped across the room and pulled open the door.

Nancy stood there, dressed in jeans and a T-shirt, tennis shoes and a baseball cap, and a shy smile. "Good," she said. "I didn't wake you."

"Is something wrong?" he asked.

She shook her head. "No. Everything's fine. Are you going to take your walk this morning?"

"Of course. I never miss it."

"Would you mind if I came with you?"

He stepped into the hallway and worked an arm around her shoulders. "I can't think of anything I'd like more. Let me get the coffee started before we leave—I like to have a cup when I get back."

She glanced at his untied boot and smiled. "Why don't you finish getting ready while I do the coffee?" And when he opened his mouth to protest, she held up a hand. "I *can* do the coffee. It's decaf, isn't it? Margaret said that's all the doctor lets you drink."

He kept his face blank as he nodded. If Nancy wanted decaf, that's what he'd serve—but only because of her baby. And he'd make sure he got to the Bluebird every morning for a cup of the real stuff. "Just be sure to use the coffee in the canister."

She started away, then looked back over her shoulder and raised her eyebrows as if he'd said something suspicious. "Okay. Are there other choices?"

"I'm not allowed other choices."

Her lips twitched. "I see. I think I'll use the coffee in the canister." With one last smile over her shoulder, she disappeared into the kitchen.

Fred went back to his boots, pleased that this time his fingers didn't freeze up on him. By the time he'd tied his boots, Nancy had the coffeepot ready and the automatic timer set.

He led her out the back door and through the yard to the trail. Dust puffed from their feet as they followed the path toward the southern tip of the lake, and they walked in silence for the first several minutes.

As a girl, Nancy had often stayed overnight with Fred and Phoebe, and she'd usually joined him for his morning constitutional. Fred had always enjoyed her company—her chatter had cheered him, her smile had warmed him, and her eagerness to see, feel, and smell everything they passed had sounded a chord deep within him.

But today tension radiated from her. She didn't mention the sunrise or the way the lake's placid surface glittered or the mossy, fresh smell of the forest. She walked quickly, eyes straight ahead, shoulders back.

Fred matched her pace and wondered why she'd wanted to join him. Since she obviously didn't have much to say, she probably just wanted company.

He let the silence ring between them until they rounded the southern tip of the lake. Then he could stand it no longer. "The lake sure is low this year—did you notice?"

She spared it a glance. "It is, isn't it?"

"It's getting late enough in the year, we ought to start getting some afternoon rain," he speculated.

She tried to look interested. "Yeah. I guess so."

"Only problem is, we'll start getting thunderstorms. And with the forest this dry, the lightning could spark fires."

She knit her brows together in a look of concern. "I hope not."

He obviously hadn't kindled much interest, so he gave up on casual conversation and let the forest work its magic. Chipmunks chattered at them as they passed, and birds called down to them from the treetops. Aspen leaves shivered in an almost invisible breeze, and waves melted softly on the shore of the lake.

When they reached the narrow spot on the path, Fred held back and let Nancy go first. She marched through the brush, head held high, until the back of Summer Dey's cabin peeked through the trees at them.

She looked over her shoulder with a half-smile. "Does that cute guy with the Doberman still live here?"

Fred stepped over an exposed root and shook his head. "The Holbrooks moved away a few years ago. The lady who lives here now is an artist—Summer Dey."

Nancy laughed. "You're kidding? That's her *name?*"

"As far as we know."

She waited for him to close the narrow distance between them, then took his arm and leaned her head on his shoulder. "You know what? I've missed taking walks with you."

"There's no reason you can't still join me once in a while, even if you have grown up."

"I know." She sighed as softly as the breeze. "Sometimes I wish I hadn't. Sometimes I wish I'd always stayed three or four." She sighed again as he guided her under a low branch. "I've made such a mess of things. Of my marriage. My life. I never planned for it to turn out this way."

Regret served no useful purpose, and Fred hated hearing it in her voice. "We all make mistakes, sweetheart."

"You're trying to make me feel better, aren't you?"

"I'm just telling you the truth."

She shook her head and pulled away slightly so she could look straight into his eyes. "Where did you go last night?"

"I had some business to take care of. Douglas didn't leave you alone, did he?"

"No, he stayed there all evening." She looked troubled. "I hate being such a bother. I know Margaret's concerned, but you really don't have to babysit me."

"We care about you. We're not babysitting, and you're not a bother."

"You almost make me believe it." She worked up a smile. "I really appreciate you letting me stay with you."

He squeezed her hand and smiled down at her. "You're family, Nancy. You're right where you belong."

They walked several more feet before she spoke again. "Margaret thinks you're trying to figure out who killed Adam—did you know that?"

"I know she's got her suspicions."

"Is it true? Are you trying to figure it out?"

He scowled. "Are you spying for her?"

"No. I'm curious."

He studied her face and her eyes grew serious. "All right then, it's true," he said.

"Have you found out anything yet?"

"A little. Not much."

"Like what?"

"Nothing concrete."

"Like what?" she demanded.

"I don't think—"

She stopped in her tracks. "Please don't, Uncle Fred. I have the right to know. He *was* my husband, after all. And Enos won't tell me anything." The frailty that had been there two days ago had been replaced by something stronger, and Fred was glad to see it.

"I asked you yesterday whether Adam was having an affair. Was he?"

She shook her head. "No."

"You're sure about that?"

"Positive."

Fred wished he could share her certainty. "What do you know about his relationship with Brooke Westphal?"

He could tell he surprised her with that question. "What relationship with Brooke Westphal?"

"According to Brooke, they often worked late together."

Nancy shook her head. "That's not true—at least it wasn't before we separated. I don't know what he did after."

"So they *could* have worked late the last couple of weeks?"

She nodded reluctantly. "I guess so. You don't really think he was having an affair with her?"

"I think it's a possibility."

"Well, he wasn't." Nancy took a step or two away and studied a chokecherry branch as if she'd never seen anything more interesting.

"How can you be so certain?"

She didn't answer for several seconds, and when she did her voice came softly. "Adam had strong feelings about infidelity. He didn't approve, and he would *never* have cheated on me."

"He wouldn't be the first person to do something he disapproved of."

But she shook her head with grim determination. "Not Adam. Not that. If Brooke says they were working, they were. What else have you learned?"

"Apparently he had an argument with Mitch Hancock just before he died. And one with your dad. And he got a telephone call on the night of the murder, and then he made one . . ." But as he spoke, he realized how little he actually knew, so he shrugged and let his voice trail off.

Nancy considered his answer. "What did he and Mitch argue about?"

"I'm not sure. I haven't talked to Mitch yet."

"Are you going to?"

"I plan on it."

She nodded and studied the tops of the aspen trees. "When?"

"I haven't decided yet. Soon."

"Who do you think did it?"

"I don't know," he admitted. "The more I learn, the more confused I get."

"But you don't suspect me?"

"No, I don't."

She smiled, just a gentle curving of her lips, but relief and gratitude burned in her eyes. "What about Mitch?"

"It's a possibility, I suppose. There are half a dozen possibilities, but nothing adds up. Mitch claimed he was at the office early on the morning of the murder to deliver test samples to Adam, and it's possible he was lying. But even if he *is*, what possible motive could he have?"

She shrugged. "Then how about Brooke? She's lying about having an affair with Adam—why would she do that?"

"Actually, she denies it. I heard the rumor from someone else."

Nancy's brows knit. "Who?"

"Pete Scott's wife."

She groaned. "Tiffany? Oh, hell. Half of the county will have heard about it by now. What about Charlotte Isaacson? What did she say when you talked to her?"

"She's the one who made me wonder if Mitch was lying about the tests. She claims the results go straight to Philip—that Mitch wouldn't have gone to work early to deliver tests to Adam. According to Brooke, Charlotte and Mitch have been seeing each other the past few months. Did Adam ever mention anything about that to you?"

"Mitch is probably the boyfriend I heard Adam talking to

Charlotte about." She looked thoughtful. "You know, I don't think Adam liked Mitch very much."

"What makes you say that?"

"I remember him complaining about Mitch being closed-minded. About the way he kissed up to Philip. It drove Adam crazy." She smiled at some memory. "Adam believed people should earn what they get—Mitch thought you could manipulate it." She stared into the trees for a minute before she shook herself as if to bring herself back to the present. "Brooke. Mitch. Charlotte. Anybody else?"

"A man named Roy Dennington."

"Who's he?"

"I saw him at EnviroSampl the day of the murder, and I know he's a land developer. Other than that, I don't know a blasted thing."

"Is he a black man?"

Fred nodded. "Why? Do you know him?"

"No. But I remember hearing that a black man was trying to buy Shadow Mountain."

"The man's race was an issue?"

"I don't think so. In fact, I don't even remember how I knew that." She took a couple of steps away as if trying to remember something, then turned back eagerly. "Listen, Uncle Fred, I just had a great idea. Let me help you."

"Help me what?"

"Find out who killed Adam."

Fred shoved his hands into his pockets and shook his head. "But I'm not *investigating*."

She looked skeptical. "If you say so. But you are doing *something*, and I want to help."

"I've asked a couple of questions, that's all."

"Then that's what I want to help with."

But Fred didn't want Nancy to hear unfounded rumors and speculation—not in her condition. "I don't think it's a good idea. Not with the baby—"

She frowned. "You mean you want me to stay behind because I'm pregnant?"

"Well . . . yes."

Her face darkened. "You think I'm too delicate?"

Obviously a bad choice of words. "Not delicate, exactly—"

"Believe me, I'm no more delicate than you are."

"I know that—"

"And I'm not so stupid I'd do anything to hurt the baby."

"I never said you would."

"Not in so many words, but I know what you're thinking."

He humphed and walked a few steps away.

But she danced after him, acting more like herself than he'd seen yet. "I'm serious, Uncle Fred."

"So am I."

"If you can do it, so can I."

"No."

She grabbed his arms and made him face her. "Look, I spent the last two days lying in bed and feeling sorry for myself, but that's not going to help me, it's not going to help Adam, and it's not going to help my baby."

He shrugged away from her, but he liked hearing the life in her voice.

"Let's talk to him. Right now."

"Who? Mitch?" Fred shook his head. "He'll be at work."

"It's Saturday," she argued. "And I'm going with you."

"No you're not."

"I'm not asking for permission."

"What if he's the killer? What will you do then?"

"Then I'll make sure nothing happens to you," she said, but her eyes danced at her joke.

He humphed again. "Your mother would have my hide."

Her eyes grew serious. "I need to do this. Please."

He hesitated.

"Look," she argued. "I'm not hysterical, and I'm not going to flip out if you let me come along. I loved Adam, but we weren't *in love* with each other anymore. I've made a lot of mistakes the past few months. If he'd lived, maybe I could have made some things up to him, but the only thing I can do now is make sure his killer doesn't get away with it."

"Your mother will have my hide," he repeated.

She grinned. "And Margaret will have mine. But I won't tell if you won't."

He looped an arm around her shoulder and led her back onto the path. "I'll think about it."

She sighed heavily, but she didn't argue.

They walked past Doc Huggins's house and turned around just before the Kilburns' place. Fred pointed out places of interest and changes in the scenery, Doc's new toolshed and Mary Kilburn's new car. He named trees and undergrowth, made sure Nancy saw the poison oak a few feet off the path, and stopped to listen to a woodpecker doing its job.

Nancy pretended an interest in the toolshed, admired the color of Mary's car, paid strict attention to the poison oak, and made appreciative noises over the woodpecker as if she suspected he was testing her.

Fred didn't mention Adam or the murder again until the back deck of his own house came into view. Then he stopped and faced her with the most solemn expression he could muster. "I guess I can't talk you out of this foolish idea."

She shook her head.

"If I let you come along, you have to play by my rules."

"Absolutely," she promised.

He growled low in his throat as if he hated conceding the victory. "First things first," he said. "First, coffee. *Then* we'll talk about paying a visit to Mitch Hancock."

fifteen

Fred drove slowly down Mountain Home's Main Street while he and Nancy scoured road signs for the one marking Sprucewood Lane. According to her, it would lead them straight up the mountain to the Sprucewood Condominiums where the telephone book said they'd find Mitch Hancock.

Time was, Fred knew his way around this town. He still knew the basic layout but, like everything else, Mountain Home had changed in the past couple of years. Now, unfamiliar streets curled off the main drag like pencil shavings, and there was no rhyme nor reason to the way they'd been placed.

Fred frowned over at Nancy, frustrated by the search. "How much further?"

"It's right around here somewhere," she said slowly, and a second later she pointed. "There it is. Over there—see? Sprucewood Lane."

Fred inched to the center of the street and flicked on his left turn signal. He waited while an old blue Chevy pickup crawled past and then followed the narrow road until it ended in the parking lot of the Sprucewood Condominiums—a scrabbling, gray collection of buildings that had been stuck together at odd angles on the side of the mountain.

The minute he cut the engine, Nancy pushed open her door and jumped out of the car. When he didn't immediately follow, she looked back at him. "What's wrong?"

"You can learn a lot about people from the place they live, but I never could figure out what kind of person would want to live in a place like this. They're the ugliest things I've ever seen."

Nancy looked at him as if he'd lost his mind. "Are you kidding? They cost a *fortune*."

"Now *that's* a solid recommendation."

"Have you ever been inside?"

"No."

She looked wistful. "They're really nice. All hardwood floors, huge plateglass windows, and the views are incredible." She sounded as if her list ought to impress him.

It didn't. He clearly remembered Phoebe's elation when they'd finally carpeted the living room and all the hours she'd worked trying to make the windows sparkle. "You have neighbors on the other side of your walls," he groused as he climbed out of the car. "And not a speck of privacy."

Nancy smoothed the legs of her jeans and stepped onto the sidewalk with a wry grin. "You're impossible, you know that? You don't like anything to change."

"That's not true. I don't mind change, but I don't think new automatically means better." He took a second to get his bearings. They needed unit S-103. When he saw the building with a large metal "S" stuck on its side, he struck off toward it.

She matched his stride. "I hope Mitch is home. I still think we should have called first."

"If we'd called, we couldn't catch him off guard. And we'll get more out of him if we surprise him."

She looked doubtful. "What do you expect to get out of him—assuming we catch him off guard?"

"The truth."

"And you think we'll recognize it when we hear it?"

"Absolutely." He slowed his step and looked over at her. "We'll certainly know if we don't hear it."

She still didn't look convinced. "I hope you're right."

"Look, sweetheart, we know Mitch and Adam fought before Adam died. All we need to know is why, and what that argument had to do with the murder."

"Maybe nothing."

"Maybe *everything*. Mitch is the only person we know of besides you and your dad who fought with Adam. We can't afford to ignore this lead."

"Do you think Mitch killed him?"

Fred dragged to a stop. "I don't know. Maybe."

"Why? What possible motive could he have?"

"The Shadow Mountain tests. If he was so determined to be Philip Aagard's number one man and Adam found out he was making mistakes in his work . . ." When she made a face, he broke off with a shrug. "Okay, it's weak. But we'll never know unless we talk to him."

Nancy plunged her hands into her pockets and tried to look determined. "Then let's go talk to him."

"Good. But we follow my rules, remember?"

She nodded. "I remember."

"That means I do the talking."

"I know."

She sounded so much more cooperative than his own children would in similar circumstances, Fred studied her face to see if she was hiding something. He saw nothing but genuine anticipation, so he took her elbow and set off down the sidewalk at a brisk clip. They passed several units, rounded a sharp curve, and found themselves in front of number 103.

Its front door peeked out from a shadowed recess, but a narrow patio set off to one side managed to capture the morning sun. A table with umbrella and several padded lawn chairs held center stage. The patio door stood open, but Fred could see no sign of Mitch.

Remembering Brooke Westphal's claim that Mitch and Charlotte were keeping company, Fred tried to imagine Charlotte here. He had no trouble. Like Nancy, she'd be impressed by this place. But Charlotte would also be impressed by anyone who owned it.

Doing his best to keep one eye on the open patio door, Fred stepped into the shadows and rang the bell. Within seconds, heavy footsteps sounded on the other side, and Mitch Hancock opened the door.

One glance convinced Fred that all Mitch's charm lay in his worldly possessions. He wore blue corduroy shorts but no shirt, and his soft belly hung in folds over the waistband of his pants—fertile ground for the crop of wheat-gold hair growing there.

He smiled when he saw Fred, but his eyes widened in surprise when he saw Nancy. "Nancy? What are you doing here? What's going on?"

Determined to take immediate control, Fred stepped forward. "We'd like to ask you some questions."

Mitch didn't even hesitate. "Sure. Come on in. Can I get you something? Coffee? Ice water?"

Though coffee sounded tempting, Fred didn't want to turn this into a social call. "Nothing for me, thanks."

Nancy shook her head, obviously taking her vow of silence seriously.

Mitch led them into the living room, a long, narrow room with Nancy's beloved hardwood floors, a fireplace set into one wall, and an incredible view of the condominium unit across the way. A large blue couch stood in front of an open window, and several easy chairs clustered nearby. Mitch gestured vaguely toward the furniture and dropped into a chair beside an end table that held a coffee cup and an ashtray brimming with cigarette butts.

Fred waited until Nancy claimed one of the chairs, then lowered himself into one that didn't look too low.

Mitch leaned back in his chair and sent Nancy a sad smile. "I can't tell you how sorry I am about Adam. Are you doing okay?"

She managed a trembling smile in return. "I'm all right."

"God, what a mess. I still can't believe it. Have they figured out who did it?"

Nancy shook her head. "Not yet."

"Do they have any ideas? Any leads? Any suspects?"

"Not that I know of. But then they're not telling me very much."

Mitch shook his head slowly. "This is the damnedest thing, you know? One day you're working right alongside the guy, and the next—" He broke off suddenly and his face flamed, obviously embarrassed by the direction he was taking. "Oh, man. I'm sorry."

When Mitch paused to light a cigarette, Fred scooted

forward in his chair. "It's always a shock when someone dies unexpectedly. We're trying to find out why Adam was killed."

Mitch exhaled a cloud of smoke and looked confused. "What about the police? Aren't they still investigating?"

"Yes, of course they are."

"Well, then, I don't understand." Mitch looked from Fred to Nancy several times. "Why are *you* trying to figure it out? And why come to me?"

Fred didn't want to put him on guard, so he smiled. "Actually, we're just trying to clear up a couple of things that are a little confusing."

"Like what?"

"Well." Fred leaned a little closer. "We've heard that you and Adam had an argument the day before he died."

If Fred's announcement had any impact, Mitch didn't show it. He dragged deeply on his cigarette and looked thoughtful. "We might have, I guess."

"What about?"

Mitch shrugged. "I don't remember."

This was the second time in as many days Fred had heard someone say that, and he didn't believe Mitch any more than he'd believed Porter. "How can you not remember? If I'd fought with a man who was murdered less than twenty-four hours later, I'd remember."

Mitch stared at him for half a beat, then chuckled as if he'd suggested something amusing. "First of all, we didn't *fight*, we argued. And I don't remember because Adam and I probably had half a dozen arguments every day."

Fred shot a glance at Nancy to see if that answer surprised her as much as it did him, but she didn't give anything away. He turned back to Mitch. "What did you argue about?"

Another shrug. Another puff. "You name it. Look, Adam and I worked closely together. Everything he did impacted me directly. If he was half a day late getting me samples, my tests were half a day behind schedule." Mitch readjusted his position on the chair and leaned forward in his eagerness to explain himself. "If I start the tests late, the results are delivered late, and Philip climbs all over *me*." He dragged again and stubbed out the cigarette. "I don't mind eating trouble when I'm the one who screws up, but I'll be damned if I'm going to take the blame for somebody else's mistake."

"Like Adam's," Fred suggested.

Mitch nodded and looked satisfied with Fred's ability to understand. "Yes. Like Adam's."

"And it happened often?"

Mitch lifted one shoulder. "If not exactly that, something else. And it was getting steadily worse."

For the first time since they'd arrived, Nancy reacted. "Worse how?"

Mitch looked a little surprised by her question. "It was no secret the two of you were having problems," he said slowly. "And that affected Adam's performance. He brought it all to work with him, and his mind just wasn't on his job."

"So that's why he had to work late?" Fred asked.

"Work late? No. I—" Mitch broke off and looked confused. "How would I know why Adam worked late?"

"Well, I just assumed—" Fred managed a bit of confusion himself. "You said you worked so closely together."

Mitch scowled at him. "As far as I know, Adam didn't work overtime. What makes you think he did?"

"According to Brooke Westphal, they worked late together."

Mitch's eyes rounded in surprise. "Really?" He leaned back against the chair. "Why?"

"Brooke said they were retesting samples."

"My God. Did she say why?"

"She said she didn't know. That Adam never told her."

Mitch snorted a laugh and dug into his pack for another cigarette. "Well, I believe that. Adam always had to be top dog." He lit up and looked out the window for several seconds, before he asked, "If she didn't know what he was doing, why was she there?"

"I thought it was because Adam didn't work in the lab and didn't know how to run the tests."

Mitch stood and ran a hand over his chin. "This doesn't make a whole lot of sense to me." He flicked in the general direction of his ashtray. "Adam had no business checking up on any of us. If anyone was going to double-check test results, it would have been Philip." He shook his head, paced a few steps, and looked back at them with an agitated expression. "I mean, this kind of thing would have been *way* outside Adam's chain of command."

Fred struggled to understand what this meant. Had Brooke lied to him? Had she and Adam really used the lab as a rendezvous spot?

Nancy leaned forward, eager for reassurance. "Couldn't Philip have asked Adam to conduct the tests?"

Mitch shook his head. "*I'm* the lab supervisor. And even if Philip wanted someone to double-check us, why would he ask Adam? Adam didn't know his way around the lab."

"Then what do you think Adam was doing?" she asked.

Mitch looked back at Fred with pleading eyes. "I don't know."

But Fred knew, and he thanked his lucky stars he'd already prepared Nancy for the rumors about Adam and Brooke.

Mitch sent an apologetic look in Nancy's direction. "I'm sure I'm wrong."

"I want to hear what you think," she said.

With a sigh of resignation, Mitch gestured widely and sent ash drifting across his path. "Look, I have no reason to doubt Brooke's claim that she ran tests for Adam. And I believe she didn't know why. Brooke's easygoing, easily led—easily manipulated. If Adam said he needed help, she'd have been there. With bells on . . ."

Now where on earth was he going with this? Fred shot a glance at Nancy, but her face gave nothing away.

". . . but I don't think he was retesting samples, and I don't think Philip sanctioned it."

"Exactly what are you accusing him of doing?" Nancy's face might not betray any anxiety, but her trembling voice did.

Mitch turned to her. "I'm sorry, Nancy. I'd give anything not to bring this up, but ever since the day Adam was killed, I've been trying to figure out why Roy Dennington's hanging around."

Taken by surprise, Fred repeated, "Roy Dennington?"

"Yes. He shouldn't have been anywhere near Enviro-Sampl, but all of a sudden he's calling, making appointments with Adam, showing up at the office, for crying out loud—"

"Have you seen him lately?" Fred asked.

Mitch nodded. "Yes. Last night at the Four Seasons, of all places. The thing is, I can't figure out what he's doing here. Why here? Why EnviroSampl? Why *Adam?*"

That was the sixty-four-thousand-dollar question, Fred thought. "And you think you know why?"

"If Adam was sneaking into the lab after hours, yes." His brows knit together in a solid line. "Tell me, did Brooke know what property they were testing?"

"Shadow Mountain."

Mitch's face froze. "I see. You're sure?"

Fred nodded.

"Did she say what they found?"

"No. I don't think she knew what Adam was looking for."

Mitch paced a few steps toward the front door, then whirled back to face them. "Look, Nancy, I'm sorry about this, but I think—" He shook his head and paced away again. "God, I can't even *imagine* it could be true," he muttered.

Losing patience with hints, Fred worked his way out of his chair and put himself squarely in the younger man's path. "It's obvious you think you know what Adam was doing, so why don't you just tell us?"

In obvious agony, Mitch looked at Nancy again. "I hate to even speculate."

"Just tell me," she said.

Mitch drew in a tortured breath and smiled weakly. "I think maybe he was doctoring the files."

This answer was so different from the one Fred had been

expecting, he wondered if he'd heard right. "You think *what*?"

"I think he was altering the results of tests we'd performed on the Shadow Mountain property."

sixteen

Fred's heart skipped a beat, and Nancy sank back into her chair looking pale and shaken. "That's impossible," she whispered.

Mitch hunched over until his belly folded in on itself. He looked miserable. "I can't think of any other reason for him to be in the lab after hours."

For the first time in days Fred found himself wanting someone to accuse Adam of infidelity. What was that old saying—better the devil you know? He'd grown accustomed to the idea of Adam straying. Of Adam in love with Brooke and wanting a divorce from Nancy. But *this*— This came out of the blue and knocked him flat.

And he could see by the look on Nancy's face, it had the same effect on her. She hadn't even suspected something like this. She'd vehemently denied the possibility that Adam was cheating on her, but the accusation that he'd been involved in something illegal left her speechless.

Working to keep his voice steady, Fred asked, "Why would he do that?"

"Well—" Mitch hedged.

Fred's patience finally snapped. "You've already said the worst, don't beat around the bush now."

Mitch dropped back into his chair. "Like I said, I've been wondering what Roy Dennington's doing here. The only thing I can figure is that he's interested in buying a piece of property. Right?"

Fred nodded.

"Naturally, he's not going to be able to buy anything really valuable, so he looks at Shadow Mountain. That place is too contaminated to pass EPA standards, so what does he do?"

"He doesn't buy it," Nancy said.

Mitch waved her words away. "No! He's got one shot at the game up here. He *has* to find a way to build on the only property he can afford."

"What makes you think he can't afford anything else?"

"He's a wanna-be. Plain and simple."

Mitch must have seen something in Roy that Fred hadn't, or he knew something he wasn't telling. "You know that for a fact?"

"It's pretty damned obvious if you think about it. Besides, you know how it is in a place like this. You hear things—" Mitch broke off with a shrug.

"So you think Roy Dennington was desperate to get his foot in the door, that he somehow got to Adam, and Adam was altering test results so the property would look clean enough to meet EPA standards?"

Mitch nodded. "Maybe."

Fred looked to Nancy. "But why? Adam didn't need money, did he?"

She didn't answer, but she clutched her stomach and looked as if someone had hit her.

For her sake Fred wanted to deny Mitch's story. But he couldn't, because for the first time the pieces he held started forming a picture. Porter claimed that Adam had changed in the last year, but did Porter suspect this? Was that why he and Adam fought?

Fred moved to Nancy's side and asked again. "*Did* Adam need money?"

Tears welled in her eyes and spilled over onto her cheeks. She held herself and rocked back and forth. She didn't answer, but she didn't need to. Her reaction gave Fred his answer. He dragged in a steadying breath and tried to tamp down the sick feeling that rose in his throat. Mitch's story was suddenly all too easy to believe.

He faced Mitch squarely. "Do you have any proof?"

"*I* don't. But I'd bet you money Philip will be able to

trace it on the computer." His face softened. "I'm sorry,
Nancy. I hate to be the one to tell you——"

She stood and made a valiant effort to hold herself
together. "It's not your fault."

Mitch started to say something else, but Nancy'd had
enough. Muttering excuses and thank-yous, Fred managed
to get her outside and to lead her back to the car. Neither
spoke.

He knew they'd have to talk about Mitch's accusations
sooner or later, but he wanted to give her time to think, time
to pull herself back together. Besides, he didn't have the
slightest idea what to say. He needed a little time himself.

Nancy kept her head down and her arms folded tightly
across her middle as she walked. Fred knew she'd felt guilty
about Adam before this, but if Adam's need for money
somehow related back to her, she'd assign herself even
greater responsibility for his death.

After helping her into the car, Fred settled behind the
steering wheel. "Are you going to be all right?"

She flicked her eyes at him. "I don't know," she admitted.
She looked weak and obviously shaken, and Fred cursed
himself for bringing her along.

"I'm taking you home." He used his firmest voice to keep
her from arguing.

She didn't even try. Leaning her head against the seat, she
closed her eyes. "All right."

That reaction worried him more than an argument would
have, and he wondered if maybe he *should* talk to her. Now.
Before she drew some unhealthy conclusions.

He backed in a wide arc and drove halfway back to town
before he could find a way to start. "I'm sorry you were with
me to hear that."

If she heard him now, she gave no sign. Her face looked
pale, her lips thin and bloodless.

"Tell me why Adam needed money," he asked softly.

She didn't speak, but she shook her head as if denying
there was a need.

But Fred had seen her reaction to Mitch's story, and he
didn't believe her. "I want to help you more than anything,

sweetheart, but I can't unless you're willing to tell me everything."

She didn't answer. Fred flicked his attention from the road for half a second and saw her turn away from his gaze. At least she was listening.

"Well, then, why don't I tell you what *I* know. If I get anything wrong, you fill in the blanks."

Still nothing.

He took a deep breath and plunged on. "You and Adam had a happy marriage up until about a year ago. Now, from what I can gather, the only thing that changed was that Adam got a new boss. He started working more hours, talking to you less about what he was doing— Am I right so far?"

Her head moved a fraction of an inch.

He decided to take that as a yes. "The marriage got a little shaky, and before you knew it, you'd drifted apart. You weren't spending much time together, you felt like you never talked—"

He waited until she moved her head again.

"Then you got pregnant. Now, I know you two had been trying to have a baby for some time before that. And Doc says Adam was thrilled about it. Yet you claim Adam didn't want the baby once he found out it was on the way."

She turned back to look at him, and the haunted expression in her eyes jolted him. "He didn't."

"Then why did Doc think he was?"

"Doc?" Nancy laughed bitterly. "Doc can't imagine anyone not wanting a baby."

She had a point there. Maybe Doc had assumed Adam felt the way *he* would have. "So Adam asked you to get an abortion."

She nodded.

"Why didn't he want this baby?"

For half a beat he thought she'd answer him. Instead, she licked her lips and looked straight out the windshield.

"Was it because of money, Nancy? I know kids don't come cheap—"

This time a sob escaped. She balled her hand into a fist and bit one curled finger. "It's all my fault he's dead."

"Listen, sweetheart. No matter what Adam thought he needed the money for, he didn't have to commit . . . whatever the hell you'd call what he did to get it."

He thought he'd make her feel better, but her eyes snapped with anger when she faced him. "It's *my* fault, Uncle Fred. Mine. I pushed him to this."

"No, sweetheart—"

She glared at him. "Don't keep saying that. You have no idea."

He held his temper in check for the few seconds it took him to pull to the side of the road and jam the car into park, but then he faced her with a few sparks of his own. "You know what, Nancy? You're right. I have no idea. I'm doing everything I can to help you, but I feel like I'm in a high-stakes game, and I'm playing with a deck that has a few cards missing."

Her jaw worked, but she didn't say anything.

"Well, I'm not going to do it anymore," he said. "Either you start telling me the truth, or I pull out. Right here. Right now."

She sent him a sideways glance. "I can't."

"Fine. I'm through trying to help." Reaching for the gearshift knob, he yanked it back into drive and pulled back onto the highway.

She sat beside him, stiff and unyielding. Unwilling to give an inch.

He drove quickly, taking the curves with a little more speed than usual, which meant he had to trust his brakes more than wisdom allowed. But today he didn't care. He meant what he said. He was through. He'd angered Enos, worried Margaret, and enlisted Douglas in a conspiracy— all for nothing.

He reached Mountain Home quickly and let the car crawl through the stop at the intersection with Main, making certain no other cars were coming before he gathered speed and headed toward Cutler.

He shot an angry glance at Nancy, but she didn't even acknowledge him. Fine. He'd lost sleep and worried himself nearly sick about her. And for what? She didn't trust him with the simple truth. She wouldn't even talk to him.

Even in town he drove too quickly, but he was anxious to reach home. Anxious to sit in his rocker and prop his feet up and read the paper all the way through. He shot past the chiropractic clinic well over the speed limit and saw the white Blazer too late to slow down.

A second later it flew onto the road behind him with its red and blue lights flashing and its siren at full volume.

"For hell's sake," he muttered and pulled to the side of the road again.

Suddenly interested, Nancy looked over her shoulder and sent him a cautious look. "Were you speeding?"

He let a muffled growl serve as his answer and lowered the window as Robert Alpers swaggered up to the Buick.

Robert peered into the window. "Where's the fire?"

Fred didn't intend to indulge in empty-headed chitchat, so he didn't say a word.

Robert shrugged as if Fred's refusal to answer made no difference to him. "Better let me see your license and registration."

Fred bit back the response that rose to his lips. He hadn't had a ticket in over forty years, and he didn't intend to let some eager young buck ruin his record. But he wouldn't argue now—he'd take it up with Enos later. He dug into his pocket for his wallet.

Robert pushed his hat back on his head and looked across the seat at Nancy. "Hello there, Mrs. Bigelow. How you doing?"

She gave him a thin smile and muttered something about how fine she was.

No reasonable person would believe it, but it appeared to satisfy Robert, who looked back at Fred. "I saw you come into town a while back. Where've you been?"

"I wasn't aware I had to clear my agenda with the sheriff's department." Fred shoved his license and registration under Robert's nose for inspection.

But Robert didn't take it. He looked over his shoulder as if he saw something fascinating behind him. "You know, I watched you run that stop sign back there . . ."

"I didn't run any stop sign," Fred insisted.

". . . but I told myself not to get all worked up over it. And I wouldn't have if you hadn't come tearing through town like the devil was at your heels." He looked back at Fred with a smirk. "Now, where did you say you'd been?"

"I didn't say."

With a sorry shake of his head, Robert held out his hand for Fred's documents and studied them thoroughly for several seconds.

But when the inspection went on longer than necessary, Fred found his patience wearing thin. "For Pete's sake, Robert. A body'd think I was an axe murderer, the way you're acting."

Robert pulled out his ticket-writing paraphernalia and clipped Fred's license where he could see it. "Well, now, Mr. Vickery, I don't think you're an axe murderer. But I do think you'd be wise to watch your stops a little closer and pay better attention to the posted speed limit." He held out the ticket for Fred to sign.

Fred had half a mind to refuse it, but he slashed his name across the bottom and shoved the whole blasted thing back.

With an annoying smile, Robert returned Fred's license, registration, and the ticket and leaned over so he could see Nancy one more time. "You take care, Mrs. Bigelow. Let us know if there's anything we can do for you."

"Thanks, Robert, but everything's fine." This time when she spoke, her voice sounded a little less brittle.

Robert patted the side of the car and walked back to his Blazer and sent Fred an impertinent salute as he pulled away.

Seething, Fred allowed himself a couple of seconds to calm down before he reached for the gearshift.

This time Nancy's hand shot out to stop him. "I'm so sorry, Uncle Fred." Tears lined her voice and made it soft and thick, the kind of voice that never failed to melt his heart.

He looked at her just long enough to see that the tears had moved into her eyes as well. When his own eyes threatened to mist over, he jerked his gaze away.

"You're right," she said. "I owe you the truth."

So much of his anger had evaporated in the last several seconds, he had trouble keeping the gruff edge to his voice. "Well, I think you do."

"I just can't—" Her voice caught. "I just don't want my parents to know."

"To know what?"

She pulled in a steadying breath and twisted her fingers together. "Adam and I tried to get pregnant for the longest time, but it just never happened. We finally went to a specialist in Denver who told us we'd never have a baby—not naturally, anyway. Adam couldn't. His sperm count was too low. There was a procedure he could have had, but it cost a fortune." She touched two trembling fingers to her lips as if she could make her mouth form the words easier.

Fred didn't move, didn't speak, almost didn't breathe.

"He knew how much I wanted a baby, but we didn't have that kind of money. I begged him to ask his parents, or to let me ask mine, for a loan. I would have been willing to do anything for a baby. Instead, he started working more, staying later and later at the office. Not for money—he was on salary—but to avoid me. He even told me that."

She looked up at Fred, and the pain he saw in her eyes wrenched his heart.

"I hated him being gone. We fought about it all the time." Her voice faded for a second, and she drew a breath to strengthen it. "I started finding ways to occupy myself. Classes. Volunteer work. But nothing really helped."

A pause, a sideways glance, a deep breath before she rushed on. "And then I met Kelley Yarnell. We became wonderful friends. I could talk to him about anything. One night after Adam and I had a horrible fight, I went to Kelley, and . . . well . . . one thing led to another. We had an affair. It didn't last long, just a couple of months. I loved him and I know he loved me, but Adam was my husband

and I still hoped we could fix things between us. I didn't
want to lose him."

She paused as if she expected Fred to say something, but
he couldn't speak.

"So I broke it off with Kelley, and he ended up moving
away to make things easier for me. I didn't see him again
until a couple of days ago. And suddenly, when I needed
him most, there he was. Just like always." She buried her
face in her hands as if she couldn't face Fred now that she'd
confessed.

Still unable to trust his voice, Fred reached across the seat
and pulled her into his arms, but at his simple offer of
comfort she began to cry harder. He held her tightly and
rocked her against his chest until her tears slowed and she
pulled away to look at him.

"I was so certain you'd hate me for what I did."

"People make mistakes all the time," he said. "Rumor has
it I've even made one or two."

Her lips almost curved into a smile. "I don't believe it."

He patted her hand and smoothed the hair away from her
wet face. "So the baby is Kelley's, right?"

"Yes."

"And Adam knew that. That's why he wanted you to have
an abortion?"

"I didn't tell him about Kelley until I realized I was
pregnant. There was no way I could pass the baby off as
his."

"No. And it's a good thing. A lie might have smoothed
things over for a moment, but it would have haunted you
forever, and you would have had problems down the road."

"He told me there was no way he'd raise another man's
child. I begged him, but he said the only way we could stay
together was if I got rid of the baby. He left home to give me
time to think about it. He even called and made an
appointment at an abortion clinic for me. All I had to do was
go. A few minutes and it would have been over." She sighed
softly. "But I couldn't do it. Not even for Adam."

"And when he found out you didn't keep the appointment, he came to your parents' house and demanded a divorce."

She nodded. "And then today, when Mitch said Adam was altering test results, and I realized he was trying to get money—" She ran her hands across her abdomen.

"You think it was so you could have *his* baby?"

"What else could he have wanted the money for?"

With all his heart, Fred wished he could offer another suggestion. Instead, he felt as if another puzzle piece had just snapped into place.

seventeen

Fred had forgotten all about Harriet's plan to visit Nancy today until he turned back into the driveway and caught a glimpse of her waiting for them on the front porch—which meant Porter had left her while he went to meet Fred.

From Nancy's quick intake of breath, Fred suspected she'd either forgotten or hadn't known about her mother's visit. She'd been crying intermittently all the way back from Mountain Home, and he wondered how she'd explain her condition to Harriet—especially since she'd managed to keep every other aspect of her life a secret.

Maybe it was just as well to get it all out in the open. Then everybody could get on about the business of healing.

Putting on his heartiest smile, he jumped out of the car and strode toward the house. "Harriet, I'm sorry we kept you waiting."

It took her a couple of seconds to get to her feet from the step, testimony that age was trying to drag her down with the rest of them, but she smiled back. "Oh, that's all right. I knew you'd be right back."

She had more faith in them than they deserved, and Fred wondered if he looked as embarrassed as he felt. But she really wasn't paying attention to him. Nancy had caught her attention.

Using as much finesse as concern allowed, she pushed past him and pulled Nancy into an embrace. "You look tired, sweetheart. Are you all right?"

Fred willed the girl to tell the truth—even a piece of it. But she just nodded and closed her eyes when she leaned on her mother's shoulder.

"Maybe this isn't a good time for me to visit. You've already been out—" Harriet led her toward the front door while Fred worked with the lock and shot repeated glances back at Nancy as if by doing so he could convince her to talk.

"No, Mom. This is fine. Where's Dad?"

"Oh, you know your father. Off on some secret mission. Goodness knows he doesn't tell *me* anything when he decides he needs to go somewhere. He'll be back soon, I'm sure."

Not too soon, Fred hoped. He didn't want Porter to give up on him and leave the Copper Penny before he could get there.

Harriet plunked down on the couch and patted the seat beside her. "So, where'd you two go?"

Fred lowered himself into his rocker and made a production of adjusting himself in the proper position while he waited for Nancy to answer.

Nancy sat beside her mother and shrugged in Fred's general direction. "For a drive. Uncle Fred thought I needed to get out."

"Well, he's right." Harriet nodded in agreement with herself and smoothed her pantlegs with hands that looked too old to belong to her. "Maybe you and I should go somewhere tomorrow. I'll bring my own car, and we can drive down into Granby—unless that's where you went today?"

Nancy shook her head. "No, it wasn't. Granby will be fine."

Harriet cocked her head at Fred as if he might be a better source of information. "So, where *did* you two go?"

He kept his eyes trained on his footstool. "Nowhere special. Just up the mountain a bit."

But Harriet's shoulders squared as if she'd just been told a lie, and she looked from one to the other in silence. "All right. What is it you're not telling me?"

Fred looked at Nancy, as if to signal her to start spilling a little of the truth. But Nancy avoided his gaze and shot to her feet and walked to the dining table that had been her grandmother's. She picked up a picture and studied it, then another.

For a woman who was about to jump out of her skin, Harriet showed remarkable patience. She must have been through this kind of thing with Nancy before.

At long last, Nancy turned to face her. "We went to talk to a man Adam used to work with."

"Oh? Who?"

"Mitch Hancock. I don't think you know him. Anyway, he said some things about Adam that I'm having a hard time accepting."

Harriet's eyes darkened. "Like what?"

Nancy shrugged and looked to Fred as if she wanted him to answer for her. But he knew she didn't. Not really. He'd say far more than she wanted him to. He nodded encouragement.

"He thinks Adam was being bribed to doctor the results of some of the testing they were doing on Shadow Mountain."

Harriet laughed. "That's ridiculous." But when neither of them laughed with her, her face sobered almost instantly. "That's *ridiculous.*"

Fred wished he could agree with her.

"Why would Adam do a thing like that?" she demanded.

Again Nancy looked to him for help, and again he kept his mouth shut tight.

Nancy shook her head and looked down at her hands. "I don't know, Mom. I don't think it's true, but I'm so upset about everything else—the murder and everything—it really bothered me to hear him say it."

"Well, it's not true," Harriet decided. As if to prove it, she stood and planted her fists on her hips. "It's absolutely not true, and I think there ought to be a law to keep people from going around saying things like that."

She looked so much like Phoebe, Fred couldn't help but smile. She'd had the same fierce determination to make life go her way; the same belief that once she decided a thing, that made it so; the same fire in her eyes once she set about making something true.

"I guess there probably is a law," he said.

"Well, then, somebody ought to do something about it."
That settled, her mind shifted direction with lightning speed.
"Did you two eat lunch while you were out?"

Nancy shook her head and looked relieved that they'd left
the subject for the time being. "No."

"Well, you've got to keep your strength up. What have
you got, Fred?" And without waiting for a response, she
pushed open the kitchen door and marched through it.

"I'll go help her," Nancy said.

Fred struggled out of his rocker and checked his watch.
He could still make it to the Copper Penny if he hurried.
"Don't make anything for me. I've got an appointment."

Nancy stopped midstride. "With who?"

"It's nothing you need to come along with me for," he
said. "The best thing you can do is stay here and keep your
mother busy."

"Are you trying to protect me again?"

"Of course not," he lied.

"We have a deal, remember? I'm going with you whenever you start asking questions about the murder."

"Of course I remember." He brushed a kiss to her cheek.

Looking only slightly appeased, Nancy followed Harriet
into the kitchen. Fred slipped out the front door and hurried
down the driveway.

He reached the Copper Penny a minute before noon and
scoured the parking lot for Porter's car as he walked through
it. He didn't see the car, but he did see his son-in-law's truck
in its usual spot. At noon. On one of his busiest work days.

Fred battled his rising resentment toward Webb. For some
reason he couldn't understand, Margaret wasn't ready to
give her husband his walking papers. The guy was a
halfhearted husband at best, and Fred couldn't help but wish
the marriage had broken up long ago. Except for the kids.
Sarah, Benjamin, and Deborah were the light of Margaret's
life and the only good thing to come from her marriage. For
their sakes, Fred usually swallowed his disapproval.

But when he pushed open the bar's door and Webb's
laughter rushed out to greet him, he lost the fight. He

stepped into the bar and let the door creak shut behind him while his eyes adjusted to the shadows.

Neon beer signs glowed from the walls and candles flickered at the tables. Whether because he hadn't been sleeping well or because he'd just spent an emotionally wrenching morning, Fred marched past Albán Toth behind the bar, past half a dozen empty tables, past the pool table, and came to a stop at Webb's table.

Webb sat with his back to the door, so he didn't see Fred at first, but his companion did. Quinn Udy had been in trouble with Fred more than once as a boy, and now he slid down on his tailbone and sent Fred a sheepish look Webb didn't notice.

The table already had one set of empty beer bottles in its middle, and a freshly delivered round waited for attention. With his hair tousled as if he hadn't bothered to comb it all day, his moustache badly in need of a trim, and his shirttail hanging out, Webb looked every inch a loser, and Fred wondered for the millionth time what Margaret saw in him.

Webb leaned back in his chair and kicked his boots onto the chair across from him. "—then she asked whether it might be the little starter thingie and I didn't even crack a smile. I just said, 'Lady, if your little starter thingie needs work, I'm your man.'" He broke off with a suggestive chuckle that left no doubt as to his meaning.

Quinn ducked his head and looked away.

Fred leaned down to Webb and asked, "Did you work on it?"

Webb dropped his feet and whirled around in surprise, but he recovered quickly. "Well, Dad Vickery. Fancy running into you in here."

"Fancy."

"Why don't you pull up a chair and join us?"

"No. Thanks. I just wanted to hear the end of your story. Did you work on it?"

Webb sent an amused sideways glance at Quinn and didn't even have the grace to blush. "It turned out to be the distributor cap."

"Not the little starter thingie?"

"Nope. Sure you don't want to join us? I'll buy you a beer."

"I'm sure." Fred made a point of checking his watch. "You been home for lunch yet?"

Webb's eyes shifted away. This time Fred had scored a hit. "Not yet," Webb admitted. "But I'm leaving in a minute."

"Well, when you get there, tell Margaret I'll be stopping by. I need to talk to her about something."

"Sure thing." Webb kicked back and took another swallow of beer as if he intended to stay awhile.

"If I get there before you, I'll be sure to tell her that funny little story about the starter. Now, how did it go again?"

A chuckle escaped Quinn, but Webb scowled darkly and jerked a baseball cap from someplace under the table. Jamming it onto his head, he stood. "No need. I'll tell her myself. I'm heading home right now."

Fred didn't comment.

With one last resentful look at Fred, Webb dropped a few bills to the table. "I'll catch ya later, Quinn." He lifted his arm to get Albán's attention. "Hold that next round, Albán. I didn't even notice the time."

Fred watched him leave and wished he could find some pleasure in this victory. He might have won this small skirmish, but he knew Webb was winning the war.

He turned back toward the bar slowly and caught Albán Toth watching him. Albán stood just under six feet tall and had the kind of face that would be distinctive as he aged—broad forehead, a fine straight nose, and an expansive smile. His hazel eyes carried their usual welcome, and his olive skin bore the unmistakable glow of summer.

"Is everything all right?"

"Just great."

Albán filled a glass with ice water, placed it on the bar in front of an empty stool, and jerked his head toward the door. "It's a good thing you don't make such quick work of all my customers." His voice bore just the softest trace of an accent—an almost imperceptible V where a W should have been, the slight trill of an R—tribute to his Hungarian ancestry.

Fred scooted onto the stool and took a healthy swig of water. "That one needed to go home."

Albán swiped at a spot on the bar with a towel. Someone, maybe the original owner way back when, had covered the surface with thousands of pennies and shellacked them in place, and Albán took great pride in keeping it polished.

"That one *is* spending a little too much time here lately," Albán said and scraped something off the shellac with a fingernail. "But enough of that. You're here for lunch? It's *paprikás* today. You'll love it."

Fred took another mouthful of water and prayed that *paprikás* wasn't as spicy as the last concoction of Albán's he'd tried. "All right, I'll give it a try. Have you seen Porter Jorgensen around?"

"He was here a few minutes ago. Said to tell you he'd be back." Albán pushed a bowl of peanuts in Fred's direction and leaned an elbow on the bar. "So what's up? You and Porter aren't exactly regular customers."

"We're just out for lunch."

Albán looked disbelieving. "Maybe. But you're really here for some other reason. What is it?"

Fred took a handful of nuts and popped a couple into his mouth. "He's my brother-in-law, and we wanted to get together. This seemed like a good place."

"And he drove thirty miles to meet you?"

"No, he brought Harriet down to see Nancy."

Albán cocked one eyebrow and chuckled. "And you're meeting him here. Not likely. You might fool a lot of people around here, Fred, but you don't fool me for a second."

Fred met his gaze with a smile. "I don't try to fool anyone."

"No, of course you don't." A shaft of light split the darkened room, and Albán looked toward the door. "Here's your lunch date."

Porter blocked the sunlight in the open door, looking uncertain and uncomfortable. Fred waved him over and the door swung shut behind him, bathing the bar in semidusk again.

Advancing on Fred like a man with a mission, Porter hitched himself onto the next stool. "Well, I'm here. Let's get this over with."

Fred gave the room a once-over to make sure nobody had moved in too close. "I told you I went to EnviroSampl yesterday."

Porter nodded and accepted a glass of ice water from Albán, but he waited until the other man moved away again before he spoke. "Yeah. And?"

"And like I said, the receptionist told me you'd argued with Adam a couple of days before he died. What about, Porter?"

Porter gulped half the glass of water and scooped up a handful of peanuts. "It's a family matter."

"I am family."

"Immediate family."

Fred pushed the bowl away. "Don't you understand what serious trouble you could be in?"

"I'm not in any trouble."

"Dammit, Porter, your son-in-law wound up shot to death less than twelve hours after your second fight with him. Who in the hell do you think the sheriff considers his prime suspect?"

Porter pulled the peanuts back and leaned a little closer. "I didn't kill Adam, and you know it."

"Blasted fool. Of course I know it. But does Enos? Or have you made yourself look so guilty he won't look any further once he finds out what you've done? Now what did you argue with Adam about?"

Porter checked behind him. "That woman."

"What woman?"

"Brooke What's-her-name."

"Westphal?"

"That's the one. I saw the two of them together one night. Late. I wanted to know just what the hell was going on."

"And?"

"He denied it, the son of a bitch."

"You didn't believe him?"

"Hell, no, I didn't believe him." Porter reached across the bar for a bowl of pretzels. "I saw them together."

"Maybe it wasn't what it looked like."

"Of course it was. Adam had no business being out so late with a woman who's not his wife. Whispering in her ear—" Porter broke off in disgust.

"Maybe it was business. They did work together."

Porter chewed thoughtfully, but after a few seconds he shook his head. "No."

"It could have been."

Porter stopped chewing. "What do you know that I don't?"

Fred didn't have the time, the inclination, or the authority to recite the whole list. "I've heard one or two things."

"Such as?"

"I talked to Brooke Westphal. She claims they were working together."

Porter barked a laugh. "That's what he tried to say."

"Well?"

"Well, what? Isn't that what *you'd* say if you got caught cheating?"

Conceding that it probably was, Fred took a pretzel and thought for a couple of seconds. "Yesterday you said you thought Philip Aagard killed Adam. Why do you think that?"

Porter motioned Albán back and lifted his glass for a refill. "While I was there, Philip came in. Started shouting at Adam, accusing him of all sorts of things, including using the office for unauthorized activities—and we all know what *that* was, don't we?" He nodded his thanks at Albán and swigged another mouthful. "Anyway, Adam tried to say he'd been working, but Philip said then why didn't the computer show him logged on? And he warned Adam the funny business had better stop."

Fred's pulse flickered. "How did Adam explain that?"

Porter snorted. "He said it was a misunderstanding. That Philip didn't know what he was talking about. Now, I ask you—" He broke off without asking a thing.

"Nothing else?"

"Nothing. Then, the next night, Adam barges into *my* house and demands a divorce from my daughter. And the next thing I know, somebody's shot him. So what would you think?"

"You're sure about what Philip said?"

"Yeah. Why?"

Fred tried to fit this piece into the puzzle in his head. Philip must have found out about Adam's late-night lab work. But would he kill Adam because of it?

Maybe. Fred supposed stranger things had happened.

Porter checked his watch. "You going to get something to eat here?"

Fred nodded. "Figured I'd better. It's *paprikás* day."

"Really? Sounds good." Porter looked interested for a few seconds, then his face dropped. "But I promised Harriet I wouldn't be gone long. What were they doing when you left?"

"Fixing lunch."

"Then she'll have made me a sandwich. And one for you, too."

Fred shook his head. "I told Nancy not to bother."

Porter wrapped both hands around his glass and grinned. "That doesn't mean anything. You mark my words, there'll be a sandwich there for you. And the way Harriet's been acting lately, I'd better go eat mine."

Good. The Jorgensens could use some time together. Fred smiled. "Tell Harriet I'll be along in a bit."

Porter opened his mouth to say something else, but just then the outside door jerked open and Margaret stormed inside. He clamped his lips together and shot a look at Fred. "Looks like you've got trouble."

Fred watched her approach. Her eyes glinted, she held her posture rigid, and she clenched her jaw in fury. No doubt about it—something had upset her.

He pushed away his glass and cursed himself silently for confronting Webb. He might have known there'd be repercussions, and he should have suspected that Margaret would be the one to pay the price.

eighteen

Margaret stopped long enough to brush a kiss onto Porter's cheek before she hopped onto the stool beside Fred. "What are you doing here?"

"Talking. Ordering lunch." Fred looked to Porter for backup.

Porter nodded enthusiastically. "*Paprikás* day."

Albán slid a plate in front of Fred that held a concoction Fred assumed must be *pakrikás*, a mound of thinly sliced cucumbers that smelled suspiciously like vinegar, and those tasteless little dumplings Albán had made him try once before.

Margaret still looked disbelieving. "The two of you are having lunch? Here? How nice." She pulled in a deep breath as if struggling for control, obviously lost it, and turned on Fred. "You're doing it again, aren't you?"

He didn't bother to ask what she meant, and he didn't bother to answer. He didn't want to actually *lie*.

She didn't appear to notice his silence. "I ran into Doc this morning. He asked whether you'd been sleeping any better."

Fred made a mental black mark next to Doc's name.

Margaret's face darkened. "If you're not sleeping, it means you're obsessed with something. And let me guess what."

Fred chewed another pretzel, but he didn't like her tone of voice. Not one bit.

"Where else have you been today? I dropped by to see you earlier, but nobody was home."

He reached for the peanuts. "Nancy and I went for a ride."

"To Mountain Home?"

The speed of her information network amazed him. "Yes, to Mountain Home."

She dropped her head into her hands, and her voice lost a note of its anger. "Oh, Dad. When Enos called me, I thought he was joking. At least, I *hoped* he was. What were you doing up there, and how did you get a speeding ticket?"

Porter's eyebrows shot up. "A speeding ticket?"

Fred added Robert Alpers and Enos to the list of people he was currently out of sorts with. "It was all perfectly innocent, Margaret."

"I might have known you'd say that. It's *always* perfectly innocent." She reached for one of his hands and held it in hers. "You're not supposed to do this kind of thing. You know what Doc said about getting overly excited."

"But I'm fine."

"Yes, for the moment. But what if something happens to you while you're off chasing murderers?"

"Nothing's going to happen."

"You have heart trouble—you can't pretend you're all right."

"I feel great."

"You're *not* great."

Fred shifted on his seat and held her gaze. "Margaret, if something was wrong with me, I'd know it. If I felt bad, I'd slow down."

She made a noise and tried to turn away.

But he held her shoulders and made her look at him. "I'm not going to sit in my rocking chair and stare out the window like some old man for the rest of my life."

"Which won't be long if you don't stop."

Porter leaned forward and reached across the bar to get her attention. "I've got to agree with your dad, honey. Don't try to put him out to pasture yet."

"I'm not trying to put him out to pasture," she insisted. "I'm trying to keep him around. I've already lost my mother, I don't want to lose him, too."

"Can't imagine what good you think I'll be in my rocking chair," Fred muttered.

Porter shot him a glance designed, he supposed, to shut him up. "Just do me one favor, Margaret. Ask yourself what it is you love most about your dad. Figure out *why* you want to keep him around. Frankly, he's so blasted ornery, I don't see it." He slapped the counter, amused by his own joke, and slid from his stool. "I've got to go before I have Harriet to deal with," he said, but he reached into the peanut bowl again.

He seemed to have made a point with Margaret. She looked at Fred sadly, and for a long moment he thought she might agree. Well, good. It was about time she saw things for what they were.

He turned toward her, ready to hear her admit Porter's point, ready to accept her apology graciously.

She slid from her stool and looked at him.

He smiled his encouragement.

From behind her back, Porter nodded at Fred. Obviously, he could feel a concession coming, too.

Margaret shot a glance at each of them, but settled on Porter last. "*That* is the most ridiculous thing I've ever heard you say, Uncle Porter. I can't believe you're encouraging him."

"Now listen, Margaret—" Fred began.

"You two are like peas in a pod." Exasperation tinged the edges of her words. "I have half a mind to give up on both of you." Whirling away, she stomped across the bar and out the door.

Porter watched until she'd disappeared and the door closed behind her. He looked at Fred with raised brows. "Something bothering her?"

Fred nodded slowly. "Sure looks like it."

"Something wrong at home?"

Porter obviously recognized the symptoms. Fred just nodded.

"I guess we shouldn't hope the son of a bitch drops dead—"

Fred knew Porter meant his words as a joke, but it was a

stupid thing to say out loud. Especially since Fred could have understood someone wanting to do away with a son-in-law who caused so much heartache.

Porter patted his back. "Look, Fred, I've got to go. I don't want Harriet going up in steam." He cast another glance at the door as if anticipating a repeat attack.

Fred shook his head. "No, you don't. Go on. I'll be along."

Porter looked a little reluctant to leave, but his concern for Harriet and Nancy finally tugged him away.

Fred took an experimental bite of *paprikás* and signaled Albán for another glass of water. To his surprise, it tasted better than it looked. A little spicier than he usually liked, but he'd eaten worse. Still, he didn't expect *paprikás* to replace chicken-fried steak on his list of favorites.

Glancing toward the door, he took another bite. Every time Margaret's life at home got out of control, she tried to exert more control over him. And if giving in wouldn't cost him his own happiness, Fred might give in to her a little more often.

He took another bite and pushed his plate away. No appetite. No sleep. He'd better get to the bottom of this mess soon. When he stepped out of the Copper Penny a few minutes later, Fred had to wait at the door until his eyes adjusted to the sunlight. But he needed a few seconds to pull himself together anyway.

It looked almost certain now that Philip Aagard had found out about Adam's illegal testing and confronted him with it. But if that happened the day before the murder, why would Philip sneak back the *next* night to kill him? Seemed to Fred, tempers would have cooled a bit by then.

Maybe Adam refused to stop. But then why not turn him into whatever authorities had jurisdiction over that sort of thing? Why not fire him? Fred scratched his chin and stared up Main Street as if it might give him the answers.

Finally, well adjusted to the bright sunlight, Fred stepped up onto the boardwalk. His confrontation with Margaret made him long for a little solitude, but he wouldn't find it at home. Besides, he wanted to give Nancy time with her parents.

He walked aimlessly, uncertain where he wanted to go. He'd almost reached the corner of Aspen Street when heavy-booted footsteps approaching from around the corner brought him up short. It sounded like Enos.

Well, good. He wanted to discuss that blasted speeding ticket, anyway. He planted himself where he knew Enos would have to stop to avoid hitting him and waited.

A second later Enos rounded the corner and pulled himself up short. "Good billy hell, Fred. You scared me out of a year's growth."

Fred yanked the speeding ticket from his pocket and waved it at Enos. "I want to talk to you about this."

Enos chuckled. "I heard about your trip through Mountain Home this morning."

Fred scowled at him. "Sounds like word's gotten out. Somebody in the sheriff's office must have a big mouth."

Since he couldn't deny it, Enos obviously chose to ignore Fred's observation. "I don't suppose you want to tell me what you were doing up there?"

"I don't suppose it's any of your business. Now what are you going to do about this?"

"Not a blasted thing. Tell me who you know at the Sprucewood Condominiums."

"What were you doing? Following me?"

Somehow Enos managed to look innocent. "One of my men just happened to be driving by when you came out."

"Which one? That overly excited young whelp?"

Enos shook his head. "No, it was Grady. So? What were you doing there?"

"What in the Sam Hill was *Grady* doing up there?"

"Grady was doing his job. Now, quit trying to change the subject and tell me why you were there."

Fred supposed there was no harm in telling Enos *part* of it. Maybe it'd make him feel better. "I took Nancy to visit someone."

"Mitch Hancock?"

For tar sakes. "If you know so blasted much, why do you even bother to ask me?" Fred started across the street.

As if they were somehow attached, Enos matched his stride. "You know you're interfering in a police investigation. Again."

"I'm not interfering in a doggone thing."

"I almost wish I could believe you. But you don't just *happen* to visit somebody connected with a murder. You went to Mitch Hancock's because you expected him to tell you something. Now, what was it?"

That was backward praise if Fred had ever heard it, but he decided to accept it anyway. He paused half a beat just to keep Enos wondering, then said, "I expected him to tell me why he fought—or argued—with Adam the day before the murder."

Enos looked impressed. "And did he?"

"Yep. But he claims they argued a lot. Over almost everything. He says Adam's work had been slipping the last little while, and since his work affected Mitch directly, he and Adam argued regularly."

"What else?"

Fred didn't answer immediately. Not because he didn't plan to tell Enos what he knew, but he didn't want to just blurt out his suspicions. No sense making Adam look like a crook unless he had to.

Apparently Enos interpreted his silence as a refusal to answer, because his scowl darkened. "You'd better not hold anything back, Fred."

As if he'd *ever* held anything back when Enos needed to know it. "I'm not hiding anything from you," he snapped. "Just trying to figure out how to phrase it, that's all."

"Why don't you just tell me?"

Fred stopped under the shaded overhang of the Kwik-Kleen and glanced around to make certain they wouldn't be overheard. "All right. It looks like Adam might have been changing the results of certain tests they ran in the lab at EnviroSampl."

Enos's face puckered. "Where'd you hear that?"

Keeping his voice low, Fred explained what he knew,

taking care to step around any mention of Nancy, the baby, the abortion, or the medical procedure Adam apparently wanted to have. If somebody proved Adam was altering test results, Enos would need to know why, but that story wasn't Fred's to tell.

When he got to the end, Enos shoved his hands into his pockets and looked away. His jaw worked for several seconds before he managed to speak. "I can't believe it."

"Well, I certainly don't *want* to—"

Shaking his head vehemently, Enos took a couple of agitated steps away. "I absolutely don't believe it. Adam wasn't that kind of guy."

Remembering Enos had a high emotional stake, Fred softened his tone. "People have been known to do surprising things."

Enos whirled back to face him. "Are you trying to tell me Adam needed money so desperately he'd do something like *that*?"

They were treading dangerously close to territory Fred couldn't enter, but he nodded anyway. "Maybe." He moved closer and clapped a hand on Enos's shoulder. "Look, maybe it's not true. Maybe Adam *didn't* do it. Maybe he had another reason altogether for working late."

Enos looked miserable. "Well, I hope so." He gave an embarrassed laugh and shot a glance at Fred. "You know, I've heard some things I thought I didn't want to hear on this case, but I'd almost rather find out Adam and Brooke *were* having an affair than this."

"That makes two of us." Fred leaned against a rough wood post and stared out onto the street. "So what's next?"

"For you? Nothing. Honestly, Fred, I can't let you race around the country like some hotshot private investigator. You're going to get hurt one of these days, and if that happens, Maggie'll never forgive me. Hell, I'll never forgive myself."

Fred figured Margaret would eventually forgive Enos anything, but he didn't waste breath pointing that out. "I'm not going to get hurt asking a few questions."

Enos laughed. "All you ever do is 'ask a few questions,'

and you've already managed to get yourself into some pretty deep trouble that way. Or has that slipped your mind?"

Fred pushed away from the post. "I'm here, aren't I? Nothing's happened to me."

"Yeah, but not because of anything *you've* done." Enos's face softened just a tad. "Look, Fred, I wouldn't be happy to have anybody poking around one of my investigations, but considering your health—your age—"

"My health is fine," Fred snapped. "And my age shouldn't have a blamed thing to do with it."

Enos looked a little sheepish. "Maggie worries about you," he said, as if that explained everything.

"Let her find something else to worry about." Fred started down the broadwalk again, hoping that would put an end to a painful topic.

But the invisible string between them jerked Enos after him. "Well, that's just great. You've got a daughter who loves you and worries about you. And what do you say?"

"She wants to chain me to my rocking chair and turn me into an old man."

"She wants to keep you alive."

"Like a bird in a cage. What kind of life is that?"

"Maggie doesn't want to put you in a cage," Enos said in a voice that sounded as if he was dealing with a slow-witted child.

Fred humphed his response. Enough said. Arguing wouldn't get them anywhere. They'd been through it too many times already.

But Enos apparently didn't want to give up yet. He obviously enjoyed sounding like a broken record. "*I* don't want to put you in a cage, either—" he began, but just then the door to the laundromat opened, and Summer Dey stepped outside clutching a basket full of black clothes all heaped together.

Blessedly, Enos snapped his mouth shut on the rest of his argument.

A smile lit Summer's face when she saw them standing there. She wore hiking boots, socks, shorts, and a T-shirt—

all black, as usual. Fred had never seen her in any other color. She claimed that only by staying depressed could she successfully produce her paintings. And that wearing nothing but black helped keep her spirits low.

Fred had seen her work and thought a wardrobe change might improve it, but she apparently sold enough of the silly things to keep her in the black.

"Ah, Fred," she said. "You *did* come. My spirit guides told me you would."

It had already been a long, hard day, and Fred didn't want to deal with Summer or her guides. But he worked up a smile anyway. "Afternoon, Summer."

"I'm so glad to see you. I've been waiting for you to come ever since Janice Lacey told me you wanted a reading."

Fred's smile evaporated. "I never said I wanted a reading—"

Summer reached out a hand to stop him. "Your higher spirit self knows what it needs."

His higher spirit self knew what it *didn't* need, too. And it didn't need any of Summer's psychic poppycock.

But Enos grinned as if he'd heard a grand joke and spoke before Fred could frame another response. "You want a reading? You know, that might not be a bad idea."

"Absolutely not—"

"Get a little direction for your troubled soul."

"I know who's causing the only trouble my soul is experiencing," Fred said with a pointed glance toward the troublemaker himself.

Enos pretended not to notice. He turned a serious face back to Summer. "You don't have time to do it right now, do you?"

Fred backed away a step. "Can't do it. Not now."

But Summer tucked a hand beneath his arm and held fast. "My next appointment canceled. The way has been opened for you to receive the direction you crave."

The only direction Fred craved was a way out. He shook his head and pulled his arm away. "Can't stop now. I've got to get home to Nancy."

Summer looked concerned. "She still has a long way to go but she is much better. It's your soul that's seeking enlightenment."

Enos struggled to keep a serious look on his face. "Then by all means, let's enlighten it."

Summer tilted her head as if somebody in the treetops were whispering to her. "Yes. You want to know about Adam Bigelow's murder."

All at once, Enos's face grew serious. "Now, I don't want you to encourage Fred in that direction."

"Adam caused his own death," she said with a dazed smile. "He found the truth, and the truth killed him."

Fred's heart tap danced high in his chest at Summer's words. What truth? The truth about Nancy and her baby? About Kelley Yarnell?

Enos shoved his hat back on his head and looked every inch the sheriff. "What truth, Summer? If you know anything about Adam's murder, you'd better tell me right now."

"I know only what my guides have shared with me. What *Adam* has communicated through my guides."

"Have you seen anything? Heard anything? From *real* people?" Enos demanded.

Summer's eyes snapped down from the trees, and her face filled with color. "My spirit guides are as real as you and me."

"Do you *know* anything?"

"I only know Adam was killed because he learned the truth," she said and turned back to Fred. "The truth was hidden beneath a mountain of lies. And you're so close to that truth you must watch that you don't step over it." She broke off and studied him for a long moment. "You aren't coming for a reading, are you?"

"I'm afraid not."

She smiled a forgiving smile and touched his arm gently. "No matter. One day you will. I feel it." She lowered her voice to a near whisper. "Watch for the place where truth and delusion meet. That's where you'll find Adam's killer."

As if she'd flipped a switch, her eyes seemed to focus and

her smile to brighten. With a toss of her head and a hitch of the laundry basket, she turned toward The Cosmic Tradition.

Too stunned to speak, Fred watched until she'd crossed the street. Enos must have been equally affected because he kept his mouth shut until she'd gone a full block.

Finally, Enos dragged in a breath. "What in blazes do you think she meant?"

"I think you're a blasted fool if you even worry about it," Fred said.

Enos turned slowly toward him as if he'd read something in Fred's voice. "You know something, don't you?"

"Nonsense."

"You do. I can tell."

"Let's just say I have my suspicions—assuming you believe all that hogwash."

"I'm not saying I do, but she sure sparked something in you. What was it? And about who?"

"I don't like to say," Fred hedged. "It may be nothing."

Enos sighed heavily and used that tone of voice that suggested he'd said this a dozen times or more already. "Listen, Fred, I know you don't want to make an innocent person look guilty, but you can't keep information from me that might have a direct bearing on this case."

"If I find out it has a direct bearing, you'll be the first to know."

Enos planted himself smack in front of Fred and looked him square in the eye. "Oh, no, you don't. You tell me what you suspect and let me check it out."

If it weren't for Nancy, Fred would. No doubt about it. Instead, he said, "I can't."

"What do you mean, you can't? Listen, I'm trying like hell to be patient with you, but you're not making it easy."

"I mean I can't. I'm sworn to secrecy. I've promised that I won't tell anyone."

"You have to tell me."

Fred shook his head and met Enos's gaze. "I'm a man of my word, Enos. I can't. All I can do now is go to the person and convince them to tell you."

Enos studied him for an eternity. "It's got to be Nancy. Nobody else could have gotten you to agree to keep your mouth shut."

Fred tried not to react, but he didn't like the way Enos's mind jumped to such accurate conclusions, and he didn't like being so all-fired easy to read.

"It's Nancy, isn't it?" Enos demanded.

Fred still didn't answer.

With a noise that sounded like a growl, Enos said, "All right. I'll give you your own way *this one time,* but I don't like it. You bring her in before I leave the office tonight. Otherwise, I'm coming to your place."

Fred glanced at his watch. "Just until six o'clock? That doesn't give me much time."

"It's all I can offer, Fred. I'm trying to catch a murderer here. Take it or leave it."

"I'll take it."

With a satisfied nod, Enos turned away.

Fred knew he'd pushed Enos a little further than wisdom might suggest. But he really had no choice. And in spite of Enos's shortsightedness when it came to Fred's abilities, he had at least granted him until the end of the day. Fred cleared his throat and called after him. "Enos?"

The younger man turned back.

"Thanks."

Enos didn't answer, but he sketched a tiny salute using two fingers and the brim of his hat before he crossed the street.

nineteen

Racing against the clock now, Fred hurried home down Lake Front and let himself in through the front door. The living room stood empty and silent. No sign of Nancy. No sign of Douglas. No sign of Harriet and Porter.

He looked into the kitchen and found nothing but a note from Harriet telling him where to find his sandwich, so he headed toward the bedrooms. Three doors stood open, but the one to Margaret's room—the one Nancy was using—was closed.

Leaning his ear against the door, he listened for sounds of movement. Nothing. He knocked softly, but when no answer came, he opened the door and peeked inside. Nancy lay on her side facing the wall, and her back rose and fell so rhythmically, Fred knew she must be asleep.

He debated waking her, but she'd looked so worn when they came back from Mountain Home, he decided to let her rest another hour. He'd just have to be his most persuasive when she woke up.

Tiptoeing back to the living room, he settled into his rocking chair with his reading glasses and the *Denver Post*. But his mind refused to concentrate on the newsprint. Instead it danced around the clues he held.

Why had he let Summer Dey's suggestions affect him? Was he starting to believe her nonsense? No. Of course not. But he spent several minutes reassuring himself he hadn't slipped over the edge of common sense, and that Summer's suggestion—meaningless words chosen at random—had simply tapped into his own fears that Adam had discovered the truth about Nancy and Kelley.

Glancing at his watch again, he suppressed a groan. Only five minutes had passed, but it felt like an hour. Maybe he should wake Nancy after all. They had to talk about Adam, the baby, and Kelley Yarnell before Enos showed up on their doorstep.

He pushed to his feet and walked halfway across the living room before he stopped himself. He had plenty of time, and she'd been through hell already today. She needed her rest.

He walked back to the front window and stared out over the yard. He wished in vain he had someone he could trust to talk it all over with. Someone who could inject a note of reason into his thought processes. Someone like Phoebe. She would have known just what to say.

Feeling at loose ends, he crossed to the door and stepped onto the porch. He lowered himself to the front steps, just the way he always had while Phoebe'd dug in the flower beds. He could almost see her there on her knees, smudges of dirt on her nose and chin, her hair wisping out from under a broad sun hat.

He pulled in a deep breath of fresh air and closed his eyes. He imagined her sitting back on her heels with a scowl and asking if he didn't have anything better to do than stare at her. He'd have told her he couldn't imagine there was anything better to do. And she'd have pretended to think him foolish, but her lips would have curved into a smile, and she'd have gone back to work while he talked.

Half expecting to see her there in reality, he blinked his eyes open, but the flower beds stood empty and untended, evidence that even his best efforts to keep them up were insufficient. Pushing back to his feet, he stepped into the yard, checked the height of the grass, turned on the hose and used his finger over the water stream to spray the bleeding hearts and lupine Phoebe'd planted under their bedroom window.

And he thought. Of Margaret. Of Nancy and Adam. Of the baby. Of Kelley Yarnell.

Kelley Yarnell. The father of Nancy's baby. By her account, a kind man. Considerate. There when she needed him. But hadn't Adam also been—until he learned the truth?

Fred turned the spray onto the lilac bush at the north edge of his property and wondered how he would have reacted under similar circumstances. If Phoebe had confessed to taking a lover, to carrying another man's child. He wouldn't have reacted with kindness and understanding. He'd have been furious. He'd have felt betrayed.

So had Adam's reaction been out of line? Or simply the reaction of a man who loved his wife? Try as he might, Fred couldn't fault Adam for his anger or for his refusal to raise the child.

Fred studied the rest of the yard and decided the clump of scrub oak and aspen trees in the front corner looked dry. Tugging the hose a little further, he sprayed them and released the nutty, mossy forest smell of the dirt and the trees.

And his thoughts turned back to Kelley Yarnell. He seemed like a nice young man. Honestly concerned about Nancy. Why, even the morning of the murder, he'd been right there—

Fred let his finger off the hose and stared into the trees. *Even the morning of the murder?*

If Kelley had moved away from the area to make life easier for Nancy, what was he doing here the morning of the murder? And how had he found out about it so quickly? Fred let the water run into the dirt as he calculated, replayed their conversations in his head, and hoped he'd missed something.

Finally, he hurried across the lawn and turned off the water. Slipping back inside the house, he grabbed his keys and scrawled a quick note to any one of the kids who might find it. Less than three minutes later, he pulled out of the driveway.

He just hoped Nancy would sleep for a long time, because he didn't think she'd find any comfort in what he expected to learn at the Columbine Inn.

*   *   *

Less than half an hour later, Fred turned into the parking lot and found an empty space outside the lobby. The Columbine Inn sprawled across the lot in a U shape, with one set of rooms looking over the center court and the lobby and another larger set opening off the back.

With sinking heart, he realized there must be a hundred rooms or more. Suddenly, his chances of finding Kelley Yarnell looked dismal. But he refused to let that discourage him.

He climbed out of the car and searched the parking lot for Kelley's car on his way inside. He didn't see it, but maybe he'd parked around back. Or maybe he'd gone out somewhere. Fred refused to even let himself think he might already have checked out.

Inside, a tall red-haired boy of about twenty-five smiled at him from behind the front desk. "Can I help you?"

"I'm looking for one of your guests. A Kelley Yarnell. Can you tell me where to find him?"

"Sure thing. What's the room number?"

Fred leaned on the counter and tried to look trustworthy. "I was hoping to get that from you."

The boy's smile slipped. "Oh, I'm sorry, sir. I can't give that information out."

"It's quite important."

"I'm sorry."

"Can you tell me if he's still here?"

"Yes, sir." The boy pounded at a computer keyboard for a couple of seconds and nodded. "He's still registered."

"But you can't tell me his room number?"

"No, sir."

Fred battled frustration for a second. "What do you do if someone calls for one of your guests?"

"Generally speaking, they know the room number."

"But what if they don't?"

"Then we can put the call through, but we can't tell you the room number."

"So if I step outside and call you from a pay phone, you can put me through to his room?"

The young man nodded.

"What if I asked you to just call his room and tell him I'm here? Could you do that?"

The boy looked hesitant. "Well, I—" Then a little more confident. "Well, I guess that would be all right."

"All right, then, let's do that." Fred slapped his hand on the counter and waited while the boy picked up the telephone and dialed.

"Mr. Yarnell? This is the lobby, sir. I have someone here who'd like to speak with you, but he doesn't have your room number." A pause while he listened, then he looked back at Fred. "What's your name?"

"Fred Vickery. Tell him we met at the gas station the other day."

The boy relayed the message, mumbled something else and replaced the receiver. "He's in 115, sir. Around back. Ground floor. About the middle of the long center section. You can go out through these doors here if you're walking around." He nodded toward a set of doors set off to one side.

"You've been a big help, son." Fred started away, then turned back. "One more thing. Can you tell me if Roy Dennington is still registered?"

The wary look returned to the boy's eyes, but he punched at the computer and nodded. "Yes, sir. But I can't tell you the room number—"

Fred waved a hand to ward off his concern. "Wouldn't even think of asking. You did say Mr. Yarnell is in room 115?"

The boy nodded.

Fred hurried outside and around to the back of the inn. Sure enough, Kelley Yarnell's car stood in a space not far from the room numbered 115. He must have been watching out the window, because the door flew open before Fred could even lift a hand to knock.

The young man looked as if he'd just shaved and showered. Little track marks in his wet hair showed where the comb had been, and his aftershave still smelled bottle-fresh. He stepped aside to let Fred enter and fastened the last button on his shirt. "Is something wrong? Is that why you're here?"

"In a manner of speaking," Fred said, but when the young man's face lost all its color, he went on. "Nothing's wrong with Nancy or with the baby. Yet."

A pause, the return of a little color, and a look of intense embarrassment. "You know about the baby?"

"I know about you, and about the baby."

Two double beds stood side by side with nothing but a small table between them. Kelley dropped to the foot of one and looked miserable. "You must think I'm an absolute son of a bitch."

"I think you and Nancy made a serious mistake."

Kelley didn't look up. "But Nancy's all right?"

"For the moment." Fred perched on the foot of the other bed and tried to catch the young man's gaze. "I need to ask you some questions."

"All right. What?"

"Nancy tells me you moved out of the area, is that true?"

He nodded. "I'd been offered a job in Colorado Springs, and when she found out about the baby and decided to stay with Adam, I accepted. I certainly couldn't stay here." He smoothed his hair with his palm. "You know, I really thought I could walk away. That I loved her enough to let her stay with Adam and raise my baby as his . . ." His voice trailed away into silence.

"But you were wrong?" Fred prompted.

Kelley laughed without humor. "Big time. I haven't been able to think of anything else since I left. I love her so much it hurts. And then there's the baby—"

"Did you know Adam wanted her to have an abortion?"

Another miserable nod. "I tried to leave her alone, but something always pulled me back. When I found out what Adam wanted, I begged her not to do it. I asked her to leave him and marry me, but she wouldn't. Too much guilt, I guess." He jerked to his feet and stalked to the window. Shoving aside the curtain, he looked outside. "I don't think she wanted an abortion, but she had all that history with Adam, and I couldn't compete with that."

It seemed to Fred he'd competed quite well, but he didn't comment. Instead, he asked, "When did you come back here?"

"Tuesday."

"The day before Adam was killed?"

Agitated, Kelley dropped the curtain and fell into a chair by a round table in the corner. "I found out Nancy had an appointment with an abortion clinic, and I just couldn't let her go through with it. It's *my* baby, after all."

"So you came back."

A nod.

"Did Nancy know you were coming?"

"No. I tried to call her the first day, but she wasn't home. That night I walked over to the Silver Mine for a beer and ran into a friend of mine. We had a couple of drinks and talked for a while. She told me Adam and Nancy were separated and that Adam was staying at his office."

So Kelley had known, too. Fred tried not to look overly interested, but he feared his voice would give him away when he asked, "Who told you?"

"Charlotte Isaacson. I've known her for years. We used to be neighbors."

The connection chilled him. "What did you do when she told you about the separation?"

"Celebrated. Got plastered, if you want to know the truth." Embarrassment colored his face, and he looked down at his fingernails. "I called Nancy the next day in the morning. She seemed ready to listen and agreed to meet me that night after she had dinner with her parents."

"Then what?"

"Then I hung out for a few hours. Then I called Adam."

"Why on earth did you do that?"

"To stop him. He wanted her to kill my baby. Doesn't anybody get that? We're talking about *my* baby. It wasn't even a big secret anymore." Kelley jumped up again and gestured broadly as he talked. "Adam laughed at me. Told me I'd lost Nancy and *the kid*. He claimed Nancy'd agreed to have the abortion, that she was going that afternoon, and that by the time I saw her again, the baby'd be gone." His jaw clenched with remembered fury, and the color in his face changed from embarrassment to anger.

"What then?" Fred asked softly.

"Then? Then I tried like hell to find Nancy, to stop her from doing something she'd regret the rest of her life."

"Did you find her?"

He shook his head. "No. So I got drunk again. I figured she'd gone through with it, and I was planning to give up and head back home."

"When did you find out the truth?"

Kelley hesitated and looked away. "Not until later."

"Later that night?"

Kelley nodded as if that sounded good. "Yeah."

"Before Adam was killed?"

His eyes shifted. "No. After."

"Did you see Adam the night of the murder?"

The young man's face froze. "Why do you ask that? You think I killed him? I'll admit nobody had a better reason than me to want Adam Bigelow out of the way, but I *didn't* do it."

"Then who did?"

"Somebody with a lot more nerve than I've got," Kelley muttered. "But why are you asking me? I don't know."

Fred pushed to his feet and stepped into the young man's path. "I think you'd better tell me everything, Kelley. Right now. You and Nancy are in too much trouble to play around any longer. The sheriff's given me until six o'clock to bring Nancy in so she can tell him the whole truth. That'll include you and the baby, and you might think there are no more secrets, but she's carrying around a whole heap of them. The only way I'm going to be able to help her is if I know the whole truth. So start talking."

Kelley turned away and buried his face in his hands. "Can't we talk about this with Nancy?"

But Fred had worked himself into a fine state, and he didn't intend to wait. "You tell me a story I can believe, and we'll see."

"It *is* the truth," Kelley almost shouted, then pulled himself under control and folded his arms across his chest.

"Look, the only thing I didn't tell you was that I came back because Charlotte wrote and told me Nancy and Adam were separated. But the rest is exactly what happened. I got in on Tuesday night. I went to the Silver Mine for a beer, and Charlotte was there. She told me everything then—about how Adam wanted Nancy to get an abortion and how she already had an appointment."

He broke off and balled his hands into fists. "I was furious—with Charlotte, with Nancy, and especially with Adam. So I called him. Told him I wanted the baby, even if he didn't. I told him if he and Nancy wanted to stay together, fine. But *I* wanted the baby." He paced toward the bathroom and swung back. "He told me staying with Nancy wasn't an option unless she got rid of *the kid*. That he wasn't about to raise some *little bastard* for a lowlife like me." Kelley laughed bitterly. "So I told him that was fine, that I'd be happier if he gave them both up. And he said that would only happen over his dead body. Next thing I knew, he was dead."

A chill raced up Fred's neck. "Who else knew he said that?"

Kelley lowered his head and didn't speak for a long moment, and when he finally did, it was to give the answer Fred feared most.

"Nancy."

Fred waited to speak until the roaring in his ears subsided a little, then he asked, "You told her?"

Looking as if he'd rather die himself than admit it, Kelley nodded. "I was drunk."

"When did you tell her? Wednesday night? After dinner with her parents?" When hopefully Adam was already dead and Nancy's knowledge of his ugly words held no threat.

But Kelley just shook his head slowly. "Actually, Nancy came here Tuesday night. Somehow Adam found out she'd come to see me—that's why he finally demanded a divorce."

Fred struggled to hang on to the shreds of truth from all the stories he'd heard. "She came here the night before the murder?"

"Yes. But we didn't *do* anything. We had to talk. To decide what we wanted to do. What would be best for the baby. We thought we could keep it quiet—that Adam wouldn't ever need to know we'd seen each other again."

"But he found out."

Anger flashed across Kelley's face. "Yeah. Somehow."

"Any idea who told him Nancy'd been here?"

"There's only one person I can think of, but I don't have any proof."

"Who?"

"Charlotte. It had to be her. Nobody else even knew I was around."

"Why would she do that?"

"You figure it out. I sure as hell can't." Kelley twisted away and slammed his palm onto the wall. "All I know is, she set me up, man. Right from the beginning."

Fred thought about Brooke's claim that Charlotte had been eager for a relationship with Adam. And for the first time, he gave the idea serious consideration. And he wondered just how far Charlotte would have gone to get what she wanted.

twenty

Fred walked slowly around the Columbine Inn on his way back to the Buick. He checked his watch and calculated his travel time. It was just after two o'clock now. Allowing himself more than an hour to Mountain Home from here, half an hour with Charlotte, and an hour back to Cutler, he'd still have a little time to work on Nancy if he needed to.

He replayed his conversation with Kelley as he rounded a corner and started down one side of the U. Did he believe the young man's story? Yes. Most of it. But even people who thought they were telling the whole truth tended to downplay important points and emphasize others and to alter the picture without even realizing it. Four children and forty years with the school district had taught him the value of hearing all sides of a story before he passed judgment.

A few feet ahead of him a door opened, and a tall black man in a gray pin-striped suit stepped out onto the walk. He pulled his room door shut, double-checked the lock, and started toward a late model Lincoln just a few feet away.

It probably was too much of a coincidence for this to be Roy Dennington, but Fred quickstepped after him anyway. "Excuse me. Mr. Dennington?"

The man turned and studied Fred with evident curiosity. "What is it?"

Scarcely daring to believe his luck, Fred closed the gap between them. "Could I have a minute of your time?"

"Do I know you?"

Fred extended his hand with a smile. "My name's Fred

Vickery. I happened to see you the other day at Enviro-Sampl."

Roy folded his lips together and scowled down his nose at him. "I see. You don't work there?"

"I'm Nancy Bigelow's uncle. Her husband Adam was killed . . ."

"Ah. Yes. Of course. How can I help you, Mr. Vickery?"

Fred struggled for half a beat to phrase his question. It required delicacy. Tact. He couldn't just blurt it out.

Roy frowned impatiently.

"It's been suggested that you were offering Adam bribes to doctor the results of the Shadow Mountain tests."

Roy's face worked its way through confusion and anger before his brow straightened and he laughed aloud. "That I *what*?"

Fred's turn to look confused. "That you were interested in the Shadow Mountain property and that you might have offered a kickback to Adam if he could make the tests pass EPA standards."

Roy leaned against the hood of his car and looked amazed. "You're joking." A pause. "You're not joking."

Fred shook his head. "No." But at that moment, he certainly wished he were.

"Where did you hear a ridiculous thing like that?"

Rather than divulge his source, Fred returned a question. "Then it's not true?"

"Absolutely not."

"You're not interested in Shadow Mountain?"

"I didn't say that. I've got a great interest in the mountain. With the right investors, the right kind of money, that place could be bigger than Aspen."

Over Fred's dead body, but he didn't want to tempt fate by saying so. "Then you *are* interested."

"Very."

"Can I ask whether you've made an offer?"

Roy pushed himself up from the car and walked to the driver's door. "No."

"No, you haven't made an offer?"

A headshake. "No, you can't ask. My financial dealings

are strictly confidential—especially in the early stages."
Roy slid behind the wheel and jammed the key into the
ignition. "Now if you'll excuse me."

But Fred grabbed the door before he could pull it shut.
"When was the last time you talked to Adam Bigelow
before his death?"

"I never talked to Adam Bigelow."

"Never?"

Roy looked impatient. Put out. Ready to leave, and
annoyed with Fred for preventing him from doing so.
"Never."

"But I thought you were there the morning of the murder
because you had an appointment with him."

"I was. I had an appointment with him that morning
because his secretary called my office to set one up, but I
don't have any idea why he wanted to see me."

"Why *Adam* wanted to see *you*?"

"That surprises you?"

"I thought it was the other way around."

Roy managed to look slightly amused. "I guess you
would if you thought I was bribing him. Listen, you want to
know what I was doing there, ask his secretary. She's the
one who called my office. Now, do you mind? I've got an
appointment, and I'm already late."

Fred's head buzzed with unanswered questions, but he
stepped away from the car and let Roy pull his door shut
before he shot out of his parking spot. By the time he
followed Roy Dennington onto the highway, the Lincoln
had already disappeared from view.

When Fred passed the One-Stop on his way back through
Cutler, he checked his dashboard clock and cursed under his
breath. Already two-thirty, and he had so much he wanted to
do before Enos expected Nancy in his office.

His stomach grumbled about giving it only three bites of
paprikás for lunch, but he didn't have a minute to waste. He
drove past the Bluebird Café at a snail's pace. But when he
caught a glimpse of Pete Scott's new wife in the window all
hesitation vanished. Might as well stop for lunch—there

was no time like the present to find out about the appointment she'd made for Adam with Roy Dennington.

He whipped around the corner onto Estes Street, found a shady spot for the Buick, and hurried back to the Café. Half a dozen heads turned as he stepped inside. George Newman had probably been in the same spot since before lunch. Arnold Van Dyke leaned up from his seat and shouted something about the drought into Grandpa Jones's ear. Bill Lacey sucked soda through a straw and looked relieved to see Fred instead of Janice coming through the door. Douglas sat on a stool next to Grady Hatch, and Grady was perched in his usual spot by the kitchen where he could talk to his mother as she worked.

Douglas swallowed the bite he'd been working on and turned around on his seat. "Hi, Dad. What are you doing here?"

"I need lunch, and this seemed like a good place to get it."

Douglas took another mouthful and checked his watch. Chewing, he seemed to consider Fred's answer, as if he needed to pass approval before Fred could take a seat. "Want to join me?" He nodded toward the empty seat next to his.

Fred shook his head and patted the small of his back. "Don't like the counter, son. I'll just go on over to a table." He turned to leave, but Douglas started stacking silverware on his plate and scooted a cup of something icy toward the edge of the counter. "Then I'll come sit with you."

Glancing over his shoulder, Fred looked to see whether the new Mrs. Scott had moved. She hadn't. "No. Stay here. You're right in the middle of your meal. Besides, I don't want to interrupt you and Grady—"

Grady patted his stomach and waved a hand at him. "I'm almost done, and I need to get back to work in a few minutes anyway."

Fred tried to work up a smile. "Well, all right then, son. I'll go get us a table."

The larger room stood empty except for Pete and the new Mrs. Scott near the window, and one other young couple huddled at a back table studying a map as if their lives depended on it. Choosing the booth next to the Scotts', Fred slid onto the seat facing Pete. Wishing he could remember the new Mrs. Scott's name, he tried to find an excuse to start a conversation.

With his headful of dark hair that always looked too big for his narrow face, and a pair of wire-rimmed glasses pinching his nose, Pete looked dull and bookish. Fred thought he'd been a perfect match for the first Mrs. Scott—Elizabeth—who'd been dull and bookish herself, and who'd run off a few years ago with the electrician who rewired their basement.

Pete didn't dovetail as well with his new wife. He was at least ten years older in age and eons older in interests, but she seemed content, and he seemed thrilled with his good fortune.

Douglas tromped into the dining room carrying his half-eaten lunch. "Hey, Pete. Welcome back."

Fred remembered his wife mentioning something about Pete being gone, so he echoed Douglas's sentiment.

Pete looked delighted that they'd noticed his absence, but he put on a wary expression and wagged his narrow head. "By the skin of my teeth."

Rolling her eyes in mock exasperation, his wife smiled over her shoulder. "He's been moaning since he got home last night, but doesn't he look *great*?"

Fred thought he looked the same as always, and he'd never thought of *great* as a word he'd use to describe Pete's appearance, but he didn't say so. Instead, he held her gaze. "How are you holding up? Are things any better at the office?"

"Since the murder?" She shuddered. "I don't want to think about it anymore. It gives me the willies. I'm just glad today's Saturday so I can get away from it for a while."

Douglas slid in across from Fred and sent him a curious glance as he arranged his silverware.

Immediately losing his self-absorbed expression, Pete managed to look protective. "Then don't think about it, sweetheart. And we won't talk about it." And he sent Fred a pointed look.

Fred decided to ignore it. "I just ran into Roy Dennington a few minutes ago."

Douglas wedged his sandwich into his mouth and bit off a chunk as Pete frowned and sent Fred another look, a little more intense than the first. Fred made a point of not noticing that one either and watched Mrs. Scott instead.

But she looked confused. "Roy Dennington? Where have I heard that name before?"

"I understand he's a land developer," Fred suggested.

Though she stared at him out of blank eyes, she pretended to understand. "Then I must have heard his name at work."

Pete reached across the table and patted her hand. "Let's not talk about it, honey. Okay?"

Fred frowned at him. They had to talk about it. Now. "I'd imagine that's where you heard it, all right. He was at EnviroSampl the morning of the murder, you know."

Confusion clouded her face. "No. I didn't know," she said slowly. But all at once she jumped around to face Fred a little better. "Wait a sec. Is he that black guy? The one in the suit?"

Now they were getting somewhere. "That's the one."

"Yeah." She nodded. "I did see him."

Pete scowled darkly. "I *thought* we decided not to discuss it."

Pete might have decided, but Fred certainly hadn't. "I just need to ask you a couple of things about that morning—" he began, but broke off when Lizzie stopped by with a fresh pot of coffee. Chafing at the interruption, he flipped over his cup.

Lizzie filled it, pulled her pencil from behind her ear and a pad from her pocket.

"Hot turkey sandwich," he ordered quickly. "And give me mashed potatoes with extra gravy."

Douglas stuffed his mouth full again, but he lifted his eyebrows as if he thought Fred needed to explain his choice.

Fred didn't. A man ought to be able to order what he pleased—complete with extra cholesterol *and* fat—without having to make up excuses.

Never one to waste time on small talk, Lizzie replaced her

pencil and took away the coffeepot, but in that short time the Scotts had already drifted into another conversation, and when Pete noticed Fred watching them, he nearly broke his neck trying to avoid eye contact.

For half a second Fred considered waiting until he could talk with the new Mrs. Scott alone. But if he couldn't tie the murder to EnviroSampl by six o'clock, he'd have to put Nancy's trust on the line.

Fred leaned forward in his seat and coughed to catch her attention. Even Pete couldn't fault a man for carrying on a conversation he didn't start.

Pete raised his voice and leaned a little further into the dialogue with his wife.

Fred cleared his throat.

Both of the Scotts seemed to have developed hearing problems, but Douglas munched a little more slowly, and Grady turned around in his seat on the other side of the Café.

Douglas wiped his mouth with a napkin. "What are you doing?"

"I must have a frog in my throat."

"Drink some water."

Fred drank and kept one eye on the back of Mrs. Scott's head.

Douglas lowered his fork to the table. "What *are* you doing?"

"Keep your voice down, and I'll tell you," Fred snapped. He lowered his voice and said, "I'm trying to get a few answers."

"About the murder."

"Not exactly."

"Then what exactly?"

"An appointment Adam had the day of the murder."

Douglas leaned back and let a mocking smile curve his lips. "Oh, I can see how unrelated it must be."

"If you're going to interfere, go back to the counter. I don't have time for any of your nonsense."

"Well, don't let Grady hear you asking questions."

"I'm *trying* not to."

Douglas had the good grace to flush. "You know what I mean. Grady says Enos is afraid you think you can make a habit of this."

"A habit? Not on your life. I only do what I have to."

Douglas nodded. "Oh. I see."

But Fred could tell he didn't see at all. Abandoning his effort to reason with the boy, he cleared his throat a third time.

This time the new Mrs. Scott glanced over her shoulder. Wonderful. He leaned forward and spoke just loud enough for her to hear. "So you'd never met Roy Dennington before the morning of the murder?"

She shot a glance at her husband, almost as if she had to ask permission to answer. Pete scowled darkly at Fred, but he didn't speak, so she wet her lips and shook her head. "No. And like I said, I didn't even *meet* him then."

"But you talked with him on the telephone."

Behind him, Pete's face flooded with color. "She said she didn't want to talk about it, Fred."

"Nobody *wants* to talk about it, Pete," Fred snapped. "But she might have information that's vital to the investigation."

Her eyes grew huge. "But I don't know anything."

"Just tell me why you called Roy Dennington to set a meeting with Adam. What did Adam want?"

Pete shot out of the booth, but his narrow face had colored so deeply Fred worried a little about his health. "Tiffany doesn't know a damned thing about Adam Bigelow's murder," Pete shouted.

Tiffany. Fred repeated it silently and hoped he could remember this time.

Douglas draped an arm across the back of his seat. "Calm down, Pete. He's not accusing her of anything."

"Of course not," Fred said, and held Tiffany's gaze with his own. "But I think you know things that could help find the killer. For instance, what happened when Philip learned that Adam was accepting kickbacks for gathering phony samples and altering test results on Shadow Mountain? And why did Adam ask you to make that appointment with Roy Dennington? This is a key issue—"

Pete swore loudly, and Grady slid from his stool. With a heavy frown in their direction, he hitched his duty belt up on his hips as if he meant business.

When he saw Grady advancing, Pete tugged at Tiffany's arm and tried to pull her out of her seat. "Come on, honey. Let's get out of here."

But Fred couldn't let her go. Once Pete got her alone, he'd convince her to close up completely. "Will you please tell me what you know about that appointment?" His voice came out harsher, more demanding, than he'd intended.

Tiffany whipped back around to face Fred. "What makes you think I know anything about it?"

Fred spoke quickly, urgently. "Roy said you'd called."

But before she could respond, Grady reached Fred's booth and parked himself in front of his only escape route. "Couldn't help but hear raised voices. What's going on here?"

Like a frightened schoolboy, Pete thrust an accusing finger in Fred's direction. "He's trying to insinuate that my wife knows something about Adam Bigelow's murder, and he won't leave her alone."

Grady didn't look pleased. "Is that true, Fred?"

Fred's temper frayed a little around the edges. "No, it's not true."

When Pete made a noise to suggest what he thought of that answer, Fred's temper snapped. The fool couldn't even see how important it was to find out what Tiffany knew. Pushing to his feet, he slid out of the booth straight into Grady. Surprised, Grady took a step back and gave Fred the room he needed to get around him. "I didn't *insinuate* a blasted thing. I came right out and said she knows something important."

Douglas clambered out of the booth and put an arm around Fred's shoulders as if he needed someone to control him. "Dad, don't cause trouble."

"I'm not causing trouble. I'm asking a simple question, and I'd like an answer."

Grady sent him a warning look.

And Fred sent an angry one back. "I didn't accuse her of

murdering him, for tar sakes. All I asked was whether she knew what Adam wanted with Roy Dennington—"

That finally made Grady's ears perk up. "With Roy Dennington?"

Relived that finally someone was ready to listen, Fred nodded. "She made an appointment for Adam to meet with Roy the morning of the murder. All I want to know is why. What did Adam want?"

Grady looked interested for half a second longer, but as if he suddenly remembered who he was, he pulled his face back into line and tried to look official. "Do you have Enos's permission to poke around in the murder investigation?"

Fred didn't even bother to answer such a ridiculous question.

Taking advantage of the diversion, Pete tugged at Tiffany again. This time she stood. But when he saw Fred following their every move, he shouted, "My wife isn't answering any more of your questions," and led Tiffany a few steps away.

Grady made no move to stop them, so Fred pushed past the younger man. "If I didn't know better, Pete, I'd think you had something to hide. Why won't you let your wife answer a simple question?"

Pete stiffened and turned, red-faced and almost beside himself with anger. "I want to press charges. That's libel or slander or *something*, isn't it?"

Douglas stepped forward and tried to get in front of Fred. "Now listen, you two—"

"What's the matter with him? Why doesn't he want Tiffany to talk?" Fred demanded.

Grady held up his hands and scowled at them all. "I want everybody to calm down right now. Fred, don't say another word."

"That's more like it," Pete huffed.

"You either, Pete. I want both of you to keep quiet while I talk to Tiffany for a minute."

Pete drew himself up to his full height, which didn't look like much against Grady's. "Not without me, you don't."

Grady didn't say a word, he just fixed Pete with a hard

stare and waited until the other man's posture readjusted itself. But when he turned to Tiffany, all the harshness left his expression. "Why don't you tell me about that appointment? Do you know why Adam wanted to see Roy Dennington?"

Shoving his hands into his pockets, Fred rocked back on his heels and waited for the answer. For the piece that would pull the picture together.

Tiffany shook her head.

"You don't know?" For a boy as big as Grady had grown, he could sound surprisingly gentle.

"No."

"Adam didn't tell you?"

She looked confused, anxious. "I mean I don't even know what you're talking about. I never called Roy Dennington."

Shocked, Fred shot forward. "What? But Roy said Adam's secretary called—"

Gaining a little confidence now that she'd given one answer, Tiffany shook her head again. "Well, it wasn't me," she said, and the look in her face and the set of her jaw convinced him she was telling the truth.

Pete lunged around Grady and put a protective arm around his wife's shoulders. "See? *Now* will you leave her alone?"

Fred nodded. He saw Lizzie come out of the kitchen balancing a tray at shoulder height, and he knew she had his lunch. But all at once he didn't want to take time to eat.

If Tiffany hadn't called Roy Dennington, that left only two other possibilities: Brooke Westphal or Charlotte Isaacson. And he wanted to find out which—immediately.

He couldn't imagine either woman referring to herself as Adam's secretary. Neither would have set appointments for Adam in the ordinary course of business. But if he had to guess which one had made the call, he'd bet on Brooke. And he didn't want to let any grass grow under his feet before he asked her about it.

He watched Pete lead Tiffany away, listened to Grady warn him about sticking his nose into the investigation, and agreed to almost everything the boy said, just to set his mind at ease. He ate half his turkey sandwich, fortified himself with a second cup of coffee, and threw enough money on the table to cover the bill and Lizzie's tip.

With less than three hours until his deadline, he was back in the Buick and headed toward Mountain Home.

twenty-one

Fred pulled off the highway and parked in the shade of an old spruce tree next to EnviroSampl's tin building. He didn't want to be here, but Nancy's time was already running short, and he couldn't afford to wait. And the smattering of cars in the parking lot made him hopeful he'd find Brooke here.

After crossing the parking lot, he pushed on the front door. It opened easily, and he stepped into the tiny reception area. Nobody sat at the front desk, but the door to Philip Aagard's office stood open.

Philip looked puzzled when Fred entered, but he beckoned him into the inner sanctum. "Mr. Vickery, isn't it? What are you doing here?"

"I'm trying to find one of your employees, and I'm hoping she's here."

Philip dropped into his chair and tilted back. "Oh? Which one?"

"Brooke Westphal."

"Brooke? You're in luck. As a matter of fact, she did come in today." Philip gestured toward one of the chairs in front of the desk and punched a couple of numbers on the phone pad. "I don't imagine there's any problem with you talking to her—unless she's right in the middle of a test."

He broke off and focused on the receiver. "Mitch? Is Brooke in the lab? What's she doing? Great. Have her come up here for a minute, would you? No, no problem . . . somebody to see her. Nancy Bigelow's uncle." He shot a confirming glance at Fred. "Right. We're in my office." He hung up and folded his hands on his desk. "She'll be right here."

"I appreciate you letting me interrupt like this."

"It's all right if it doesn't take long. I don't know how much she needs to get done before Monday." He frowned at Fred and asked, "There's no trouble, is there?"

Other than illegal kickbacks, falsified test results, and murder? Fred shook his head. "No."

Philip almost looked disappointed. "Tell me how Nancy's doing."

"She's all right. It's a difficult time."

"Yes, of course." Philip let a moment of understanding silence lapse. "Such a tragedy."

As if even that word could begin to convey the horror of it all. Fred glanced around behind him. "I hate to interrupt what you're doing. Do you have another office where I could wait?"

Philip looked toward the door as if he expected Brooke to walk through any second. "Just Adam's, and I can't let you use that one. I don't mind letting you talk to Brooke in here. I'm just catching up on a few things, myself."

He might not mind, but Fred didn't like the idea.

"I imagine you're here because you've heard about Adam—?"

Not entirely certain what Philip meant, Fred just nodded.

Philip's brows knit as if he were confused. "You know—in spite of everything he did, I still think Adam was basically a good man."

"Yes, he was."

"I can't tell you how shocked I was to find out what he'd been up to."

On second thought, there was no harm verifying a few facts while he waited. "Exactly when did you find out?"

Philip shook his head and looked incredibly sad. "Just recently."

"The day before Adam was killed—?"

Philip's eyes flew open. "No. This morning."

"This morning?" Fred's turn to look confused.

"I thought I knew everything that goes on here, but I had no idea until Mitch brought his suspicions to me. It didn't take long to verify what Adam was doing, and I'm completely shocked."

So it was true. Adam had altered the Shadow Mountain test results. Until this moment, Fred had harbored hope that it would prove false. "But I thought you argued with Adam before he died."

Philip pulled back slightly and stiffened his shoulders. "Where did you hear that?"

Fred scrambled to remember, but the details escaped him.

Philip jerked to his feet and paced as far as the tiny office would let him. "I don't know where you got your information, but it's absolutely false."

Fred ran through conversations he'd had over the past few days, but he'd been so busy, talked to so many people, asked so many questions, he'd begun to lose track of where he'd heard what.

With his charm nudged out of place, Philip paced toward the door. "Where in the hell is that woman? I don't know what's happened to the discipline around this place."

Fred didn't try to soothe him. Something about this conversation bothered Philip—made him nervous.

Sketchy details of conversations formed as Philip paced, until Fred remembered exactly who'd mentioned Philip's argument with Adam. Porter. And though Porter could be exasperating and could act like an idiot on occasion, Fred trusted him. If Porter said Adam and Philip argued, they must have.

Philip looked out the door as if he could make Brooke appear by force of will alone. He swore again and stomped back to the telephone. He punched numbers and nearly growled into the receiver. "Where's Brooke? I thought you said she was free."

Fred waited until Philip slammed the receiver back into place for the second time before he spoke. "I've talked with a witness who claims you were upset with Adam."

"Upset with him?" Philip whirled back to face Fred, and his voice rose a notch. "That's ridiculous. Adam was a trusted employee. Believing in him the way I did might make me stupid or blind, but it doesn't make me a murderer."

Fred kept his face completely expressionless. "I never said it did."

Philip stopped, drew a deep breath, and gave an embarrassed laugh. "No. Of course you didn't. Look, this whole thing's been a nightmare . . ." As if that explained his outburst.

Rapidly approaching footsteps broke the moment's tension, and Philip's face relaxed. So when Brooke appeared in the doorway, he greeted her with a bright smile. "Ah—here she is. Come in, Brooke. Mr. Vickery has a few questions to ask you." But instead of leaving them in private, Philip settled back into his chair.

Fred scooted to the edge of his. "Do you mind if I talk to Brooke alone?"

Philip cocked his head as if he'd just heard a new idea, but he nodded in concession. "No. Of course not. I wasn't thinking. You two stay here. I have a few things to check on in the lab, anyway. Come in, Brooke. Sit." He gestured toward the empty chair, restacked a sheaf of papers and tucked them under his arm, and with another over-friendly smile, slipped out of the office and closed the door behind him. But he left behind a whirlwind of emotions Fred couldn't begin to analyze.

Brooke approached the empty chair beside Fred's with a hesitant step. "What's wrong?"

"Not a thing. I just need to ask you one question—" He looked back at the door through which Philip had just disappeared. "—maybe two."

Brooke almost smiled. "Okay."

"Did you make an appointment for Adam to meet with Roy Dennington the morning of the murder?"

"Me? No." She looked mildly surprised. Confused. Truthful.

But just to be sure, he asked, "You're certain?"

Add a touch of annoyance. "Of course. What makes you think I might have?"

Her response sounded so genuine, Fred's spirits fell. "Dennington told me Adam's secretary called."

"Then you should talk to Tiffany. She's the one—"

Fred shook his head. "I just did. It wasn't her."

"Oh." A pause while she considered. "Do you think it was Charlotte?"

His thoughts exactly. "I guess it must have been."

But Brooke didn't look convinced. "It couldn't have been. Charlotte works hard to make sure nobody ever mistakes her for clerical staff. I can't imagine her ever setting up an appointment for Adam—for *any* of the men here."

"Maybe she didn't," Fred agreed. "I figured since you were the one helping him after hours—"

Brooke flushed at the words left unspoken. "Can you believe this? Philip's been like a crazy man all day. He called and made me come in so I could show him what Adam and I did. He even got Mitch to come in— Honestly, if I'd had *any* idea what he was up to, I *never* would have helped."

Discussing her guilt or innocence on that issue wouldn't get them anywhere. "Can I ask you about something else?"

She nodded.

"Philip just told me he didn't know about Adam's late-night tests until after the murder, but I have it on good authority they argued before. Any idea why?"

"Why they argued?" Another long pause. "No." She looked over her shoulder as if she expected someone to check on her.

"They didn't have trouble?"

She almost laughed. "Philip has trouble with everybody. He breeds stress. If he *hadn't* ever argued with Adam, that's when I'd worry. He's probably out there right now. Pacing and waiting for me to come out. I really ought to get back—"

Fred didn't want her to go. Nothing made sense. Nothing felt right. But he stood and tried to look accepting. "Yes, of course. Thanks for your time."

Her lips curved in a weak smile. "I wish I could have been more help."

"So do I."

"Maybe you ought to talk to Charlotte."

"I think I will. It can't hurt. Is she in the middle of something important?"

Brooke made a face. "*She* didn't have to come in today."

"Why not?"

She looked over her shoulder again and whispered, "You tell me. Why me and Mitch, but not her?"

Fred leaned a little closer and kept his voice low. "What do you think?"

"I think Philip's the biggest jerk I've ever worked for. Frankly, I'm surprised that *he's* not the one who got killed." She laughed a little and looked at the ceiling panels. "I shouldn't have said that—he's probably got this place bugged."

"So things have been difficult around here since the murder?"

"I'll say. And Philip's having an absolute fit about it. He can't understand why anyone's still upset. After all, it's been almost three whole days—" She broke off and shook her head in disgust. "He's absolutely impossible to deal with. And Mitch is bearing the brunt of it. And it's not helping matters that we can't find the Paradise Valley tests Charlotte ran last week."

"Some of Charlotte's tests are missing?"

"One that I know of. Who knows how many others."

All at once, Kelley Yarnell's story echoed in Fred's mind. Charlotte had wanted Adam. She'd brought Kelley back for Nancy and fed him stories about divorce and abortion until she thought everything was where she wanted it. But had she also been involved in altering the test results? Had *she* been the driving force behind Adam? And if so, what had backfired? Had it made her kill Adam in the end?

Suddenly convinced he'd found the murderer, Fred shot to his feet and quickly crossed to the door.

Brooke bolted after him. "Where are you going?"

But Fred didn't answer. He couldn't. He only knew he had to catch Charlotte before she disappeared, and that time was quickly running out.

twenty-two

Ignoring the very real possibility that he'd get another speeding ticket, Fred cruised through Mountain Home without looking at his speedometer. If Robert Alpers wanted to follow him, it might not be a bad idea. He raced down Main Street to Twin Creek Drive and shot up the mountain, all without attracting a speck of attention.

When he reached Charlotte's place, he pulled into the driveway behind her car and hurried up the front steps. The house looked innocent enough. Nothing sinister. Nothing foreboding. Yet his heart hammered against his chest and threatened to block his throat.

He pushed on the doorbell, but he didn't expect her to answer. So when the door opened away from his hand, he had to swallow his surprise.

Charlotte stood there, looking as surprised as he felt. "What are you doing here?"

He had to corral his thoughts for a second before he could form words. "I need to talk to you."

"About what?"

"Can we talk inside?"

Without a word, she turned and strode into the living room and draped herself into an off-white chair. "For heaven's sake, you're acting as if the sky's falling."

For all he knew, it might be. Steering clear of the low-flung couch this time, he chose a chair next to the front window instead. "I've got a few more questions for you, and this time I want you to tell me the truth."

"By which you imply I didn't the last time we spoke." Ice

lined her voice, but her face betrayed nothing. "All right, go ahead."

"I understand you're a friend of Kelley Yarnell's."

She crossed her legs and stared hard at him. "I've known Kelley for years. But what does that have to do with anything?"

"I also understand you told him Nancy and Adam had separated, and why."

She nodded, but she looked a little wary.

"And that you had drinks with him the night before the murder."

A shadow flitted behind her eyes. "What are you insinuating?"

"I'm not insinuating a blasted thing, I'm telling you what I know. So was it you who called Roy Dennington and set up an appointment for Adam the morning of the murder?"

Her body snapped out of its languid pose but she still tried to sound casual. "I guess so."

"Why? What did Adam want to see Roy about?"

"He didn't tell me."

But Fred had reached the end of his tolerance for the games all these people wanted to play. "You're a respected chemist," he said. "Adam's equal in every way. And I understand you're very careful to keep people from mistaking you for a member of the clerical staff. Yet when Adam asked you to set an appointment for him, you did it without question?"

"Yes," she said, but her certainty wavered a bit.

"What did he want with Dennington?"

She shot up and paced a few steps away. "I don't know. I honestly don't. To tell you the truth, I don't have any idea what's been going on around the office lately. Philip's been on the rampage. Adam was distracted all the time. And even Mitch is jumpy. It's gotten to all of us."

"What has?"

"Well, at first, I thought Adam was upset because of his marital problems, but toward the end I started thinking there was something else bothering him."

"You knew about Kelley Yarnell's relationship with Nancy?"

"Not at first. I found out about it shortly before Adam died. He was really torn up about it."

"That's why he insisted on an abortion?"

"No. Adam hated the idea of abortion, but he insisted on one because he couldn't raise that baby. It would have been a constant reminder. And Nancy wouldn't even consider giving the baby up."

"So you told Kelley about Adam and Nancy, and you urged him to come back to town."

"No! We ran into each other by accident. But, yes, I told him. Listen, I liked both of them—Adam *and* Kelley. It's not their fault they were both in love with the same woman. If anybody's to blame, it's her."

Either Charlotte was lying, or Kelley had lied to him earlier. And if Fred had to choose one to believe, he'd pick Kelley. The young man had seemed sincere. Charlotte did not. "Did you tell Adam that Kelley was back?"

Charlotte's face tightened, and for an instant Fred thought she wouldn't answer. When she did, she spoke softly. "The day he died."

"And you told him Nancy had been to see Kelley at his hotel room?"

She put a touch of shock into her eyes. "No. I didn't know that."

"I was under the impression you were the only one who knew Kelley was back in town."

"Well, I couldn't have been, could I? Somebody else had to know." Her voice sounded just right. Defensive. Outraged. Innocent.

But Fred didn't believe a word of it. "Then what did you tell him?"

"Just that I'd run into Kelley the night before." She looked away. "I didn't *mean* to tell him that. It slipped out in the conversation."

Maybe so, but only after she'd oiled the tracks. "How did Adam react?"

"Like you might expect. Angry. Hurt. Ready to confront Kelley and demand that he leave Nancy alone."

"And did he?"

Charlotte dropped back into her chair. "I don't know. Look, this wasn't the only thing bothering him."

"What else was on his mind?"

"I don't know. Things around the office really got bad about then. Philip called Adam into his office the day before the murder, and when Adam came out, he was absolutely livid. I followed him into his office and offered to help, and that's when he asked me to call Roy Dennington and set up an appointment."

"But you didn't ask why."

She looked supremely innocent. "No. And if you'd seen the look on his face, you wouldn't have, either. I figured I'd wait until he calmed down and ask him then."

"His behavior didn't seem strange to you?"

She gestured broadly and crossed her long legs. "Of *course* it seemed strange. Adam had no business meeting with Roy Dennington—or any other potential purchaser. It was an absolute conflict of interest, and Philip would never have allowed him to do it."

"Do you have any idea why Adam wanted to?"

Looking miserable, she nodded. "I do now, of course. Adam was accessing records in the lab and creating a clean set of test files on the computer under another password."

"Who told you that?"

"Mitch called me a little while ago. I can't help wondering what Roy could have offered Adam that made it worth losing everything."

"So who killed him?"

Charlotte shook her head and looked puzzled. "Philip obviously found out about the tests and ordered Adam to stop. Adam must have wanted to meet with Roy Dennington to tell him they'd been caught. He probably asked me to make the call while he got rid of stuff in his office and files on the computer."

After he got caught? Locking the barn door after the cows escaped? It seemed unlikely to Fred, but he didn't comment.

Instead, he pretended to ponder her answers for a minute. "What about Brooke Westphal?"

"What about her?"

"I understand she helped Adam with the second set of tests."

Charlotte rolled her dark eyes as if dismissing Brooke completely. "Yes, but she didn't know what he was doing. I hear Philip's furious that she accessed the lab after hours, but he doesn't blame her."

"Did she have any reason to kill Adam?" he asked, more to himself than to Charlotte.

But she hurried to answer with a short laugh. "Brooke? She'd never have the nerve."

"Then who do you think did it?"

The smile slipped from her face, and she turned toward the window. "I don't know."

But Fred had the feeling she had a very good idea. "Kelley Yarnell?"

She whipped back around to face him. "No. Kelley would *never* do something like that."

"Then who?"

"I don't know."

"Philip Aagard?"

"No."

"Mitch Hancock?"

With her face in a tight frown, she stood. "Listen, Mr. Vickery, there might have been trouble at EnviroSampl, but if you want to know what happened to Adam, you're looking in the wrong place."

She crossed to the front door and jerked it open. "Now, I really have to ask you to leave. I have a thousand things to do."

"Of course." He moved slowly toward the door, but when he drew abreast of her, he stopped. "Why did you go to work so early the morning of the murder?"

Her face might as well have been carved of stone. "I often put in extra hours. We *all* do. There's no way to get everything Philip expects done in eight hours."

"And you weren't surprised to see Adam's car there?"

"Of course not. He'd been living there, remember? His car was always there."

"And you knew about his appointment with Roy Dennington—"

Her eyes narrowed. "What's your point?"

Fred shrugged and tried to look nonchalant. "Just trying to piece everything together that happened that morning."

Charlotte's thin face colored. "Are you wondering if *I* killed Adam?" He didn't answer immediately, so she rushed on. "Look, Mr. Vickery, I know you're trying to prove that Nancy's innocent, but nobody else had a reason to kill Adam. Honestly, I think you're deluding yourself."

He faced her squarely and held her gaze for a long moment. "You're wrong. Seems to me the trouble is that too many people wanted Adam dead. And too many people are trying to protect themselves."

She drew in a deep breath, and her nostrils flared slightly. "Meaning me?"

"Maybe."

"Well, good luck," she said in a voice that suggested she wished him otherwise. "I hope you find exactly what you're looking for. Now, if you'll excuse me—"

Under the weight of her stare, he stepped outside and returned to his car. But he felt no better than he had when he arrived. Instead, he felt as if he'd been led in a perfect circle and had somehow ended miles from where he started.

twenty-three

Fred drove back to Cutler as quickly as he dared, watching for speed traps and cursing himself under his breath. Maybe he had been on the wrong track after all. Maybe he'd wasted time trying to tie Adam's death to EnviroSampl. Maybe Adam *had* been killed because of Nancy and Kelley and the baby.

Fred glared at the road and tried to understand how he'd gotten so turned around. But by the time he reached the straightaway through Bergen's Meadow, he still didn't have any answers. Increasing his speed by a couple miles per hour, he tried to work through that scenario once more.

Nancy's marriage had begun to suffer when Adam's work demanded too much of his attention. She'd had an affair with Kelley Yarnell that resulted in a pregnancy, and because Adam couldn't have children and would never believe the child was his, Nancy'd confessed the truth to him. Adam had insisted Nancy get an abortion, and when she refused he demanded a divorce.

No trouble so far. Everything fit.

So who killed Adam? Nancy?

Of course not. Even considering the affair, the baby, the arguments, and the abortion, Fred refused to believe it. Porter?

It might be a *little* easier to believe, but that didn't make it any less painful. Kelley Yarnell?

Fred lifted his foot from the accelerator and rounded a curve in the road. Could Kelley be the murderer? Fred didn't want to think so, but he didn't completely understand why. Did he honestly believe Kelley was innocent? Or did he just *want* him to be—for Nancy's sake and the baby's?

He pondered the possibilities as he drove into Cutler, but by the time he passed the Kwik-Kleen, he knew he didn't think either option fit. Adam had been murdered because of something at EnviroSampl. Fred knew it, but he couldn't prove it. And because he couldn't, Enos would end up dragging Nancy's story out into the open—unless Fred could convince him to wait a little longer. But he'd already pushed Enos to the limit of his patience; he didn't dare ask for anything more.

Turning onto Lake Front, Fred drove past the Kirkhams' big, ugly cabin, followed the winding road half a mile, and pulled into his driveway. When he saw Margaret's Chevy parked in front of the garage, he didn't know whether he should be grateful or upset. Margaret's presence offered an excuse to put off talking to Nancy, but stalling would gain nothing. It would only postpone the inevitable.

He parked beside Margaret's car and waited for her to race out the front door demanding to know where he'd been. But several seconds passed without a sign of her.

Fred climbed out of the car and headed up the front walk, wondering what else had come along to claim her attention. It must be something important if it kept her from watching for him.

He pushed open the door and peered inside, half expecting the room to be empty—for Margaret and Nancy to have migrated to the back deck. But Margaret sat alone on the couch, staring at her mother's round oak table and the jumble of pictures on its surface. And that made her failure to accost him even more unexpected.

She didn't turn around until he closed the door. Then she met his gaze with tear-swollen eyes, and when she tried to smile, her mouth trembled.

He hurried to the couch and lowered himself onto the seat beside her. If that husband of hers had done anything to upset her—Fred struggled to keep his voice steady. "What's the matter, sweetheart?"

She took a second to pull herself together. "I've been talking to Nancy."

He tried not to look relieved that the tears sprang from Nancy's life and not Margaret's. "About what? Has something happened?"

"She told me everything—about the baby, the baby's father. About Adam—" She caught back a sob and met his gaze again. "Oh, Dad. I feel so bad for her. This is such a mess."

A small word for such a big problem. "Where is she?"

"She went with Aunt Harriet a few minutes ago."

Fred slid an arm around Margaret's shoulders and squeezed in his most reassuring manner. "Well, I'm glad Nancy told you the truth. At least it's a step in the right direction."

"Can you imagine what Aunt Harriet and Uncle Porter will say when they find out?"

"Nancy's got a rough row to hoe, that's for sure. But her parents are good people. They'll be all right—eventually."

Margaret shuddered, and a few seconds of silence passed before she spoke again. "She said you'd met the baby's father. What did you think of him?"

"He seems like a nice guy—honestly concerned with Nancy and the baby. Why?"

"Do you think he killed Adam?"

"No, I don't."

"Really?"

"Really."

She breathed a sigh that might have been one of relief. "Then who *do* you suspect?"

For half a second he wondered if she'd staged this conversation to trap him into a confession of his most recent activities. But he couldn't read an ulterior motive in her face. "It could be anybody. Philip Aagard. Charlotte Isaacson. Brooke Westphal. Mitch Hancock. Roy Dennington."

"But you *don't* think it was Kelley?"

Fred leaned away from Margaret and looked deep into her eyes. "You're not trying to trap me into something, are you?"

She almost smiled. "What? A confession that you've been out trying to solve this case?"

"Maybe."

He expected a grin. Instead she shook her head and looked serious. "No. Tell me why you don't think Kelley's guilty."

"It's nothing more than a gut reaction. In fact, I was trying to figure out exactly why I believe he's innocent on the way home."

"And—"

"And I decided I have to rely on my instinct—that Adam was murdered because of something at work."

Her eyes burned with eagerness. "Like what? Do you know?"

Pressing his hands against his knees for leverage, Fred worked himself back to his feet and paced to the window. "Adam was altering the results of soil and water tests on Shadow Mountain. Best I can figure, Philip Aagard found out and called Adam on it. What I *can't* figure is why anybody would kill him after he was caught—after Philip already knew."

Margaret didn't respond immediately. When she did, her voice sounded immeasurably sad. "Are you sure Adam was doing that? It doesn't sound like him."

Fred turned back from the window to face her. "There's a buyer interested in the property—a man named Roy Dennington. It could be that he killed Adam because he didn't want Adam to blow the whistle on their deal and bring his involvement to light—but it still doesn't feel right to me."

"Maybe it was just the way you said. Maybe this Roy Dennington killed Adam to protect his own reputation."

He shook his head. "There's still something missing."

"Have you told Enos what you suspect?"

"Not yet. But he's coming by at six o'clock to question Nancy again unless I can convince her to take her story to him."

Margaret's face darkened. "How much does he know about that situation?"

"Not much. But he suspects there's more to the story than we're telling, and he's determined to find out what."

She rose from the couch and took a couple of steps

toward him. "There must be something else we can do before he gets here."

"Well if there is, I sure can't figure out what. I've spent all afternoon trying to find the missing piece."

"Have you talked to Brooke?"

Fred dropped into his rocking chair and nodded. "And Charlotte. And Roy. And Kelley— I'm telling you, I'm at my wits' end."

Margaret paced away. "Well, there has to be *something* you haven't done—some stone you've left unturned."

Well, of course there was, or he'd have found the murderer by now. But Margaret had never accepted his involvement in a case so easily, and he didn't intend to ruin the moment by pointing out the obvious.

She paced back toward him, ticking silent markers off her fingers, glancing at him every few seconds as if verifying some aspect of his story. Finally, she perched on the arm of the couch and leaned toward him. "So you believe Adam's death is somehow linked to Shadow Mountain?"

"Yes."

"Because he was accepting kickbacks from this Roy Dennington, who wants to buy the place?"

Fred nodded.

"And you're sure Roy Dennington's offering a payoff even though he denies it?"

"There isn't anybody else with a reason to want the test results altered."

Margaret shook her head as if warding off his logic. "Who gains if the property sells? If it's developed?"

"The buyer—the developer. Roy Dennington."

"And the seller. Kate Talbot."

Fred stopped rocking. After the murder of Kate's sister last year she'd been named executor of the will, and now she held Shadow Mountain in trust for her niece Madison.

"But Kate wouldn't—" Margaret began.

"No, Kate wouldn't," Fred interrupted and shot to his feet. "But she'll know just how eager Dennington is to get his hands on the property." He headed toward the telephone.

Margaret fell into step behind him. "Do you have her number?"

Fred nodded. "She wrote to me once after she and Madison got back to San Francisco, and I think she gave me her home number and one for her office." Snagging up his battered address book, he flipped through its pages and wondered where he'd managed to find a spot to add a new listing.

Margaret leaned her chin on his shoulder and studied the pages with him. After several seconds she thrust her hand forward and waggled her finger at a pencil scrawl in the upper corner of a page. "Is that it?"

Fred had no idea, but there were enough digits to be out-of-state numbers, and the notation beside them looked enough like "Kate" to satisfy him. He lifted the receiver, punched buttons, and waited for someone to answer.

"Hello?"

He thought he'd forgotten her voice, but she sounded as familiar as if he'd spoken to her just yesterday. "Kate? Fred Vickery here. How are you?"

"Fred? It's really you?" She sounded almost glad to hear from him. "What do you need?"

She hadn't changed a bit. Still wouldn't spend a second on pleasantries if there was business at hand. Well, it wouldn't hurt her to spare a moment. "How's Madison?" he asked.

"She's fine. Doing well."

Had he imagined it, or was there a little warmth in her voice? He smiled. "And you? Motherhood suits you?"

"I don't know how well it suits me, but she hasn't died from my cooking or suffered any obvious damage yet."

"I'm sure you're doing fine," he said, and when Margaret jostled his shoulder, he added, "Margaret sends her love."

"Tell her hello." There it was again, that slight softening of the voice. But it disappeared almost immediately. "So, what did you call for? Just to check up on my mothering skills?"

"Actually, I need to ask you a few questions."

Kate chuckled. "About what? Are you solving another

murder?" But when he didn't chuckle back, her voice grew serious. "Is that what you're doing?"

"I'm just asking a few questions," he insisted.

"Who died? Anyone I know?"

"I don't think so. He was my niece's husband."

"All right, I can spare a minute or two, but I've got to pick up Madison from her play group, so make it quick. What do you want to know?"

"I'm curious about Shadow Mountain. Have you received any offers to purchase lately?"

"I do have one offer on the table." She sounded a little surprised at his question.

"Can you tell me anything about it?"

"I suppose so. It's from a guy named Roy Dennington—" She broke off and hesitated for a second. "I don't think I ought to go into details about financial arrangements."

"I don't think I need them. I just want to know whether the sale looks like it will go through."

"Well, this Dennington looks good on paper. Sufficient liquid assets. Adequate financing. He's anxious to build— which suits me fine, but I know how much *you'll* hate it."

He would, but now was not the time to discuss it. "It's a good offer?"

"Very good. I'm seriously considering it for Madison. I'm not sure she'd ever want to go back there, considering what happened."

Fred figured she might be right about that. "Is Dennington anxious to get hold of the property?"

"Fairly anxious, I guess. Why?"

"Anxious enough to offer kickbacks if he could get the property to pass EPA standards?"

"Maybe, but there's no need to do that."

Her answer surprised Fred. "There's not?"

"No. There's a lot of reclamation that still needs to be done of course, especially around the quarries, but the other half of the mountain can be developed right away. If he builds wisely, he could bring in enough money to finance the cleanup on the rest."

Fred had been so certain about the answer he expected, he

had to stop and replay the one he actually got. "Are you sure he could build now?"

"Of course I'm sure. What in the hell's going on up there, anyway? You're the second person who's called me about this in the past two weeks."

"The second?" He tried to keep his voice steady, but every instinct told him he was just about to find his connection. He shot a glance at Margaret as if she could hear Kate's part of the conversation, but she only sent back a confused look and leaned a little closer to the receiver. "Who else called?" he asked.

But Kate didn't get a chance to answer. The telephone clicked in Fred's ear, and she sighed heavily. "Oh, hell. Hold on a second, Fred—" The line went dead for a few seconds before she came back to him. "Sorry about that. Now, what did you say?"

"Who else has been asking about Shadow Mountain?" He had to force himself to breathe while he waited for her to answer.

"A guy by the name of Adam Bigelow."

twenty-four

"Adam?" The blood drained from Fred's head, and his heart echoed with every beat. "Are you sure?"

"Well of course I'm sure. Why? Is that important?" She sounded distracted by her own concerns, and he could hear someone else speaking softly to her.

"Adam Bigelow was murdered last week."

Her quick intake of breath told him he'd surprised her. "You don't think it was because of the mountain?"

"I think it's highly probable. Tell me what he asked you about."

Her hand came down over the receiver again and muffled the sound for a few seconds before she came back on the line. "Can you believe this? Someone's at the door. I'm going to have to go, Fred."

"Wait! Don't hang up. Tell me what Adam asked about."

"He wanted to know about Roy's offer, and he was pretty concerned about the reclamation." She spoke quickly, almost in a whisper. "Apparently, Adam had been involved in testing the property for the EPA before. He thought a lot of it had tested clean then, but for some reason the tests this time came out showing the whole mountain contaminated. Adam wanted to know if I'd kept any of the old files."

A chill crept up Fred's shoulders and onto his neck. "And had you?"

"All of them. And he was right—like I said, there's a good half of the mountain that can be built on right now."

"So you verified Adam's suspicions?"

She muffled another interruption. "Listen, Fred, I've really got to go."

"No, wait."

"I have to go, Fred. I've told you everything I know, anyway."

He tried to sound understanding. "All right, then. Give Madison a kiss for me."

"She'll be delighted. She still remembers you."

"I'm glad."

"And, Fred—be careful."

"Of course."

Kate disconnected, and Fred replaced the receiver as he turned to face Margaret. Her eyes glinted with excitement. "So, what did she say?"

"I've had it all backwards."

But she obviously didn't want to hear his interpretation of it. "What did she *say*?"

He replayed Kate's conversation for her and added, "So Adam wasn't altering test results, and nobody was offering him money. He was rerunning those tests because someone else falsified them in the first place."

Her face paled. "Are you sure?"

"According to Kate, Adam was trying to uncover the corruption. *That's* why none of the stories ever seemed to fit."

"Who ran the first set of tests? The dirty ones?" She looked confused. "And why?"

"I don't know. But when I find out, I'll know who killed Adam."

The instant the words left his mouth, Margaret stopped collaborating with him. She shoved her fists onto her hips and shook her head as if she meant business. "*You're* not finding out anything else. We're calling Enos right now and telling him what we know."

"But we don't know enough."

Margaret backed away and nodded slowly. "Yes, we do."

"Now listen, Margaret—"

But she didn't listen. "There's absolutely no way I'm letting you take this any further."

"But we still don't know why. Why would somebody

falsify the reports? Why would anybody want to stop Roy Dennington from developing Shadow Mountain?"

She stared at him as if he'd suddenly sprouted another head. "*You* don't want anyone to build up there—what's to say somebody else doesn't feel just as strongly about it."

"Strongly enough to kill? I don't believe it." He tried to sound reasonable, but he could hear his voice climb a notch.

"Maybe not, but you're not going to be the one who figures it out the rest of the way. I mean it, Dad—"

"One more visit to Philip Aagard," he bargained.

Her eyes glinted with that peculiar golden light that had always signaled a fine temper in her mother. "No."

"Just to find out who ran the original tests—"

"No."

"A phone call—"

She turned her back on him. "I refuse to discuss it with you."

That suited Fred just fine. He didn't want to discuss it, either. Snapping his mouth shut, he started for the front door.

Margaret whirled back toward him. "What are you doing?"

"Leaving."

"Why?"

"We're not discussing it anymore." He wrenched open the front door and stepped out onto the porch.

"You're *not* going to EnviroSampl."

"Did I say I was?" He stormed down the front steps and headed toward the Buick and hoped she wouldn't force him to actually *lie* to her.

She raced around him and blocked his path. "Where are you going?" He didn't answer but met her gaze steadily until her eyes shifted away a smidgen. "Are you going to see Enos?" This time her voice sounded a little less belligerent.

"Yes." He kept his own tone gruff for good measure, but he felt better at being able to stick to the truth. He *would* go to Enos—eventually.

She looked relieved. "You know how I worry about

something happening to you." As if that explained everything.

"I know all your reasons," he growled and stepped around her. If she had her way, he'd wither away to nothing in his rocking chair.

"Don't be mad at me," she called after him.

He lifted his hand over his head, but he didn't respond. He felt her eyes on him all the way to the car, but he refused to look back, though he knew that's what she wanted.

Dropping onto the car seat, he cranked the engine to life and pulled the gearshift into reverse. Then he backed onto the road and sped away—before Margaret had a chance to realize that he'd *never* drive the short distance to Enos's office and to figure out where he was going.

For the third time that day, Fred followed the highway toward Mountain Home and tried to put together the remaining pieces of the story. He thought about Philip Aagard's argument with Adam, about Adam's late-night testing, about Brooke's part in those tests, and Charlotte's phone call to Roy Dennington. He thought about the discovery of those tests and Philip's claim that Adam had, indeed, been altering test results. But everything refused to fall into place until he'd driven over halfway up the mountain. Then, all at once, he saw the whole picture.

Philip Aagard had argued with Adam, *not* because he'd discovered Adam's deception but because Adam had discovered his. Obviously, Adam had figured out what Philip was doing, and there'd been a confrontation. That was the argument Porter'd heard. That's why Philip murdered Adam—to keep him from going public. And he'd used EnviroSampl's files and records to turn the story around and make it look as if Adam was guilty. Roy Dennington had obviously been in the wrong place at the wrong time, which made him a perfect scapegoat.

For a moment Fred wondered if he should turn back, find Enos, and tell him what he knew. But if any evidence still existed that could tie Philip to the illegal testing, Fred wanted to keep him from destroying it. He'd have to find a way to contact Enos from EnviroSampl.

Battling his instinct to drive faster, Fred checked the sun hanging just above the western mountains. Shadows had already begun to stretch across the highway and melt into the dense forest on the other side. Certainly not the time to drive like a maniac. But how long would Philip stick around on a Saturday, and could Fred make it to EnviroSampl before he left?

He kept his eyes on the road and told himself he'd make it. He *had* to. He had no idea where to look for Philip after hours.

But even before he reached the turnoff to EnviroSampl, his sixth sense warned him he was too late. And when he pulled into the empty parking lot, his heart dropped.

Still hoping against reason, he cruised slowly past the building and scanned the windows for any sign of life, but they looked back at him blankly. Now what?

He brought the car to a stop in front of the building and stared at the front door as if it could tell him where to look, but it gave away nothing.

Muttering under his breath, he pressed the accelerator slightly. He'd just turned back toward the highway when movement in his rearview mirror caught his eye. He stopped and watched as a man dressed in baggy pants and an untucked shirt backed out of a door near the back of the building, pulling a box behind him.

Mitch Hancock. What was he still doing here? Shoving the gearshift into "park," Fred climbed out of the car and walked toward the open door.

Mitch must have heard him coming because he dropped a flap of the box and whirled around. But when he saw Fred, he grinned and gave an embarrassed laugh. "I didn't know anybody was out here."

"That makes us even. I didn't know anybody was *in* there."

Mitch hitched up his pants and studied the empty parking lot with interest. "I guess I'm the only one left. What are you doing here?"

"I'd hoped to catch Philip before he went home."

"Sorry. You just missed him."

Fred tried to look as if it weren't a matter of life and death. "Do you have any idea where I can find him?"

Mitch shook his head and hefted the box to his shoulder. "No idea. Sorry." He carried the box toward a metal dumpster a few feet behind the building.

Fred followed. "You don't know his home address?"

"He lives somewhere on the way to Estes Park, that's all I know. Look, he'll be in tomorrow. Why don't I have him call you?"

"This can't wait. You don't have his home address inside, do you? Say, in a personnel file or something?"

Mitch seemed to consider. He shrugged. "Probably. Look, I'm just getting rid of some old samples to make room for a new contract we just got, but if you don't mind waiting a few minutes I'll be glad to look."

Fred's heart raced. "Dumping old samples?"

Mitch's mouth curved into a frown, but he nodded. "Philip insisted I stay late to get this done tonight."

Were these from Shadow Mountain? They must be the evidence Enos would need to tie this all together. Trying to look grateful for Mitch's offer of help, Fred nodded. "Thank you."

Mitch readjusted his hold on the box and pushed the carton inside the bin. Tugging at his wasitband again, he jerked his head toward the door. "You might as well wait inside with me. It's cooler in there."

He led the way into a large laboratory with several obviously delineated work stations and a large open vault at one end. A cluttered counter held test tubes, burners, glass beakers, containers of all sizes filled with soil and water samples, and countless other things Fred couldn't identify. It looked like an overgrown high school science classroom.

Mitch nodded toward one of the work stations. "Have a seat at my desk. I'll be done in a second."

Fred perched on the edge of a swivel chair and planted his feet to keep himself from turning. Mounds of documents and multicolored files teetered on the desk in varying heights, and he didn't want to dislodge any of them. "I didn't realize you got rid of the samples when you finished a contract."

Mitch stepped into the vault and called back over his shoulder. "Oh, yeah. They're nothing special, you know. Just dirt and water. You can find that stuff anywhere." He laughed at his own joke and tugged an empty box toward him. "So, why do you want to see Philip?"

Fred leaned an elbow onto the desk's cluttered surface and disturbed one of the stacks of documents teetering near the edge. He pulled his elbow back and watched the stack to make sure it didn't decide to fall over. "I have a few questions to ask him."

"They can't wait until morning? You must be closing in on the murderer."

Fred tried to keep his face impassive just in case Mitch decided to look at him. "Closing in? What makes you think I'm looking?"

"I've heard rumors about you. They say you solved a couple of cases before the sheriff did. So who do you think the murderer is?" Mitch sounded interested, but he didn't take his eyes from the sample bottles.

Still, Fred decided to try for a vague sort of look. Confused. "Well, I don't know exactly . . ."

Mitch worked for a long moment in silence. "I'm betting on the black guy," he said finally.

"Roy Dennington?" Mitch's guess surprised Fred.

But Mitch didn't seem to notice. "I figure that when Adam got caught cleaning up the test results, the black guy realized he'd lost his only way to pick up a piece of property in a nice place like this—" Mitch swept a row of jars into the box. "That how you figure it?"

"Close," Fred said. No matter how convinced he was of Philip's guilt, he didn't want the grapevine to broadcast his theory before he shared it with Enos.

Mitch laughed shortly. "I don't know why somebody like *that* would want to buy property up here, anyway."

"Somebody like what?"

"Black." Mitch scowled as if Fred were incredibly slow witted. "Why would *they* want to live up here?"

Fred tried not to stare at him. It had been a long time since he'd heard anyone admit prejudice so blatantly.

Mitch stopped packing the box and leaned an elbow on the shelf, but his expression had shifted subtly while his back had been turned. He looked hard. Cynical. Angry. "This is a good, clean area. It's why I came here to live. We can't start letting *that element* in, they'll ruin the place." And then, so quickly Fred wondered how it happened, the anger disappeared and a wide smile replaced it. He picked up the box and stepped out of the vault. "Let me get rid of this box, and I'll find you that address."

Fred tried to smile back, but his lips felt stiff.

With the box on his shoulder, Mitch started for the door. Once there, he tried to maneuver close enough to reach the knob, but his load made it difficult.

Intending to help, Fred swiveled in the chair and stood just as Mitch pulled open the door. "I'll be right back," he said, and disappeared into the fading sunlight.

As Fred turned back to his chair, his arm caught one stack of files and sent them skittering across the floor. Embarrassed by his clumsiness, he leaned down to pick them up.

One or two of the folders had fallen open, but it took Fred several seconds to realize that he held test results in his hand. Were they all here? Including Shadow Mountain?

With trembling fingers, he gathered the files into a pile. He cast repeated, anxious glances toward the door as he checked the labels, certain that Mitch would return before he had a chance to look thoroughly.

Storm Valley. Deer Run. Paradise Canyon. He pulled one set of test results after another into his arms and restacked them on the desk. Silver Dale. Pine View. Sundown Peak.

And then, suddenly, there it was. A thick file folder labeled Shadow Mountain. He tore open the front cover and tried to make his fingers behave as he dug through the documents. Page after page of double-talk and scientific jargon. But who'd done the tests?

Footsteps echoed outside the door as Fred reached the signature page on the first one. The knob turned, but he forced himself to look just before he dropped the file onto the desk. And there, on the bottom line, was the name he'd been looking for all this time.

Mitch Hancock.

twenty-five

Fred gathered the rest of the files and managed to shove them back into place just as the door reopened. Taking a quick step away from Mitch's desk, he pretended great interest in a picture of Brooke Westphal on skis that had been tacked to a bulletin board behind him and struggled to keep his breathing steady.

Mitch stepped inside, smiling and obviously relaxed. "Well, that's done. Come on, I'll find you Philip's address." He crossed to a small, recessed doorway and pulled it open. "Ready?"

Fred tried to look as if he still wanted the blasted address, when all he wanted was to get out of here and call Enos. As he turned to follow and his gaze swept the floor, a patch of bright blue caught his eye—one file folder that had somehow escaped his notice poked out from under the desk.

With his heart in his throat, Fred stepped away from the desk. If Mitch saw the folder on the floor, he'd realize Fred had been looking into the files. And if he'd killed Adam because of what Adam knew, Fred didn't think he'd be inclined to grant an old man the benefit of any doubt.

Praying he hadn't called attention to the file by even the slightest hesitation, Fred advanced toward Mitch wearing the heartiest smile he could muster. Thankfully, Mitch's gaze didn't waver, and he didn't see the folder. He led the way into a darkened corridor, and Fred breathed easier once the door swung closed behind them.

A couple of ceiling panels offered auxiliary lighting, but most of the building stood in shadow. "Philip's office is in the front," Mitch said, and his voice echoed off the walls.

The place looked different from this angle and in this light. Eerie. Threatening. How had Adam stayed here alone at night? Or hadn't it felt threatening then?

Their footsteps echoed as they walked through the empty building, and Fred imagined Mitch making this same walk the night he shot Adam. He wondered how Adam had felt when he heard his killer approaching.

At the end of the corridor, the front door stood before him, teasing him, offering him a way out. Maybe he could make a dash for it. He *might* make it outside before Mitch realized what was happening, but he wouldn't get far before the younger man caught up with him. And then where would he be? He'd have a hard time talking his way out of that.

No, his only hope lay in convincing Mitch that he still suspected Philip Aagard. In getting away and calling Enos for help. So he followed Mitch into Philip's office.

Mitch nodded toward a large filing cabinet in a corner. "The files are all in there, and Philip keeps the key in his desk." He slipped behind it, yanked open the kneehole drawer and dug around for a minute before he pulled out a set of keys and dangled them from his finger. Flashing Fred a conspiratorial smile, he said, "We're in business."

Fred mumbled something he could only hope sounded pleased and conspiratorial in return.

But Mitch had grown almost eager, and he didn't seem to notice Fred's sudden lack of enthusiasm. Crossing back to the cabinet, he tried a key in the lock. "Philip thinks he's got everything so secure, but he's a fool. It's a piece of cake to get into this cabinet."

Fred couldn't think of a reply.

When the first key didn't fit, Mitch gave a little laugh and tried another. "I never remember which key fits this lock."

Fred hoped he'd remember soon. He didn't think he could live through much more of this.

With a muffled curse Mitch tried another key, but before he could fit it into the lock, the key ring slipped from his fingers and hit the floor. When he bent to retrieve it, the tail of his shirt hiked up to expose a wide expanse of skin and the butt of a gun tucked into the waistband of his pants.

Fred's next breath failed him, and fear slammed his heart around in his chest like a tennis ball. He sidled a little closer to the desk and eyed the telephone. Could he reach it in time? Snag it up and punch "911" before Mitch shot him? Maybe. But then what? One shot and it would be all over. Mitch would get away, and Fred would be dead.

Obviously unaware that he'd exposed more than he'd intended, Mitch straightened and rested one arm on the cabinet. "You don't think *he* did it, do you?"

Fred fought to control his breathing and to follow Mitch's train of thought. "Who? Philip?"

Mitch nodded and his brows knit together in concern, the same kind of expression he'd worn when he'd suggested Adam had been accepting kickbacks. And if Fred hadn't known the truth, he might have fallen for this new direction just as easily as he had that one.

Mitch looked deeply concerned. "He sure doesn't want that ski resort built."

"Really?"

"No. It'll ruin access to some property he owns down in Paradise Canyon."

Fred tried desperately to look as though he believed it.

As if pondering this new, unhappy thought, Mitch worked the keys again, and when one turned at last, he tugged open the heavy drawer and shot a smile over his shoulder. "Well, *finally*." He walked his fingers over the tabs of several files. "He didn't have to worry, you know. The ski resort's not going in there."

Fred didn't trust himself to speak, so he didn't do anything more than grunt a reply.

But that apparently satisfied Mitch. "For one thing, the property's so contaminated, it'd take a fortune to clean it up, and there's no way Dennington's got that kind of money." He peered into a couple of files and looked as if he was enjoying himself immensely.

But Fred wasn't. "You know, it's getting a little late. If I can just get that address, I'll get out of your way." It took great effort, but Fred thought he managed to keep most of the urgency from his voice.

Mitch pulled a file almost out of the drawer and scanned its label. "Oh, you're not bothering me." He dropped the file back into place and began to search again. And when the top drawer failed to yield any results, he moved on to the second. "You want to know the other reason Dennington's not building on Shadow Mountain—"

Fred didn't think he did.

"Because he's black. And nobody's going to let that California woman sell Shadow Mountain to somebody like him."

Mitch's words sent a chill up Fred's spine.

"He'd just start bringing in a lot of his people to take jobs away from us. And where does he think *they're* going to live?"

Mitch looked at Fred as if he expected some exchange of thoughts, but Fred didn't want to share any of his. Self-preservation warned him to make agreeable noises; self-respect refused to let him.

Warming to his subject, Mitch abandoned his search for the personnel file. "You don't want a bunch of *them* living down in Cutler, do you?"

Fred really didn't want to answer. There was no way he could agree with the sentiment, but disagreeing might prove dangerous to his health.

But Mitch had apparently decided he wanted an ally, and he'd decided Fred would be it. "Well? *Do* you? Right next door with all their mess and their noise, and half a dozen families in the same house?" The tone of his voice demanded an answer.

"I don't really think that's an accurate picture."

Mitch gaped as if he couldn't believe his ears, but a second later his face flamed. "What the hell do you know about it? How many black families have you lived around?"

"Only a few, but they've all been fine people—"

"Well, then, you've known the exception," Mitch said as if he'd discovered an explanation for Fred's lack of sound judgment. "I could tell you stories."

Maybe he could, but Fred didn't want to hear them. He tried to look calm and understanding without feeding Mitch's irrational thought process. "There's good and bad of all kinds, I suppose."

Mitch apparently took his words as agreement. "And ones like Roy Dennington are the worst. They want to be white so bad, they'll do anything."

Nothing in Roy Dennington's manner had suggested a desire to be anything but what he was, but Fred knew arguing the point wouldn't accomplish anything—except, maybe, getting himself killed.

This time, Mitch seemed to interpret Fred's silence more accurately. Shoving the file drawer closed, he twisted his lips into a smile. "I can't find the address you want."

Fred was ready to abandon the search, himself. He forced himself not to let out a sigh of relief. "Well, it was a long shot, anyway." He turned toward the door and tried not to look too eager to get away. "Thanks for trying."

"Wait a second," Mitch called after him. "I'll have to get you back into the lab. There's a security lock." With rapid, jerky movements he relocked the filing cabinet, replaced the keys, and closed the office door behind them. As he led Fred back down the corridor, he held his shoulders rigid with disapproval, and Fred could sense tension in every step.

Though every instinct urged him to get away quickly, he forced himself to follow Mitch's pace. He told himself to hold on another two minutes—just long enough to walk out the back door to safety.

Mitch worked the keypad on a small white box and yanked open the door.

Pausing just inside, Fred made himself extend his hand and shake Mitch's, but he wanted to recoil from the touch and wipe his hand on his pantleg. He worked up a smile, but he knew it looked forced and unreal. "Thanks again," he said, but even he could hear the dishonesty in his voice.

"No problem," Mitch said in a tone that suggested otherwise.

Forcing himself not to glance at the file folder on the floor, Fred walked at a reasonable pace across the room, but the back of his neck burned where Mitch watched him. Any second, Mitch would look away, and the bright blue file folder would catch his eye. Anticipating it, Fred's heart tried to jump up his throat and out of his mouth several times.

At last, he reached the door and put his hand on the knob just as he sensed Mitch turning away. From the corner of his eye, he saw the younger man lean toward the file folder, and panic burst through the thin veil of his outer calm.

"What the hell is this?"

Fred jerked the door open.

Mitch reached under his shirttail for the gun. "Just a damned minute."

But Fred didn't spare even a second. Bolting out the door, he crouched as if he could make himself a smaller target in the early dusk and ran toward his car. But after a couple of steps he realized he'd never reach it before Mitch hit the door.

Veering sharply, he raced toward the trees. Pain shot through his feet and into his knees, but he ignored it and kept moving until he reached the forest. Diving into the early evening shadows, Fred crashed through the trees and tried to put as much distance between himself and the gun as he could.

"Where in the hell are you, old man?" Mitch's voice sounded so clear in the early evening air, Fred knew he'd already come outside.

He forced himself to slow down, to make less noise as he crept into the cover of the trees. He crouched into the shadows and ignored the twinge in his lower back. Should he keep moving? Or should he find a place to take cover?

Behind him, he could hear the sound of Mitch pushing through the foliage, and he knew he must make almost as much noise himself. Each step he took would betray his position.

Fighting fresh panic, he scoured the surrounding area until he found a cluster of trees and undergrowth that would provide him the best cover he'd probably find. He hesitated only a second before he ducked through the narrow opening between trees and crouched as low as he could.

He looked around for something he could use as a weapon, but everything at hand would be useless against a gun, and he had to assume Mitch had it cocked and ready to use.

"You can't get away," Mitch warned, and his voice sounded quiet and far too close.

A chill raced up Fred's spine, and he had to force himself to remain motionless. Even the slightest move would betray his hiding place.

Nearby, a twig snapped underfoot and a second later, Mitch stepped into view between two trees. Just as Fred had suspected, Mitch held the gun in one hand and used the other to give it support. He moved through the thicket with the practiced ease of a hunter, and Fred knew that if he caught one glimpse of him cowering there, it would all be over.

Fred tried to shrink even deeper into the foliage without moving. He allowed himself tiny breaths and forced his aching knees to hold the position he'd twisted them into.

Mitch turned toward him, and for the space of a heartbeat Fred thought he'd been discovered. But all at once, Mitch froze and looked back over his shoulder as if something behind him had caught his attention.

A second later Fred heard it, too. Footsteps and voices and shouting in the parking lot. Enos's voice calling directions. Ivan's shouting back.

"The door's open."

"You two—check inside."

Mitch ducked into the trees and Fred lost sight of him. Relief made him almost weak, but with Mitch still out there somewhere, he wasn't safe yet.

After what felt like an hour but must have been only a few seconds, someone shouted again. "They're not inside."

"Spread out. Ivan—take the back. Robert—over there." Enos's voice had never sounded so welcome to Fred in all the years they'd known each other. A few more minutes and they'd find Mitch, and Fred would be able to come out of hiding.

Straining to see through the trees, Fred watched and

waited, but he couldn't see anything, and he could no longer be certain whether the footsteps he heard were friend or foe. Shadows played across the floor of the forest, an angry creature chattered in the distance, and something moved behind him.

Before he could turn his head, a voice hissed in his ear. "You make one sound, old man, and you're dead." One arm circled his neck and secured him, the other held the gun against his temple.

It took Fred less than a second to weigh his options and to decide not to push his luck.

Mitch jerked him to his feet, and Fred's knees protested the too-rapid movement. "You're going to help me get away," Mitch whispered. "Where are your car keys?"

"In my pocket."

"Get them out."

Fred obliged and didn't fight when Mitch pushed him forward. Every step seemed to take an eternity, and before they'd gone even a few feet Mitch's tension rose to a dangerous level. Like a physical presence, it emanated from him and wrapped itself around Fred.

Fred knew he was safe for the moment—unless something or someone threatened their escape. Mitch needed Fred alive for that. But if they managed to get away, Fred knew Mitch wouldn't hesitate to kill him.

A noise to their left startled Mitch, and his arm tightened around Fred's throat almost convulsively. Fred tried to see into the forest, but with no success.

After what felt like an eternity, he caught a glimpse of the Buick through the trees. Fear pumped through his veins, and dread threatened to paralyze him. Another few feet and he'd lose any chance of escape. But somehow he kept moving.

Without warning Mitch's arm tightened again, but this time Fred could see what alarmed him. Ahead of them on the trail, Enos stepped out of the trees. *Thank the good Lord.*

Enos held his service revolver in both hands, but his face, tightened in anger and fear, looked almost unfamiliar. "Drop it."

But instead of obeying, Mitch shifted his own gun

slightly and nuzzled it against Fred's temple. "Move out of my way, or the old man dies."

Fred silently urged Enos to shoot, to take his chances and pull the trigger. But Enos held his gun steady and met Mitch's gaze with unblinking eyes.

"I mean it," Mitch shouted. "The old man's going to buy it right here in front of you. I'll blow his damned head off. Now drop your gun and call off your deputies."

Shoot, Fred begged without sound. But Enos made the mistake of looking at him. And when his gaze wavered, Fred knew he'd lost his edge.

"Shoot him," Fred croaked.

Enos looked away and lowered his gun to the ground.

"Call in your boys," Mitch demanded and pressed the gun even harder against Fred's temple.

Couldn't Enos see that Fred didn't stand a chance if they backed off?

"Ivan. Robert. Come into the clearing and drop your weapons," Enos said quietly.

They'd been there all along, weapons drawn, and now Enos was ordering them to surrender? Panic nearly blinded him as the boys stepped into view with their weapons extended uselessly.

Mitch jerked his head to indicate a spot to one side of the small clearing. "All of you move over this way. Over there—"

Without a word, Enos complied. Ivan and Robert followed his lead.

Apparently satisfied with their new position, Mitch tugged Fred around and backed through the trees toward the parking lot. Fred half expected Enos to make a move, but he stood there and watched, helpless.

Fred struggled to breathe, but fear and Mitch's arm against his throat made it almost impossible. He wondered what Margaret would say when Enos reported Fred's death to her—if *this* would be the one thing she'd be unable to forgive him.

The barrel of the gun warmed against his temple, melding

itself to him like an old friend. Mitch dragged him backward slowly. One step. Another.

All at once Mitch's step faltered slightly, as if he'd kicked an exposed root or stubbed his foot against a branch. Knowing this was his only chance, Fred ducked and twisted. Using both hands to give himself strength, he grabbed Mitch's gun hand and pushed it away from him.

Miraculously, Mitch's grip loosened on his neck, and Fred managed to slide out of his grasp. Air burned in his throat and lungs as he spun around. With force he hadn't known he possessed, Fred thrust Mitch's arm up and shoved the gun away from his head.

As if in slow motion, Mitch's finger tightened on the trigger. When the shot came, Fred felt it through his entire body, but the bullet flew wide and zinged into a tree somewhere behind them.

Without releasing his tentative hold on the gun, Fred threw himself into Mitch. He shoved his own arm across Mitch's throat and pressed his full weight into it. He let up and repeated the process again and again, like a battering ram until, at last, Mitch staggered under the assault.

Hurling himself into the younger man's midsection, Fred buckled him, then twisted the gun away and held it, in trembling hands, against the younger man's head. "Enos," he shouted. "Get your tail over here."

He could hear three sets of footsteps racing up behind him. Enos joined him, his own gun back in his hand, his face looking sherifflike again. While Ivan worked a pair of handcuffs over Mitch's wrists, Robert trained his gun on the captive.

They were all a bunch of heroes now.

When he was certain Mitch was securely bound, Enos lowered his gun and turned to face Fred. "What in the hell did you do that for?"

Astounded, Fred lowered his own gun. "Well, *you* obviously weren't going to do anything."

"I had it under control."

"The hell you say."

"Good billy hell, Fred. You think I was just going to let

him take you away? What kind of friend do you think I am?"

Fred didn't bother to offer his opinion.

Enos frowned darkly and shouted over his shoulder. "Get out here, Grady."

From the cover of the forest, Grady Hatch ducked under the branches of an Englemann spruce and stepped into the clearing. He clutched a rifle with a high-powered scope and looked as disappointed as the day he'd been cut from the football team.

"Grady was back there the whole time, Fred. And if you'd let us do our jobs—"

Fred looked away but humphed his opinion.

Grady joined them in the clearing. "I had a bead on him. I would have had him—"

Fred humphed again, but his knees sagged as relief hit him just ahead of the reality. He'd come far too close to death this time.

Enos reached up to pat his deputy's shoulder, then turned an unappreciative eye on Fred. "One of these days, Fred, you're going to get killed."

"Well, it darned near happened today," Fred snapped.

"You *can't* keep doing this kind of thing. If Margaret hadn't called me—"

"—you'd never have figured out who the killer was."

Enos glared at him.

Fred tried to glare back, but he didn't feel nearly as strong as he tried to pretend he was.

Enos holstered his gun and threw an arm around Fred's shoulders. "I can't even begin to tell you how I felt when I saw him with that gun to your head."

"Not nearly as bad as *I* felt, I can tell you that."

Enos hugged him as if he didn't want to let him go. "Margaret's going to have your hide, you know that, don't you?"

Fred knew that. But just for now, it didn't matter how angry she got with him. It only mattered that he'd survived and that she could get angry with him at all.

twenty-six

Fred held his boots in his hand and crept down the hallway from his bedroom toward the living room. Without making a sound, he peeked at Margaret asleep on the couch. She'd stayed overnight, as if she expected him to sneak out somewhere after his brush with death. As if she needed to babysit him.

He watched her for a second or two. She slept soundly, and even the early morning sunlight spilling through gaps in the curtains didn't disturb her. Well, good. She'd been far too upset with him last night, and he'd like her to sleep all day if she could.

Taking care not to step on any loose boards, he pushed open the kitchen door. But when he saw Enos at the table with a thermos of coffee in one hand and a package of Twinkies in the other, he froze in his tracks.

"What in the Sam Hill do you think you're doing?" he whispered.

Enos leaned back in his chair and grinned at him. "We had a feeling you might try something like this."

"Like what?"

Enos sent a meaningful glance at Fred's stockinged feet and the boots in his hand. "Where are you off to?"

"That's none of your business."

"It is when I promised Maggie I'd take you to Doc's first thing this morning."

Fred let the kitchen door swing shut behind him and dropped his boots on the floor. "I'm not going."

Heaving a sigh that sounded as if he felt terribly put-upon, Enos shook his head slowly. "We've been over this a hundred times—"

"I'm not going." Fred patted his chest and looked robust. "Do I look sick?"

"No. But—"

Fred lowered himself to a chair and tugged on his boots. "No. And I'm not. Period. End of discussion."

Enos's face darkened. "Listen, Fred, you went through something pretty hairy yesterday—"

Fred worked the laces into place and formed a bow.

"—and I'd want Doc to check you over if you were twenty years old and had the heart of an elephant."

"Horsefeathers."

Enos shoved away the Twinkies and stood. "You are without a doubt the most obstinate man I've ever met."

Fred didn't respond, but he appreciated the compliment.

"Do you have any idea how upset Maggie is?"

"Of course I do, but she's got to get over it."

Enos didn't like that response. "She's *not* going to get over it unless you make a few concessions."

Fred pulled on the other boot. "She doesn't want concessions—she wants total capitulation. No caffeine, no sodium, no cholesterol, no danger, no excitement— Just what in blazes does she think I want to stay alive for? Perry Mason reruns?"

"To see your grandchildren grow up."

"And have them think I'm a useless old man?"

Enos paced to the back door and lifted the curtain. "Nobody thinks you're a useless old man."

Fred finished tying the boot and pushed to his feet. "That's because I'm not. And I don't intend to be, either."

"Listen to reason, Fred—"

Fred snagged up the coffeepot and shoved it under the tap. "No, *you* listen. I've seen it happen. I saw my own mother shoved into a corner at family parties the minute she let herself get old. Everybody spent a token thirty seconds with her, gave her a kiss on the cheek, and ignored her the rest of the day." He shook his head as if he could shake away the memory. "I was as guilty as anyone else for letting it happen. But it's *not* going to happen to *me*."

Enos at least had the grace to look a little embarrassed. "Nobody wants that to happen to you."

"Fine. Then let's drop the subject. If I feel even the slightest twinge, I'll see Doc. All right?"

Enos tried to smile. "Sounds fine to me. Let's just hope your kids go for it."

Fred returned the smile. "You were a trial run. Come on and take a walk with me."

"I really should get over to the office—"

"Nonsense. You're never there before ten, anyway."

With a chuckle, Enos downed the rest of his coffee, screwed the lid back on his thermos, and nodded. "I give up trying to argue with you."

Fred pulled open the back door and waited while Enos stepped through. "That's the most sensible thing you've said in years."

They followed the trail around the south end of Spirit Lake in companionable silence. For the first time in days, the air felt cool, and early morning mist rose from the lake's surface. But dust still rose from their feet, and their legs brushed against drought-stiff foliage.

Something chattered in the distance, and leaves rustled in the breeze. But the forest worked its magic.

Enos's face relaxed after several minutes, and he looked younger than he had in quite a spell. "I'm glad I came. It does me good to get out once in a while."

"That's why I do it every day. It clears the mind. Gets the blood pumping."

Enos grinned, but something in the back of his eyes still looked troubled. It wasn't the first time Fred had seen that look. Enos's marriage hadn't ever been a real good one. The young man had tried everything to make it work over the years, but Fred suspected far more than Enos would ever tell him.

Fred lifted his face to the morning sun, and his heart ached for all the people who'd never know the joy of marriage with their best friend. All the people, like Enos, who'd settled for someone. And all the people who'd been settled for. All the people who hurt or were hurt by the one they loved.

Trying to bolster his spirits, Fred clapped a hand on Enos's shoulder and did his best to sound hearty when he spoke. "So, tell me when the arraignment's been scheduled for."

"Day after tomorrow. And you'll never guess which judge has been assigned to the case."

"Judge Roberts?"

Enos laughed outright. "Mitch will protest the draw, of course. He'll never be able to stand having a black judge preside over his case."

Fred shook his head and let the thought of Mitch's discomfort tease a smile from his lips. He couldn't think of more poetic justice. "I still keep telling myself there *has* to have been some other motivation behind this."

Enos stepped over an exposed root and his face grew serious. "Old prejudices die hard, I guess. He was so determined to keep Roy Dennington from buying Shadow Mountain, I think he would have done anything to prevent it."

Fred drew in a breath of clear morning air and walked another few feet without speaking. "But Kate's going to sell it to Roy, right?"

"Right."

"And he's planning to develop it—"

"Right." Enos looked as disappointed as Fred felt.

"How soon?"

Enos shook his head. "I don't know for sure. He was talking about moving his family in and getting established first."

Fred smiled. "Great. That'll give us a chance to make him see reason."

"I don't know. He's got plans for that mountain."

"I can be mighty persuasive."

A laugh erupted, and Enos grinned at him. "That you can, my friend." But a second later his face sobered. "How's Nancy?"

"She went home with Harriet and Porter last night. I just hope she tells them the whole truth soon."

"It still hurts to think of everything Adam went through before he died."

"And everything Nancy still has to go through."

Enos nodded. "What do you think Porter and Harriet will do when they learn the truth?"

"They'll love her. And they'll love the baby. In a few months they'll have convinced themselves the child was all their idea."

Enos kicked up a cloud of dust and looked up into the trees. "I suppose she and Kelley will get together now."

"I don't know. Any shot they've got at a good life together's hidden way down under all the heartache they've caused each other. And Adam. I figure they'll have to work awfully hard if they want to find it. And I'm not sure they'll even try."

"I guess it would be heartless of me to say I hope they don't—"

Fred shook his head. "No. Of all the people I know, I'd never call you heartless." He let silence ring between them for a second before he grinned. "But if you ever tell anyone I said that, I'll call you a liar."

Enos stuffed his hands in his pockets and studied the treetops again, but he blinked rapidly several times before he grinned back. "You sure you're okay?"

"You ask me that one more time—"

Enos laughed. "It's just that we're right here by Doc's—"

"No."

"—and his kitchen light's already on."

"Absolutely not."

"And I *did* promise Maggie."

Fred humphed at him and walked a little faster. When he'd put a few feet between them, he stopped on the trail to watch the lake. A breeze danced across its surface and ruffled the water. He breathed deep and savored the feel of the air and the smell of the forest. Mornings didn't come any better than this one.

A tiny movement on the opposite shore caught his eye,

and for half a beat, he thought he saw Phoebe waiting for him, just the way she always had. He almost lifted his hand to wave but caught himself short and gave a little laugh.

He looked at Enos to see if he'd been watching, but Enos stood in the sunlight with his head tipped back to catch the sun and looked like he had at eighteen. Fred took a step or two back toward the trail, but his heart felt a little empty.

Stopping again, he looked back at the lake. And he thought about the Native Americans' legend that gave the lake its name. How early in the mornings they'd seen the mist rising from the lake's surface and how they believed the mist was caused by rising spirits.

Fred lifted his eyes and tried to make Phoebe's image form on the shore again. Tried to picture the breeze tugging at her skirt and pulling her hair. Tried to imagine her waving to him like a young girl, even after so many years together.

He tried to see her face again. To hear her voice. But he saw only trees and rocks.

And he knew she'd gone.

"Fred? You coming?"

Fred turned back to the trail and met Enos's gaze. "I'm with you, son."